# CURTAINS

## *for Maggie*

# ENDORSEMENTS

Life changes are the ties that bind three friends together in Karen H. Richardson's debut novel, *Curtains for Maggie*. The story is a delight to read as Maggie struggles through a difficult transition that threatens her home and marriage. Though fraught with difficulties, themes of love and forgiveness are skillfully woven into the fabric of this story that definitely deserves a standing ovation.
—**Betty Thomason Owens**, author of *Still Water*, Home Found Suspense #1

Highly satisfying! *Curtains for Maggie* delivers strong characters, marriages that work, and friendships that warm the heart. I loved it!
—**Victoria Bylin**, Award-Winning Author

Maggie Nelson is that well-organized, dependable friend we all know and appreciate. When she takes a chance on her own dreams, she brings a slew of memorable characters along for a rewarding journey full of second chances, plot twists, and unexpected moments to shine. In this debut novel, Karen Richardson completely steals the spotlight. Encore, encore ...
—**Janet Morris Grimes**, author of *Solomon's Porch*, a 2022 Carol Award Finalist.

*Curtains for Maggie* takes the reader on a wonderful journey with Maggie Nelson as she discovers that she can claim more than one dream at a time. Navigating the stressors involved in moving from being a stay-at-home mother who manages her family with precision that would make most CEOs jealous to a woman who reclaims a college dream is a roller coaster you won't want to miss. This story has a beautifully authentic feel, and by the end, you'll wish you could join the ladies for conversation and coffee.
—**Gail Franklin**, Voracious reader

Romance isn't only for newlywed couples. In *Curtains for Maggie*, Karen H. Richardson invites us into the lives of three women ready to expand their worlds and meet new challenges. Readers will enjoy following their story roads around the potholes of discouragement, past the roadblocks, and up the lanes of joy to find out if those curtains come up for Maggie and her friends.
—**Ann H. Gabhart**, best-selling author of When the Meadow Blooms

# CURTAINS

## *for Maggie*

Karen H. Richardson

A Christian Company
ElkLakePublishingInc.com

# COPYRIGHT NOTICE



Cover Design: Kelly Artieri, Derinda Babcock
Interior Design: Deb Haggerty
Editor(s): Mel Hughes, Cristel Phelps, Deb Haggerty

PUBLISHED BY: Elk Lake Publishing, Inc., 35 Dogwood Drive, Plymouth, MA 02360, 2023

---

**Library Cataloging Data**
Names: Richardson, Karen H. (Karen H. Richardson)
*Curtains for Maggie* / Karen H. Richardson
304 p. 23cm × 15cm (9in × 6 in.)
ISBN-13: 978-1-64949-882-3 (paperback) | 978-1-64949-883-0 (trade hardcover) | 978-1-64949-884-7 (trade paperback) | 978-1-64949-885-4 (e-book)
Key Words: contemporary fiction; women's fiction; family drama; women's identity; Christian drama; contemporary Christian fiction; marriage
Library of Congress Control Number: 2023938105 Fiction

# DEDICATION

To my husband, Jay, my number one fan. Thank you for believing in me. To my son, Cole, I'm so proud of the young man you've grown to be. I love being your mom. Thank you both for going on this writing journey with me.

## ACKNOWLEDGMENTS

Thank you to the members of the American Christian Fiction Writers chapter in Louisville, Kentucky. I appreciate your encouragement.

Thank you to Janet Grimes for pointing me in the direction of Elk Lake Publishing. A special thank you to Mel Hughes, my editor. You have made this story so much better.

To my beta readers, Betty Owens, Harriet Michael, Gail Franklin, and Ann Hensley, thank you for reading through the various drafts and giving me meaningful feedback.

# CHAPTER ONE

The new haircut had been a mistake. Leaning her head against the top of the chair, Maggie Nelson took a deep breath as a persistent curl sprang out of place. If the success of the Festival of the Trees event was measured by sore feet, the fundraiser was a success. The proceeds would pay for all of Anchor Academy's classroom needs. The board of directors of the small private elementary school allowed one fundraiser a year. Maggie had planned, organized, and emailed for the last three months. Although the planning began before the school year, parents responded to her kind requests to volunteer and to get designers involved. It was Maggie's gift and onus, to be able to plan and bring people together for a common purpose.

"You aren't tired, are you?" Jen Stephens leaned in the doorway as a familiar grin danced across her lips.

At the teasing tone of her best friend's voice, Maggie lifted her head. "A little. How much is left to clean up?" She sat forward with a stretch.

"Don't get up. They're about finished, and I think you've more than fulfilled your volunteer duties for this event. Mrs. Fitzpatrick is in with Miss Amy counting the money and making the list of folks who left before the bidding closed. She'll have the secretary call them on Monday."

"How's it looking?" Maggie rose and picked up her clipboard. The edges of the colorful top page were as ragged as she felt.

"Pretty good. All the trees sold for several hundred dollars above the suggested starting bid."

Maggie nodded in satisfaction and adjusted her ankle-length skirt. "Let's go check on everyone. I want to get home. My bubble bath is calling."

Jen gave Maggie a little hug as they walked. Last night, the ordinary elementary school cafeteria had been transformed into a winter wonderland as the artists spent the evening decorating their Vogue-style trees. Throughout the day, parents and friends of the school had come through the unique auction. Now with the auction complete, the artists had disassembled their showcase trees. Mr. Charles, the custodian, pushed his broom across the tile floor. Tables would need to be reset for the students before Monday.

Mrs. Fitzpatrick emerged from her office. "Well, Maggie, you've outdone yourself. We raised almost twenty thousand dollars. This was by far our best fundraiser." She squeezed Maggie's hand. "I wish our school had more parents as dedicated as you and your army of volunteers."

"Thank you." Maggie managed a tired smile. "I'm so glad. The committee came together on this one in a big way."

Mrs. Fitzpatrick relaxed her grip on Maggie's hand. "Don't be so humble. You had a vision, and you led the way."

Jen poked at Maggie's stuffed clipboard. "Don't forget the clipboard, timetable, and color-coded plans. Where would we have been without Maggie's organization?" The three shared a laugh. "Maggie's humble spirit is part of what makes her an awesome leader."

Maggie shook her head. "You laugh—but even if we were making it up as we went, we knew what needed to get done."

Mrs. Fitzpatrick gave the final reassurance as she guided the two parent volunteers toward the front door. "Yes, we did, and the fundraiser was a success. Tell you what, Mr. Charles is finished. You two go and get some rest. My brother's here and can walk me out."

Like the elementary students who occupied the school throughout the week, Maggie and Jen obeyed the principal.

Crisp September air rushed in through the open door as two other volunteers left. Maggie set her armful of markers, tape, and event supplies on the desk as she pulled on her coat. "The weather helped us give everyone the Christmas spirit." A folded paper fell from her pocket as she retrieved her keys. Maggie snatched the tattered flyer from the floor, but not before she noticed Jen reading the word "theater" across the top.

"What's that?" Jen asked.

"Nothing." Maggie shoved the paper in her pocket.

Grasping her satchel, Maggie sighed at the quizzical expression on Jen's face. Unsure she wanted to have the impending conversation, she started out the door. Jen grabbed the last two cups of cider and followed.

Maggie had known Jen since college. But could she trust Jen with this crazy struggle? The flyer had haunted her for several days. Her conflicting emotions ran much deeper than the information on the flyer. They were rooted in her identity.

Maggie loaded the back of the van while Jen caught up to her. Planning the Festival of the Trees had pushed her edginess aside. Now that it was over, her restless spirit and wandering mind would have nothing to tire them out.

Maggie was about to say something to Jen when she noticed one of the designers wrestling to get a box in her car. She and Jen crossed the parking lot to see if she needed help. As the box began to fall apart, Maggie grabbed one end.

"Can we help you? There may be some fresh boxes inside." The woman kept shoving the box as if something would magically make it fit. The box won the battle as glittered decorations burst out and Christmas tree balls rolled away.

"Ugh. Sorry, I know you want to leave, but yes, I could use some help." The woman leaned against the four-door sage Toyota with "Stanton Designs" on the side. "My niece was supposed to help me, but she ended up with a school function of her own."

Maggie and Jen helped scoop the decorations up. Handing her a bundle of garland, Maggie offered, "I can go grab another box."

The lady shoved the remaining decorations in the car. "Thank you, but at this point let's just toss it in the trunk and I'll get it sorted and stored tomorrow at the office."

The three of them tucked the lights, garland, and ornaments in the Toyota's trunk with a slam.

Unsuccessfully trying to brush glitter from her red argyle sweater, the woman thanked them for their help.

"I don't think we had a chance to meet earlier. I'm Maggie Nelson." Maggie extended her glitter-specked hand.

"I'm Nora St. Claire, one of the designers. You look so familiar to me." Nora stood a petite five feet tall. Her brown hair was pulled into a tight ballerina bun.

"You do too." Maggie tilted her head to think.

Jen's eyes widened. "Wait a minute, Nora, Nora Samuels? From college?" Jen pointed to herself and Maggie. "Jen Baker and Maggie Fenwick!"

Nora jumped in. "Yes, yes. Maggie and Jen, I remember you both. Oh my goodness, it's been years!"

Jen extended her hand to shake Nora's. "It's Jen Stephens and Maggie Nelson now."

Nora drew her hand to her chest. "And it's Nora St. Claire now. I'm an interior designer. Do you work at the school?"

Jen shook her head. "No, I'm a part-time personal trainer, and Maggie is a domestic goddess." Her hands went up in air quotes. "She gives a lot of her time to volunteering."

Maggie swatted at Jen. "Watch that. I work hard—kids, the house, volunteering." The roles rolled off her tongue like they were no big deal. They were a big deal. She was so much more than her roles in life.

They stood in the parking lot under the buzzing light that kept flickering as they caught up on their lives since college.

"So, any kids with your Prince Charming?" Jen asked.

A shadow fell over Nora's otherwise spring-like nature. "No ... no kiddos. I'm not married anymore." An awkward silence brushed through the circle.

Maggie gave Nora her number. "It's so good to catch up with you, Nora. We'll pull Jen away from the gym sometime and have lunch."

"That'd be great." Nora reached in her oversized bag and gave Maggie her freshly printed Stanton Designs business card.

The three hugged and promised to get together soon.

Back at her van parked next to Jen's hybrid car, Maggie grabbed her cup off the roof. The hot cider was now cool enough to drink. Jen did the same, and then she hugged her best friend.

"How fun running into Nora. She looks the same ... skinny and well-dressed. Guess some people age well."

"She always was a striking girl. Yes, always well-dressed and put together. Funny to see her get so frustrated." Maggie opened her door to get in.

"Mag, let's catch up this weekend. I can tell something's up with you."

"We'll catch up. Promise."

As she drove home, Maggie's emotions stirred inside her like the leaves whirling in the wind. She loved that in Oakdale, Indiana, they experienced all four seasons, including the colorful leaf changes in autumn.

Her thoughts fluttered from Nora, Jen, college, and the carefree days of being young and having endless energy, to doing community theater—the stage, the roles she had played. She remembered the excitement of a production from the first script read to the final curtain.

At a stoplight, Maggie reached into her pocket for the flyer. The audition wasn't what troubled her. Why wouldn't Dan support her interest in this? Going back into the theater might not solve the real problem. *Who am I?*

Despite her weariness, Maggie cleared the clutter from the backseat, delaying going inside to Dan and the kids. She tussled the box and her satchel, but made it inside with everything. Leaving the heap in the entry, Maggie heard Dan and the kids giggling in the den. Turning the corner, she was caught by the sight of Dan between Danny and Emma. Maggie stepped in with a song the children loved.

"Three little monkeys sittin' on a fence ..." Laughing, Emma and Danny jumped up and hugged their mother. Closing the storybook, Dan stood.

"These little monkeys need to head to bed." Dan leaned over to kiss Maggie. "How did it go?"

Danny and Emma ran upstairs to brush their teeth.

"It went very well. We'll have totals on Monday, but we sold all the trees, so we know we made something. I'm exhausted and my feet are screaming."

Dan embraced Maggie. "Never doubted you'd succeed. I'm going to tuck the kids in. Can I get you something?"

"No, thank you. Tell them I'll be up in a minute to say good night. Then I'm headed to the bath."

Hanging up her coat, Maggie pulled the crumpled flyer out of the pocket. *You never doubted me?* Too tired to think about it or attempt another discussion with Dan, she shoved the thing in her purse and headed up to a warm bath and comfy bed.

Saturday morning Dan took the kids out for breakfast. This gave Maggie time to herself. She settled at the table with berry-blend tea and her calendar to plan their week. The silence was broken when the phone rang.

"Hello."

Jen's name popped on the phone screen.

"Hey, I heard Dan was taking the kids to breakfast. He called Mark to bring Brian. What if I head your way with some coffee, and we can catch up? And you can tell me about that mystery paper from last night."

"Good morning to you." Maggie smiled toward the phone. She knew Jen couldn't stand not knowing. They had been through a lot over the years. "Okay, come on over."

Thirty minutes later the doorbell rang, and Maggie opened the door. "You never ring the ..." Then she noticed Jen's hands were full.

Jen balanced their two drinks and a bag as she stepped in. "Just like you like it—steamy, mocha with whip. One orange scone for you and a blueberry muffin for me."

"You must really want me to spill my guts—chocolate and whipped cream." Maggie closed the door, and the two headed for the kitchen table.

"You did an outstanding job on the fundraiser. I'm worried about you, though."

"Thank you. As tired as I was last night, I'd do it again. It's a good fundraiser for the school, and I don't mind helping where I can."

Taking her first sip, Maggie continued, "I want to tell you what's going on, but to be honest, I feel a little crazy right now. I picked up a flyer from the Oakdale Community theater." She stirred her coffee, considering the right words. "They're holding auditions for the spring production in a few weeks, and I'm thinking about trying for a part ... but I'm not sure Dan wants me to."

Jen touched Maggie's wrist. "Mag, you don't sound crazy. You loved theater when we were in college."

"I know. At first, Dan blew it off when I started talking about it. His reaction surprised me. I kept trying to explain to him that I love being a mom and a wife, but I have this ache inside to do something that's just for me, you know?" Maggie took another warm sip. "Dan didn't understand, and then he got frustrated and started talking about how this wasn't a good time. He's got stuff happening at work, and he counts on me at home. Then I got frustrated, because he wasn't listening to me. And well, we didn't get anywhere but upset with each other. So, I stopped talking about it."

Jen nodded in understanding. "There's nothing wrong with wanting something of your own."

Maggie took a pensive bite of her scone. Jen didn't try to jump in to fix anything. The wonderful part of confiding in a best friend was being heard, not fixed. Maggie broke the warm silence. "This sounds so selfish when I say it aloud. It's not meant to be. My family is important to me. But I want to do something around my interests. I feel like being a mom and a wife are all I'll ever do. Jen, I'm feeling antsy like I could crawl out of my skin. New haircuts, manicures, and pedicures haven't cured it. I thought by the time I hit my forties, I'd have life figured out, but I don't. I feel like I'm losing my identity."

Jen lowered her steamy cup of tea. "As women dedicated to our families, it's an easy place to find ourselves in. How do we manage self-care without becoming selfish? Were you specific with Dan? Or did you kinda-sorta dance around the idea of it?"

Maggie gave a little smile. "You know me too well. I keep thinking I should put my desire to audition on the back burner until the kids are older. There is so much to do for them and Dan right now. He reminded me about the promotion he's up for at the bank." Maggie's voice caught and tears started to pool.

Jen reached over and squeezed her arm. "Maggie, you are an outstanding, dynamic woman who has more energy than ten supermoms. You don't seem like yourself. And I can count on one hand the times I've seen you cry. Wherever this desire is coming from, it must run deep." Jen nestled her cup. "I'm no parenting expert, but I think the kids need to see us doing things we love outside of being their moms. They should get to see us as whole people and not just their parents. It's like running into a teacher out in public. Kids don't think their teachers do anything but teach. Have you prayed about it?"

"I've tried. Sometimes the words feel whiny, and other times I feel like I'm sitting at the feet of my heavenly Father pouring out my heart. And you're right. I think the kids would get a kick out of it. I took them to see *A Christmas Story* last year. They loved it. And since the play is *The*

*Wizard of Oz*, they'd enjoy it." Maggie squirmed in her chair, stirring the whipped cream into her coffee. "Jen, I love my kids and Dan so much, but who am I when I'm not being a mom or a wife? Sounds crazy, huh?"

The comfort of sitting with a friend hung in the air. *Why isn't it this easy with Dan?*

"I don't know what to tell you other than to encourage you. It sounds like you and Dan need to talk more." Jen nudged Maggie's hand. "Even if you decide not to audition this time, this is something you love, and you're going to want to do it. He needs to understand your feelings. Of course, you know if you commit to something like this, it will shake up your perfect schedule, organized home, and planned life."

Maggie gave a little chuckle, "You're funny. Yes, I do like order in my little part of the world."

As the two friends finished their tasty drinks with the warmth of conversation, Maggie felt her anxiety melt away. Jen had always known what to say.

Monday evening, Dan got home from work between five-thirty and six o'clock. Maggie could count on his arrival most days. Danny and Emma were sitting at the kitchen table doing homework. Dinner would be ready at six-thirty like always. A standard issue weekday evening. He set his briefcase down and approached Maggie with a kiss. "Hello, sweetheart."

"Hi, honey. Dinner will be ready soon."

Dan kissed Emma on the cheek and scuffed Danny's hair. "What's the homework of the day, guys?"

In unison, both answered:

"Multiplication tables."

"Science project."

Both kids were eager to explain what they were doing. Emma jumped up from sitting on her knees. "I'm doing multiplication tables!"

Dan nodded to Emma. "What is one million times zero?"

Scrunching her nose, Emma replied, "We haven't gotten that far. I'm only on my fives."

"So have you already done your zeros?" Dan asked. He watched Emma's face light up.

The answer came as if a switch turned on. "Daaaaddd, that's not fair. You tried to trick me."

Dan gave Emma a side hug. "Danny, what's our project this year?"

Throwing his shoulders back attempting to stand taller, Danny sounded matter of fact. "I'm in fifth grade, Dad, so you can't help me. It has to be all my work."

"Oh, okay, so what are *you* doing?"

"I don't know. All the ideas the teacher gave were cool, but we can't use any of them. We have to come up with our own." Danny slumped.

"You'll figure it out." Dan surveyed the savory-smelling dinner. "Mag, dinner smells wonderful. Hey, didn't we have one of those books around here with a hundred science experiments?"

Maggie continued to stir the spaghetti sauce. "Yes, we do. It's on Danny's shelf in his room."

Danny perked up and ran to his room. "On my shelf? Thanks, Mom."

Turning to her daughter, Maggie doled out the pre-dinner duties just as she did each evening. "Emma, will you set the table for dinner?"

"It's Danny's night."

"I know, but he can pour our drinks and do the table tomorrow night."

Emma went about setting the table. Dan disappeared upstairs to change out of his suit. Maggie shook her head. In her well-organized world, too many things were predictable. The evening routine could be handled with her eyes closed. Since crawling out of her skin wasn't an option, and she didn't want to run away, she might as well have a serious talk with Dan about the audition.

# CHAPTER TWO

Dan sat in his recliner, lost in his newspaper. The kids were asleep in their beds. This part of the evening made it easy for Maggie to slip off by herself. But not tonight. She paused on her way to the kitchen.

"Honey, I'm going to make a cup of tea. Would you like one?"

"No, thanks." Dan replied without so much as a glance.

Maggie returned, steeping the tea bag in her flowered mug. "Can I talk to you about something? And I need you to listen with an open mind."

"Never thought of myself as closed-minded, but okay. What's up?"

Taking a deep breath—*Lord, please give me the words*—Maggie sat on the edge of the sofa and dove in. "I want to audition for a role in the spring production at the community theater."

Dan's shoulders dropped.

Not a good sign, but Maggie didn't let that stop her. "The kids are in school seven hours a day ... the house is practically running itself, and I want something more than volunteering at church and school. Something uniquely mine. I want to rediscover that feeling I had on stage in college."

Dan put the newspaper down in a crumple. "Oh, Maggie, we're having this conversation again? I asked you to wait. Let's get the kids a little older and me through this project at work. Sometime in the next year or so would be a better time."

His words stung. Maggie's face burned with hurt and anger. He wasn't listening, or maybe not hearing. There was a time when he hung on every word and encouraged every adventure. Now it seemed conversation had to fall into the category of Dan or the kids to be supported.

Maggie lowered her head, hoping to muster up the courage to fight for what she wanted.

*Fight to find yourself again!*

"Dan, please, I am losing myself. I am getting lost between being your wife, which I love, and being a mom, which I also love. I just want something of my own to do."

"Losing yourself. What are you talking about? You're the glue that holds our home and family together. Are you telling me that's not enough?" Dan stood and paced to the other end of the room, raking his hand through his hair.

Maggie shook her head. Her anger could not be contained. "If I didn't have a calendar, I would think it's 1950! You talk as if what I'm asking is crazy. You know women escaped the daily grind of carpool, laundry, and cooking a long time ago. I don't have to ask permission. I'm asking if you would support me taking on an activity of my own. I say little enough about your golf and tennis."

Dan made a hard turn. His eyes pierced Maggie's. "Hold on a minute. Golf and tennis are, more times than not, work-related."

Maggie stood and walked to the window. Blurting out what she was thinking wouldn't help. *How did we get so far off-track from being each other's fan?*

Dan joined her, putting his hands out. The tension in the room was as tight as the muscles in her shoulders.

"I'm sorry. I shouldn't have said that. Baby, I'm under a lot of pressure at work right now, and I just don't see how this could work with the kids' schedules and mine. I do count on you to carry things around here."

"Fine. I didn't say I wouldn't be able to balance both. I may need you to step in some—in the evenings. Do bath and bedtime."

"What if the evenings you need me, I need to work?"

"Then I'll ask Jen. You're making problems when we don't even have all the information—and there is the small task of auditioning. There will be plenty of talented actors who audition. I'm not the spring chicken actress I once was."

The levity gave them both room to breathe and catch the other's eyes. Leaning forward to touch forehead to forehead, both smiled.

In unison, they said, "I'm sorry." They laughed. After a kiss, Dan pulled away.

"I'm so sorry. I don't want you to ever feel like all you're good for is carpool, laundry, and cooking. You're a wonder woman, Maggie. You can succeed at anything you put your mind to. I was your number one fan in college, and I will be there with roses on opening night. I just don't know how all this is going to work."

Maggie leaned into Dan, and he held her close. "Like I said, I still have the matter of an audition. Let's take it one step at a time."

Dan pulled her even closer. Feeling the warmth of his strong arms reminded Maggie of Dan's strength in so many rough times they had faced together. This was her Dan, loving and supportive. "I'll put it on the family calendar."

Dan smiled at the mention of the family calendar. “I’m sure you will. I love you.”

“I love you. Thank you for hearing my heart on this.”

Dan reached for Maggie before she walked away, “So, uh, there aren’t any love scenes in this play, are there?”

Maggie chuckled. “I don’t think so, unless Dorothy falls for one of the Munchkin guys. They’re doing the *Wizard of Oz*. Of course, directors can sometimes add their own spin on things.” They shared a laugh, a hug, and a reassuring kiss.

With a renewed spirit the next morning, Maggie began her day of chores and marking errands off her list. She took the kids to school, then headed to the theater to get more information and sign up for auditions. Located within a few blocks of the university, the theater sat between student apartments and campus. The shaded parking lot was surrounded by well-aged oak trees. The leaves were turning colors of gold and red. The morning air was fresh like her perspective on life. A new adventure beckoned.

When Maggie opened the door to the theater, the whoosh of air smelled of musty old wood. The young girl at the desk boasted white and blue hair, a T-shirt and overshirt, jeans, and a nose piercing. Maggie’s stomach turned as she felt self-conscious about her age and how long she had been away from acting. The artsy look no longer meant baggy oversized sweaters and torn jeans. She checked her reflection in a framed production poster of Jerry Herman’s *Mame*.

“Um ... excuse me.” Maggie stepped to the desk, tucking a stray hair behind her ear.

The young girl looked up from the book she was reading and smiled. “May I help you?” Her voice was friendlier than Maggie had expected.

"Yes, yes, I'm wondering about the upcoming auditions for the spring play. What do I need to know about auditioning?"

The girl stood. "Oh, is your daughter wanting to get involved in theater?"

Another blow to her ego. Maggie grinned and made every effort to sound breezy. "No, I'm interested. I'm asking for me. I'm Maggie Nelson, and I did some acting in college and thought it would be fun to give it another go."

"I'm so sorry, Mrs. Nelson. Most of the folks who have come by are asking for their children. We're doing *Wizard of Oz,* so there's lots of young interest. I'm Sara Biddle, the theater receptionist-slash-unofficial intern." Sara's face softened. "So, you did theater in college?"

Maggie relaxed a little. "Yes, plays on campus and a few at a community theater after college."

"Why did you get out of acting?" Sara asked, pulling out a clipboard.

"Well, after college, my husband and I got married, and I guess life just started happening. His career launched and we started a family. You know ... normal life." Maggie fidgeted with a pen sitting on the counter. Was she talking too much?

"That's cool." Sara slid the clipboard across the desk. "This is our sign-up sheet. Put your name, phone number, email, and what role you'd like to audition for. The director, Jim Preston, may have you read for other parts, but he'd like to know the role you're interested in."

The role—Maggie hadn't thought about which role. What role would she like to read for? She thought for a minute while Sara busied herself reaching for a box behind the desk.

"I hadn't thought about which role. I guess one of the witches would be fun."

Sara smiled in agreement. "Sure, you would be an outstanding witch." The statement sounded so funny, they both laughed. Sara's hand covered her mouth. "Oh, I'm so sorry. I didn't mean anything by that."

"It's fine. If you asked my kids, I'm sure they would agree."

The corners of Maggie's eyes turned up as she smiled at Sara. "It's okay. I know I'm going to be a little older than most of those who will audition." She completed the information and handed the clipboard back to Sara.

"Thank you. Here's your script. If you can, we ask for a five-dollar deposit on the script to help pay for them. If you get a part, you can keep it. If not, we ask you to turn it back in." She nodded. "Community theater ... got to love it."

Maggie removed a five-dollar bill from her wallet and handed it to the intern.

"Thank you, and break a leg at auditions. They will be held here. Hey, do you want to see the auditorium?" Sara marked "paid" by Maggie's name.

"Sure. I've got a few minutes."

"Follow me." She waved Maggie forward as she set off with a perky step. "This playhouse was built in the 1920s. That's part of our challenge. With the old building, it cost a fortune to do new lights and sound. While the new lights don't weigh what the older ones do, hanging them is harder with the older brackets."

Walking into the auditorium, Maggie felt goosebumps crawl up her arms. A thought of her father surprised her, but it shouldn't have. He had loved the theater. This was their thing—the activity they had always done together. She touched her nervous stomach as she followed Sara down the aisle toward the stage. It was impossible to miss the well-worn red shag carpet and the frayed, overstuffed seats. The brass number plates were dulled by the decades of dreamers who had sat in the seats. The creak of the aged wood echoed as Sara stepped onto the stage. Maggie followed.

Turning to look out from the stage, Maggie was washed in the spotlight like the warmth of summer sunshine. Her goosebumps disappeared. The two women stood in silence. Although the air smelled dusty, it didn't matter in the spotlight.

A friendly voice broke the silence. "Hello."

Maggie turned toward the man walking out from backstage.

"Jim Preston." Sara moved to introduce Maggie. "This is Maggie Nelson. She stopped by to sign up for auditions. Maggie, this is our executive director."

Jim stepped forward, khakis and a denim shirt draped over his slender six-foot-something frame. He reached out to shake Maggie's hand. "Hello, Maggie Nelson, good to meet you." His voice was husky enough to be masculine without being overbearing. The lines at his eyes demonstrated a little age, but the sparkle in his eye radiated youth. He held her hand in the welcoming shake a little too long. It was warm and rough enough to show he worked with his hands.

Maggie returned his greeting with a smile, politely pulling her hand out of the greeting. "Good to meet you."

"Always a pleasure to meet fresh talent interested in our little theater."

"I don't know about being fresh talent." Maggie smirked. "It's been a while since I've stepped on a stage."

His eyes showed amusement. "As you know, any new talent in community theater is fresh. We tend to have the same actors audition for all our plays. Can't wait to hear you read."

With a slight nod, Maggie replied, "Thank you."

"I'll let you and Sara finish. I'm working on some broken riggings."

As Jim disappeared backstage, Sara turned to Maggie. "He is such a cool boss, totally laid back, and does everything around here—fixing stuff, directing, and running operations."

"He seemed nice, but I wish I didn't know he was going to be the one I'll be reading for. Now I'm a little more nervous about it. His name sounds familiar. Is he from the Preston family with all the historic landmark plaques around town?"

Placing her index finger to her lips and lowering her voice, Sara said, "Yes, but he doesn't talk about it at all. We never say anything. Not sure what the deal is with his parents and grandparents." Breaking out of her secret tone, she went on. "Anyway, he won't be the only one at auditions. He invites a couple of the board members to be there. We have several with theater experience. Other board members just come to the meetings and make donations."

At the door to the auditorium, Maggie nodded as she took in the familiar feel of an auditorium, a stage, and the dusty smell of an old theater.

*Yes, this feels good.*

# CHAPTER THREE

Jen breezed into the gym, tucking her blonde locks back in a hair band, and wearing her favorite pink yoga pants and a T-shirt from the spring color run. The weather was still deciding if it was summer or fall, so today was a T-shirt day. She made a quick stop at the front counter for messages. Daisy Morris, the gym receptionist, greeted her. Daisy always seemed happy to see everyone coming in.

"Hey, Jen," Daisy said in her singsong manner, "Kevin wants to see you."

"Okay," Jen said as she stepped behind the desk to the wall of cubby mailboxes. "What's going on?"

"Don't know. He was working on the schedule for the next couple of months and is considering the New Year's rush."

Checking her mailbox, Jen sighed.

*Kevin's going to want me to take on more classes or take a bunch of middle-aged couch potatoes through a spring boot camp. Not sure I'm up for it. I'll catch him later.*

Kevin Jones carried his six-foot-three-inch stature well. He was in shape, as was necessary for the job, but he wasn't one of those guys with biceps like tree trunks who lumbered when he walked. While he made sure the gym shop had the latest in activewear in the small shop, he seemed to be stuck in the '70s, always wearing a matching sweat suit jacket and pants. Where did people buy velour anymore?

"Good morning."

Jen closed her eyes. *Caught.* She turned around to see him flashing a toothy smile. He carried himself with overconfidence.

"Good morning, Kevin. Daisy said you wanted to see me. Here I am."

"Can you step in for a minute? I want to talk to you about the schedule."

She looked around and shook her head. "Uh, I need to get ready for my Rock-Hard Abs class."

"I checked. That class isn't for an hour, and I'll have Daisy help with setup."

She obediently walked into his office and sat.

"Jen, I get the feeling you're a little bored with your class routine. And I was looking at a couple of options for you. You're sharp, and our clientele respond to your encouragement."

*Clientele* was the term Kevin always used for the members of the gym. He tried hard to make it sound more upscale than the month-to-month member gym it was. The difference was Kevin owned it with some local investors. It didn't have the national franchise name or glamor. And it didn't have the national marketing budgets others had, so they had to work hard at getting and keeping members.

"Thank you, Kevin. I don't know if I'm bored as much as thinking of ways to enhance my job as a personal trainer. I like working here. But January will be busy. I'm not excited about the first-of-the-year rush we get, because it fizzles in early February. It's more fun to work with folks who are committed longer term."

"I agree. And between you and me, we need more members to stick."

"Everything is okay with the gym, isn't it?"

"Sure, we're fine, but to compete, we must stay ahead with our offerings. Remember, the big national gym chains are handed marketing plans and sales materials from the national office. We have the flexibility to create our own." Kevin sat down at his desk and picked up a stapled set of papers and handed them to Jen. "So, I've drafted an idea to expand our fitness classes and personal trainer services by offering monthly classes on other relevant healthy lifestyle changes. Classes on nutrition and cooking for good health. I thought we could bring in a nutritionist to teach. Also, I was thinking of reaching out to the local high schools about doing a class for parents on nutrition and lifestyle for their children who are athletes. I'm ramping up our membership plans as well."

Reviewing the stapled pages, Jen nodded. The ideas were not the usual kinds of beginning of the year, goal-busting classes.

"Wow. I like this direction. It's different, and it gives members more reasons to come in and be involved. I'm wondering about the student athletes ... if we can't do something workout-wise for them in their off-season. Especially for the smaller schools that don't have weight rooms and decent facilities." Jen leaned forward and took a pen from Kevin's desk to make some notes.

"Sounds like a great idea. It's going to take some legwork, though, to find out who to talk to and meet with them."

Jen wasn't sure if she was about to get volunteered to help with her "great" idea. The gym didn't pay much, and that would put a lot more on her plate. But it sounded like a fun challenge.

Kevin began the pitch. "I'm going to need some help putting a plan together and in motion."

Here it came. Working part-time was her choice. Mark had supported her in working either part or full time.

"To do it right, I need to put someone in place who can be a negotiator and who can speak on behalf of gym operations, so they aren't having to run back to me for decisions and to get something scheduled."

Jen could tell "the ask" was coming. Her face gave her suspicions away.

Kevin held up his hand, halting her. "Hang on. Yes, I'm about to ask something of you, but you need to hear the entire offer."

She sat back in the consignment store wooden chair, prepared to hear him out.

"I presented my idea along with a preliminary budget to our investor group last night. They were impressed and are willing to invest the money we need ... including funds for me to hire someone to help execute the plan. Would you consider being my assistant general manager, keep whichever classes you like teaching the best, and work with me to implement our new program?"

Not the offer Jen was expecting.

"I'll handle the student athlete program. You plan and market the personal fitness and healthy living classes. And yes, there is a raise involved," Kevin added.

"Wow. Sounds interesting. I wasn't thinking about a change, but I like the ideas you've started with." Jen looked back at the document. "Might be fun."

"Jen, you've been with us since we opened the doors on our struggling enterprise. You're doing a wonderful job engaging our clientele, and you seem to care about their fitness goals. Any of the business operations you don't understand, I can help you learn."

"I don't know much about the operations. I've never dealt with budgets and ..."

"I'll show you all that. It's easy. Our outside accountant does the hard part. Rose in billing will still do the bookkeeping. All you'll need to understand is the budgets and how to evaluate whether the programs are making money."

This ordinary day was becoming extraordinary. Jen knew this would mean more time at work—full time. But the idea sounded exciting, a more holistic approach.

"Kevin, this sounds terrific, but I'm going to need to talk to Mark about it."

As if knowing her concerns, Kevin further offered, "I know this would bump you up to full time. What if I gave you the flexibility you need to make sure Brian is taken care of? As long as you get the job done, it doesn't matter to me if you need to leave to pick him up or have him here some. I trust your professionalism and work ethic."

"Are you sure you don't sell cars on the side? My first thought was how this would work with Brian's school schedule." Jen pulled a pencil from behind her ear and toggled it between her fingers. "Any chance you could give me a job description with the salary offer for me to discuss with Mark? I want to be sure of your expectations before I make the decision." Jen tucked the pencil behind her ear. "It does sound fun though."

Kevin laughed, "No, I don't sell cars, but I may have to if I can't build this business a little stronger. I think you and I could work well together. I've started a description." A smirk highlighted his dimples. "And I've started an offer letter for you to take home today. Stop by on your way out, and if I'm not here, I'll leave everything with Daisy. It will be in a sealed envelope. You are the only one I've discussed this with. If you decide to take this position, we will hold a staff meeting."

The word *we* echoed through her thoughts. After five years in her present job, this position would be a promotion over her peers.

"Okay, fair enough. Thank you for the offer. Mark and I will talk tonight."

"If you're talking, and other questions come up, call me. I'll be at home. I know this may seem like I'm moving fast, but I've been thinking about this for a while. To be honest, mentioning you to the investors was a big part of their enthusiasm for the plan." He walked to the door. "I need to know something tomorrow." Another dazzling smile. "But no pressure."

"Thanks." Jen returned the smile. "No pressure."

Daisy raised a curious grin at Jen as she and Kevin walked out of his office. A closed-door meeting was rare.

"You all were in there for a while. Everything okay?" Typical puppy-dog curiosity from Daisy.

"Everything is fine. We talked about the schedule. Did you have a chance to set up for my class?"

"Yep, you're ready to tighten some flabby abs."

Jen loved Daisy's youthful spirit. It reminded her of herself a few years ago and still some now.

Her fitness and yoga classes went well. She felt a new energy with her students. Did she want to leave this role? Like Maggie back in the day, Jen had had to work to help pay for college. She taught step aerobics, and Maggie waited tables.

She and Maggie had met during their freshman year while standing in line to sign up for the work-study program. Jen was very much a free spirit, standing in line juggling books and forms. Maggie noticed her disheveled balancing act and offered help. Their friendship budded, and now neither one could imagine life without the other. Jen was Maggie's voice of adventure and no worries. Maggie fostered a little order in Jen's world.

As promised, the envelope was in her mailbox at the end of the day. Tucking it into her bag, Jen headed to the school to pick up Brian.

*Lord, what am I to do with this opportunity?*

Pulling into the school parking lot, Jen spotted Maggie's car and an empty space next to it. Stepping into the gym to pick up Brian, Jen saw Maggie on her way out.

"Hey, Mag, let me grab Brian, and we'll walk out with you."

Juggling the science project materials Danny had thrust in her arms, Maggie called over her shoulder, "Let me meet you at the car."

"Be there shortly." Jen turned to the teacher with the clipboard. "Brian Stephens, number 712."

Maggie's kids were in the van as Jen and Brian approached.

Brian looked up at his mom. "Can I go see Danny and Emma while you and Ms. Maggie talk?"

With hands exaggerated on her hips, Jen looked at her son. "How did you know we would want to talk?"

"Oh, Mom, you always talk, talk, talk, in the parking lot." Brian teased.

"Is that so? Yes, climb in, and you kids can talk, talk, talk." Jen returned the mocking.

Brian ran over to Maggie's van.

"Hello, Brian, how was your day?" Maggie asked.

Half-ignoring her as he climbed in the van, Brian said, "Fantastic, Ms. Maggie."

Jen reached in her car and pulled out her smoothie from the gym snack bar.

"Let me grab my coffee, and I want to hear about your day. You seem excited about something." Maggie lifted her coffee from the cup holder and closed the driver-side door. The kids were talking and playing in the back of the van with the side door open.

Jen looked anxiously at Maggie.

"Give it up, girl. What is going on? You know you could never play poker." Maggie quipped.

"I know. But I've had to keep a straight face all day, and now I'm out of there, and it's killing me. I wanted to call you, but I was afraid someone would overhear. It was hard enough whispering a call to Mark from the locker room."

"Let's have it! What's your news?"

Jen explained the meeting with Kevin.

"This conversation was different." Jen's words accelerated, and her hands danced about. "I've been offered a promotion to assistant general manager to help Kevin roll out healthy living programming. He offered me a raise, and said I could keep teaching my favorite classes, and have flexibility with Brian. He wrote a job description and an offer letter for me to discuss with Mark."

Maggie nodded with every detail. "That's wonderful. It's a perfect fit! So, you'll be bumped up to full time?"

"Yes, but I think the flexibility and pay increase will make it work."

"How wonderful. Congratulations. Your excitement tells me you want to accept."

"It's kinda strange. At first, I thought he was going to try to get me to take on more work. Or this was one of his crazy ideas for marketing ..." Jen shrugged. "This one he really thought through. I like the possibility of taking a more holistic approach with our gym members. But Mark and I need to talk and pray over it. This is definitely a 'we' decision." She took a sip of her drink. "It might be fun to do something different."

"When he sees how excited you are, he'll be on board," Maggie said.

"You're right." Jen continued. "It will be a change, but it seems to fit my interests."

Maggie offered, "Well, let me know if you need help with Brian. I could pick him up and bring him to you at the gym."

"Thanks. I know they've offered me the freedom to schedule around him, but no doubt there will be days I'll need to call you." Her voice trailed off like the cool-down on the treadmill. "Enough about me. What about your schedule change? We may have to back each other up. What's new with the audition stuff?"

"Not a lot. I've started reviewing the script and the passages I want to audition with."

Jen looked over to check on the kids. "So what part are you going to read for?"

"I think one of the witches."

"Oh, the kids'll get a kick out of that."

The two friends chatted back and forth until it was obvious the kids needed to get home. Their two families were almost as close as Maggie and Jen. The kids played together as if the three were siblings, but their threshold was limited. The three kids jumped out of the van.

Just a little out of unison, they demanded, "Can we go over to the playground?"

Maggie and Jen looked at each other.

"Sorry guys, not today. I saw Mrs. Fitzpatrick leave, which means the gate's been locked."

Crestfallen, the kids started to head back to the van.

"Come on, Brian. We need to get home." Jen turned to Maggie. "Thanks for listening. Say a little prayer for me. I need to be sure this is a good move."

"You got it." The dear friends hugged and headed for their respective vehicles.

On the ride home, Jen sang along to the music on the radio. Brian shook his head at his mom. Her talk with Maggie left her feeling more excited about the new job. She was more confident that this was what she wanted. *Now if only Mark will agree with me.*

# CHAPTER FOUR

Jen had dinner on the table, taco night, when Mark came through the door. Tossing his keys in the bowl by the door, he sidled up to Jen as she arranged the bowls of toppings on the counter. "Hello, beautiful."

Jen gave him a quick kiss and a tight hug, then started in with her exciting news. "Hey to you. I'm so glad you're on time. I've got a ton to talk to you about."

Mark let go, his eyes curled with a smile to follow. "Okay, no 'how was my day?' It's all about you tonight."

Jen swatted at him. "Oh, you. Kevin gave me the envelope with an offer letter and job description. I haven't opened it yet. Wanted us to look at it together."

"Should I be worried? He's always had eyes for you, you know."

She grimaced and dived in. "He has not."

Mark stroked his chin, fuzzy with the start of a beard. Jen had complimented him after it started. That was enough encouragement to let it grow. "Hmm, not sure about that guy." He wrapped his arms around his wife. "It was hard to hear everything you were saying on the phone earlier. But what I did hear sounded interesting."

Jen began to share more about the job, including what she had whispered into the phone that morning, her words and gestures flying. "He wants me to work with him to establish the topics, secure the speakers, and promote healthy living programs." Jen stirred the sour cream. "It's a holistic approach that may help new members stay engaged. This will give a little something extra for our current members too. He says there's a raise involved. I can choose to keep any of my favorite classes I'm teaching now, and I still have the flexibility to pick up Brian in the afternoons."

Holding up his hands, Mark stopped Jen. "Hold on a second. First, this is going to take you to full time. Sweetie, I didn't think you wanted to work full time."

Jen stepped back with dimpled eyebrows and shrugged her shoulders. Mark picked up the mail from the counter. It was times like these that her free spirit got away from her. "Well, I hadn't thought much about the time, other than having to make sure I schedule things to pick up Brian. You're right, I wasn't looking for full time, but I like the concept. Although there may be some Saturdays ..." Mark stopped sorting the mail and glanced directly at Jen. She stopped talking. These were all the details they needed to talk out. Mark always asked the hard questions and was terrific at helping her break down opportunities to make the best decision.

"Weekends, Jen. Really? You want to work weekends?" Mark's nodding was changing to a little frustration. Jen reached in her bag and handed him the sealed envelope.

"No, it's one Saturday every now and then. It will be a change for us. And if it's only a Saturday here or there, that's okay with me, if you and I both have peace about the job overall."

Mark handed the envelope back to Jen. "This is your opportunity. You open it first, and then, we'll go over the details together." He waited for Jen to open the envelope. "I'm not trying to be a party-pooper here. It's obvious you're excited about this. I just want to be sure no one is taking advantage of you. This role does sound like something you'd be good at."

The document she pulled from the envelope was three pages plus a cover letter. Jen read the letter with a bulleted list of general job duties and the salary. She smiled and handed it to Mark, while she read through the job description. "It looks like everything he described, including the flexibility with Brian. And the raise could help us with some of our other goals." Jen set the document down. She reached across the table with her slender fingers and interlocked with Mark's strong hands. Their eyes met, and both took a deep breath. She was excited. He was being cautious. Looking into his green eyes, Jen spoke earnestly. "Let's back up, though. Are you okay with me working full time if I want to?"

Mark's voice softened. "Of course, if this is something you want to do, I'm all for it. I want you to be happy in any work you do, part time or full time, gym or no gym."

Over dinner, Mark, Jen, and Brian talked about other things, like Brian's day at school. After the dishes were picked up and Brian was in bed, Mark and Jen were alone again and could continue the conversation. They came together on the details. Jen needed to have the weekends clarified so it didn't start as every now and then, only to grow to every weekend. She didn't want to sound demanding, but she wanted to be sure the schedule worked. Mark assured her it was completely appropriate to get clarification and ask for more specifics on any of the job expectations. That night in bed, Jen's thoughts tossed and turned as much as she did. She went over and over the conversation she would have with Kevin. Mark reached for her hand.

"Nervous?"

"Sorry. A little. I'll settle down."

"It's going to be fine." Mark pulled her close in the darkness of their room and whispered a prayer for calm, confidence, and clarity. Listening to his prayer, she drifted off to sleep.

Daisy was in her spot with her perky smile. "You're in early."

With a peaceful spirit she knew came only from Mark's prayer and support, Jen greeted Daisy. "A little. I need to talk with Kevin before I get into my classes."

With a quizzical tilt of her head, Daisy commented, "Funny, Kevin was in early today too. Is something going on?"

Jen smiled, walking past Daisy's post at the reception desk. "Settle down. Everything is fine. He and I have some things to talk about before the day gets going."

Standing straight and ready to hopefully finalize the details and accept the job, she knocked on Kevin's half-opened door.

He looked up from his desk and the stack of papers he was reading. His computer was making the beeps and sounds of booting up. "Good morning. Did you and Mark talk last night? Do you have a decision?"

"Hold up a second. We spoke, and I've got a few questions."

Sitting down, Kevin gestured for Jen to close the door. "Have a seat. What are your questions?"

"Well ..." She began. "The salary works, but are there other benefits? And I want to be sure we're on the same page as far as weekends. I'm committing to full time. I'd like to be sure that the 'every now and then' weekend doesn't get out of control."

"Oh, I'm sorry. Yes, there are benefits, including vacation days, and we have an investment program for retirement savings. Vacation days begin accruing as soon as you say yes. Any weekend time will be designed around the way you set up the programming. So, if you know one weekend is better than another, schedule it to fit. Also, if we have a weekend event, I'm good with you trading time during the week so you're not working over forty hours in a week."

Some quick math in her head. "Okay, about the vacation days ... As an hourly employee, I had one week. Being fulltime and managing Brian on school breaks, would you consider an additional ten days?"

Kevin sat back in his chair with a grin. "You are a tough negotiator."

She sat back in her chair, as if they were at a stand-off, and hoped she hadn't overstepped the negotiations.

Kevin noticed. "It's okay—I'm joking. The investors want you to take this position. In addition to the increase in pay, yes, we can do a total of three weeks' vacation, but I would ask that you not take them during our busiest months of January and February if possible, and of course, we will do the retirement fund match I included in the letter."

A raise, three weeks paid vacation after the first year, and three percent to retirement. It was a good offer and better benefits than she and Mark had speculated. A peace washed over her like a cleansing breath at the end of yoga. *Lord, here we go.* Standing with confidence, she reached out to shake Kevin's hand.

"I'll take it."

With a pleased look, Kevin stood and shook her hand. "Thank you. I'll have Daisy get the staff together about eleven-thirty before the noon rush of clients. In the meantime, do you want to see your office?"

"Office? My current office is my locker and whatever corner of Daisy's space I can squeeze into."

Kevin led the way across the lobby, past the juice bar, to a door that Jen thought went to an old storage area. For all the time had Jen worked there, the open door had led to the dusty smell of cardboard boxes. The window had been covered with packing paper so gym-goers couldn't see inside. Now, opening the door released a waft of cinnamon air freshener. Kevin flipped the light switch to reveal a small office with a window that looked out at the cardio machines. Jen slowly walked in.

"We can have your locker moved in here if you like." Kevin chuckled. "I had the cleaning crew clear out the junk and move your desk in. The tech company is coming to set up your phone, so you'll have a direct extension, or Daisy can take messages like she does now when you're in class. Your computer should be here this afternoon."

Her eyes got bigger with each item Kevin mentioned—a phone extension, a computer. Walking over to the desk and chair, she could see they had been purchased new and not from one of Kevin's office auction sales.

"Have a seat. Try out your new space. Make it as personal as you like, but I would ask that the pictures you hang are framed. If you want a bulletin board, we can have one hung."

Kevin's pet peeve was when a bunch of stuff got stapled or taped to the wall. The papers got crumpled or outdated and no one remembered to take them down. He'd had an encased bulletin board hung and Daisy was given the responsibility of making sure the information was timely.

"Let me get into the job, and then I'll let you know if I need a board."

"Fair enough. Your work is going to need an office, with the phone calls and planning you will need to do. I hope this works for you. If the cardio area gets too loud for you, close the door." Kevin offered.

Jen tried to restrain her excitement—a benefit package and an office!

Daisy walked in, "There you all are." She stopped when she saw Jen behind the desk. "Wow, you've got an office?"

Kevin turned to Daisy in a direct manner. "I need you to call a staff meeting for eleven-thirty. It shouldn't take too long."

Daisy's nose scrunched and her head tilted to the right. Kevin spoke a little more directly. "I need you to do this now. It's already nine-fifteen, and I want folks to know about it before they plan to leave after their morning classes. We'll meet in the juice bar." Daisy turned on her heel and left the doorway. Kevin hesitated. "Daisy, come back here. I'm sorry if I was rude. Were you looking for one of us?"

"Yes, there's a guy from the phone company here, and I didn't know what he was talking about."

Nodding, Kevin said to send him to Jen's office.

"Oh, right, okay. Didn't know." Daisy wilted as she walked away.

Kevin turned back to Jen. "Her feelings are hurt way too easily. And according to my wife, I can be a little impatient when someone isn't thinking the way I am. Jen, it thrills me that we're going to work on this new phase of the business. I've got a couple of files to send you to review. You may not have planned to start on this today, so how about we talk tomorrow afternoon. I need to know what you want to do about your class schedule. Your first task may be getting a part-time person in here to teach the classes you don't want."

Kevin left Jen alone in her office. *Her office*. She wasn't quite sure what to think about this setup. She had never had an office. The closest thing to a desk she'd ever had was to pull a chair up to the end of the reception desk Daisy used. She walked over to the matching file cabinet and yanked on the handle. Having nothing in the drawer, it flew open with a clang. The sound startled Jen. Looking around to make sure no one outside her door heard, she pushed it closed. The phone installation guy stood respectfully at her door. Had he heard the clang of the drawer?

"Ms. Stephens?"

Around the gym, she was Jen. Only Brian's friends called her Ms. or Mrs.

"Yes, I'm Jen. What can I do for you?"

"I'm here to hook up your phone extension."

"Sure, let me get out of your way. I need to go get ready for class."

"I should be done by the time you're back. I have a couple of options on the phone number. Do you want to choose?"

"Choose my number? Sure, what are my choices?"

As he bent over, the tools on his tool belt clanged, and his lack of a regular belt revealed the band of his Fruit of the Looms. He began to unscrew the plate over the phone outlet. "Well, all the phone lines here have the same first three numbers. You can choose the last four. Your choices are 3323 or 0523."

Jen knew at once. "I'll take 0523."

He stood up, looking surprised at her decisiveness. "That was quick. I don't usually offer a choice because most women—please don't be offended—take forever to choose. Some have to write it down or act like they're dialing it."

The morning had gone well, Jen was feeling so blessed, and the number 0523 made her think of Brian—his birthday. An easy choice. Stepping out of the room, Jen looked back at her small office as if it might disappear without her in it. The clock in the main gym reminded her that the spin class started soon. She was hoping to call Mark, but it had taken longer with Kevin than she thought. Her stomach flopped when she thought about the staff meeting. Having back-to-back classes this morning would help take her mind off it. Everything seemed to be happening so quickly. *Am I ready for this? Will my instructor friends care or think I'm too uppity for them? I'll call Mark later ... from my new office.*

# CHAPTER FIVE

Maggie checked her look in the mirror and adjusted her brown curls behind her ears that displayed simple gold knot earrings. She was old enough to be the mother of many of the cast members. No need to try and look twenty something. She settled on jeans and a middleweight tan sweater that boasted wooden toggle buttons at the top of the V-neck opening. Her jeans fell somewhere between hipster and mom jeans. At five-foot-nine inches, she gained a half inch when she slipped on her low-heel ankle boots. The jeans and boots emphasized a tall, slender appearance. A navy jacket completed the ensemble. A glance in the mirror, deep breath, and she was satisfied with her look—casual, but not too casual.

With a bottled water and her script on the passenger seat, Maggie's index fingers tapped along with the hits of the '80s on the radio as she drove to the theater. Her thoughts bounced between *What am I doing?* to *I can do this* all the way there. Slowing down for a string of traffic on the interstate, Maggie checked her watch. Plenty of time. She changed the channel on the radio and found a song she knew the words to, so she began to sing as loud as she could. The effort helped her get a deep breath and relax her breathing, besides just being fun. The music took her back to her high school and college days, her younger self.

Pulling into the theater parking lot, she noticed there were a lot more cars than on her first visit. Competition. Maggie checked her teeth and hair once more before stepping out of the car with confidence and heading for the entrance.

Sara was at her post and recognized Maggie. Her hair was an unusual color combination this time—pink and purple. It matched her oversized sweater. She greeted Maggie with a teasing smile. "I'm so glad you made it. Wasn't sure if you would chicken out."

Taking another deep breath while shaking her jacket off, Maggie replied, "Nope, didn't chicken out. I'm ready to take the stage."

Coming around to take Maggie's jacket, Sara gave her some directions. "Here's your audition sheet. I completed it based on what we talked about. Did you change your mind about the witches?"

"No."

"Okay. Now, be ready—they may ask you to read from both the good witch and the bad witch parts."

"No problem. I rehearsed some on both."

"I'm sure you'll do well. Just go on into the auditorium, and when they call your name, hand Jim your sheet." Reaching for a hanger off the rack, Sara said, "And, Maggie, break a leg."

Exchanging smiles with Sara, Maggie gave a pull on the auditorium door and stepped in.

The seats were peppered with a variety of actors, old and young, male and female. Maggie was caught by the musty smell again. Choosing the second row on the left side of the aisle, she settled in. Jim gave her a grin. There was a woman who appeared to be older than Maggie sitting next to Jim with her own set of notes. Maggie smiled at both, remembering Sara telling her about guest directors who helped Jim with auditions.

After watching three auditions by actors who had done this more recently than twenty years ago, Maggie felt the butterflies bloom in her stomach. Then her name was called. She stood, handed Jim her audition sheet, and walked up the tattered red carpeted stage stairs. Turning toward the directors, she felt the warmth of the spotlight. The butterflies flew away, and she began.

Hunching over and wringing her hands, Maggie moved her eyes back and forth in a squint. *Evil. I am evil.* She began her lines as the bad witch. She had memorized a short part of the scene before the flying monkeys were released. When she was done, she stood tall and took a deep breath as the other actors applauded.

Jim smiled and nodded. "That was good. Can you shift gears and give us something of the good witch?"

Maggie agreed to and took a couple of steps to the side, shaking off the evil demeanor and turning on her sweetness. Three minutes later, she finished her monologue with a sway of her hand as if waving a wand. Applause scattered across auditorium from the other actors waiting to audition.

"Thank you, Ms. Nelson." The woman next to Jim said in a blunt and dismissive manner, allowing the *s* in "Ms." to last too long. "We'll let you know."

Maggie took the woman's indifferent tone as her cue to exit. "Thank you."

The other actors seemed to know each other and chatted between auditions. Not knowing if she should wait around or leave, Maggie decided to forgo the awkward standing around with no one to talk to. She quietly retrieved her jacket and headed for her car. The butterflies were back, whirling around as if they couldn't decide which way to fly. Not unlike Maggie and this whole idea of a role in a play. What was she chasing? Her youth? Was she being selfish? Was Dan right, the timing was not good now?

*Maybe I won't even be chosen. That would help with the decision.*

Alone in her car she whispered a quick prayer, "Lord, if this isn't right for me or my family, please show me in some obvious way."

It was still early for carpool, but Maggie didn't have enough time to go home. Deciding to treat herself to a coffee, she pulled into the coffee shop near the school.

# CHAPTER SIX

Settling into a corner table, Maggie noticed the variety of patrons scattered around. There were the coeds huddled around a table, their phones and laptops buzzing. The businessmen with laptops and briefcases at hand. And the two harried mothers trying for a conversation while placating their toddlers.

The jingle of the bell at the door drew Maggie's attention. Doing a double take, she realized it was Nora. She had been the consummate sorority girl in college—impeccable outfits, brown hair always pulled in a tight ballerina knot. She could have made Princess Di feel frumpy. Upon further observation, Maggie concluded that Nora had aged well. Fifteen years out of college, she had a few smile lines at the corners of her eyes showing, and she was still dressing to the nines. Maggie remembered Nora as being friendly, but they were never close.

Smirking, Maggie thought about how Jen and Nora had been like oil and water—Jen in her all-natural, simple beauty and Nora with her regimen. Maggie always felt somewhere in between the two, not having the simple, natural looks of Jen, but not wanting to be a slave to her wardrobe and makeup like Nora seemed to be.

Placing her order, Nora looked around and noticed Maggie. Some personalities were unforgettable. Nora darted toward her with a sunshiny smile. "Hi, Maggie."

"Nora. Good to see you again. Want to join me? I've got a few minutes before carpool."

"I'd love to. Let me run to the ladies' room."

The two enjoyed a quick visit, catching up on details neither remembered about the other. The conversation turned to families.

Nora blew on her coffee. "I know you have at least one child, or you wouldn't have been volunteering at Anchor Academy. Boy or girl?"

"I have one of each. Danny is in fifth grade, and Emma is in third."

Nora's coffee order was announced. "Let me get my coffee."

As she watched Nora add just the right amount of cream and sugar, Maggie wondered what her story was. Why wasn't Nora married? Guys in college always seemed to be at her beck and call. She was pretty and had a kind heart. And as Maggie recalled, she was a talented artist.

Nora returned to the table. "And you married Dan, right?"

Since Nora took the lead on the questions, Maggie had to follow. She told her about marrying Dan right out of college and starting a family. Not having much to add outside of being a stay-at-home mom, and volunteering at church and the kids' school, Maggie turned the conversation. "Enough about me. Tell me where you work?"

"I've recently taken a job at Stanton Designs." Nora smiled. "You wouldn't remember, but I was an art history major in college. I went back to school a few years ago to get an interior design degree. Better fit, and more job opportunities."

*Why did it take her so long to go back to school?*

"I love the work we do," Nora went on. "We're designing the interiors of the loveliest homes in Oakdale."

"I remember you being a talented artist. What do you like to do when you're not working?"

Nora looked down at her coffee. Stirred it slowly before she answered. "It's been a rough several years." She continued to stir.

"I'm sorry." Maggie sat back in her chair. "I didn't mean to pry."

The sadness rolled across Nora's face. "No, you're not prying. It's just ..." Nora shifted in her chair. "My husband, Seth, died five years ago. I know it sounds like a long time, but I'm just now starting to feel like the grief is lifting. Finishing interior design school and getting a job has been a huge step forward for me."

Maggie's hand drew to her heart. "Oh, Nora. I am so sorry. How terrible."

"It's okay. Every day it gets a little easier. The first couple of years were awful. You see, he was killed in the line of duty. He was on the police force. The case took what felt like forever to solve. It made it hard to heal. Once the case was closed, and I wasn't hearing about it all the time, I felt like I could start to rebuild my life." Nora looked away. The pooling tears subsided.

Maggie sat quietly. What did you say to such a tragedy? A young couple's life torn apart.

The silence was broken by a crying baby at the next table. Maggie shook her head. No children. They hadn't had time.

Nora dabbed the one escaped tear, took a deep breath, and recovered her smile. "Bet you're glad you ran into me and my sob story. I'm so sorry to bring the mood down."

"Heavens no! You've been through something no one should have to go through. I'm so sad your time with Seth was cut short."

"It was a ... a struggle. But God is faithful. He has been my strength. I've managed to get a career going, and to answer your question about the rest of my time, well ..." Nora paused and smiled again. "My evenings and weekends are a little quiet. I have some church friends I see every week. We do lunch after church. Other than that ... not a lot going on. I'll rebuild a social life again. It's difficult to be around people who don't know about Seth."

"You don't want to feel like you have to explain." Maggie reached across the table and touched Nora's arm. "Thank you for telling me. I'd love to have you over sometime for dinner. Maybe get Jen and Mark."

Nora patted Maggie's hand. "Thank you. I loved running into you and Jen at the Festival of Trees."

Maggie noticed the time. "Oh, Nora, I'm sorry, I've got to get going. The time has flown, and I'm going to be late for picking the kids up."

Nora stood. Maggie reached over and gave her a hug. "Do you still have my number from the other night? Call me so we can catch up some more."

Maggie headed out the door, leaving Nora to settle back in the chair.

Pulling into the carpool line, Maggie saw Jen in the car ahead of her. When Jen looked up into her rearview mirror, she waved and signaled to Maggie to pull into the other lot after she got the kids. Maggie waved back and followed her instructions.

"Well, you didn't call me. How'd it go?" Jen stepped out of her car toward Maggie.

Her encounter with Nora had pushed the audition back in her thoughts. "Oh, that. It went well, I guess." Maggie shook her head, "I have no idea, and it's been so long since I've auditioned or been on stage. That Jim guy I met the other day was kind and said thank you. I couldn't get a feel for the woman director. She looked serious and never cracked a smile." Maggie shrugged. "Who knows?"

True to her encouraging personality, Jen offered, "I'm sure you did magnificent. What part did you read for?"

"Both the good witch and the wicked witch."

Jen smiled at her friend and nodded, "Yeah, you've got a little of both in you." The two laughed. Their three kids had jumped out of the car and were tossing a ball around in the grass.

Maggie gave Jen a little elbow nudge. "You've got more of an adventure going on than I do. Tell me about the job and your conversation with Mark. Was he supportive? Did you accept? I need details."

Jen beamed with excitement. "I took the job! After we talked it through, Mark was on board and encouraging about the whole thing. I was ready to just jump in, but he gave me some good questions to ask and some details to double-check before accepting. And when I went in, Kevin agreed to all my requests."

"Sounds intriguing. When do you start?"

"Right away. Mark, Brian, and I are going over after dinner to set up my office."

"An office, wow," Maggie said with a teasing grin. "Do you have a secretary too? Am I going to have to go through her to schedule time with my best friend?"

Jen shook her head with a small wave of her hands. "It's not like that at all, and you know it. Too much more corporate and I wouldn't have taken it. But I do have an office with phone and a computer. Because you're so dear to me, I'll give you my direct line. The part I'm looking forward to are the programs we're developing to give our clients healthier living options."

"I'm so excited for you. Please let me know if I can help with picking up Brian. Even if you have me drop him at the gym with you." Maggie gave Jen a hug. "Congratulations."

"I have no doubt I will be congratulating you in the next day or two on getting your part."

"We'll see. I hope I haven't jinxed myself with starting my list of how I'm going to manage home and rehearsals. Kids, load up, we need to get going."

"Call me tonight no matter how late. I want to hear as soon as you know." Jen waved as Brian climbed into her car.

# CHAPTER SEVEN

Dinner was the same routine as always. Maggie fixed dinner, the kids did their homework, and right on the button, at six o'clock, Dan came through the door. Maggie's immediate thoughts turned to June Cleaver from the show in the 1950s and '60s. Should she have her pearls and pumps on? It all felt so predictable, and what was her role in all of it?

*Capable mom, reliable wife.*

"Hey, sweetie." Dan greeted her as he dropped his briefcase by the door to the garage.

"Hey. How was your day?" *I do sound like June Cleaver. Why didn't I just end it with "dear" and set up the whole 1950s scene?*

Danny and Emma were excited to tell their dad about their day. Loosening his tie, he joined them at the table.

Stirring the vegetables and checking the roast, Maggie couldn't keep from checking the time every few minutes. It was after six, and there were no calls from the theater. She had even checked their website on the off chance the roles had been posted. Since getting home with the kids, she hadn't been able to stay busy enough to not wonder about her audition. Dan hadn't asked about it when they talked during the day. And the kids were oblivious to the whole thing. She had told them she was going to audition or "try out" as Danny kept saying, but they didn't realize it had been today.

The phone interrupted her thought, and Maggie jumped, flinging green beans out of the pot. Dan looked up and smirked. "Why are you so jumpy? It's just the phone." He got up to answer.

"Hello. Sure. Can I tell her who's calling?"

Handing the cordless phone to Maggie, Dan gave her a doubtful look. "It's some guy named Jim?"

"This is it." Maggie took the phone. She looked around for a way to talk privately. *I need to be in the other room. No, that would look too dramatic.* Dan turned his attention to the kids and Maggie turned her back to them.

"Hello, this is Maggie."

"Maggie, it's Jim Preston from the theater. I hope I'm not interrupting dinner."

"No, we haven't sat down yet." Maggie couldn't say anything else for fear of blurting out, "Just tell me, did I get a part?"

"Sorry to keep you waiting all afternoon. Mary and I had some very hard decisions to make."

"I'm sorry, who is Mary?" Maggie asked.

"Oh, you didn't meet her. Mary was there during the audition. She's a theater professor at the college who comes and helps me with auditions and, sometimes, with the productions."

Maggie made no comment for fear of saying something about how blunt and borderline rude she thought Mary was.

"Anyway, I've got an offer for you, and I hope you're not disappointed. I'd like you to be our stage manager and the understudy for the good witch."

Maggie felt her heart fall into her stomach. Stage manager. Understudy. Tears threatened to make an appearance. She hadn't considered an option other than a primary role.

"Hear me out. I'm sure you're disappointed. My challenge is it's going to be spring semester and several theater majors from the college procrastinated and didn't audition for any community plays. Now, they're trying to graduate, and they need a role. And because we get a lot of our resources from the college, I'm sort of forced to give them roles. I could use someone with experience and organization to help me run the production."

Maggie was trying to hear his explanation while her thoughts were bouncing around from disappointment to relief. Now he wanted her to be involved without being in the play. Maybe this was a better way to return to the theater. She didn't know how to answer. She should talk to Dan. This was a different commitment.

"Maggie, are you there?"

"Oh, I'm sorry. Yes, I'm here. So, you'd like me to stage manage and learn the role of the good witch."

"If you would, I'd appreciate it. I know it's not what you started out thinking, but I think you'd make a great asset to our production team."

"Thank you, Jim. That's kind. Do you mind if I call you back? I'd like to talk this over with my husband."

"Certainly. You can call me as late as eleven tonight or in the morning. Let me give you my cell number. First reading will be next Monday, but if you take the stage manager job, you and I need to get together this week."

Maggie took his number and promised to call him back. Hanging up, she wasn't quite sure what she felt about this new direction. Her prayer had been for a clear direction. *Was this clear?* It was a clear offer for a specific role for the spring production. It just wasn't what she was thinking. It was hard enough talking to Dan about auditioning. Now she wasn't going to be in the play but would have a much bigger role. Dan looked up, expectant, when Maggie turned around. She wasn't smiling, she wasn't crying.

"Are you okay?" He approached her.

"Yes, that was Jim Preston from the theater with my offer."

Dan hit his palm to his forehead. "Oh, yes, your audition was this morning. I am so sorry. I forgot to ask." Maggie shook her head and burst into tears.

"You forgot because you didn't want me to do it anyway!" Running from the kitchen, Maggie left Dan and her kids with dropped jaws.

As she threw herself on her bed, Maggie didn't understand the tears either. But they kept coming. Thoughts of her father crept in. He was always good at helping her sort out her feelings when they didn't make sense. The tidal wave of emotion left her swimming in confusion. Gasping for air, trying to regain her focus and confidence in who she was, she rolled over, sat up and reached for another tissue. There was a soft knock on the door.

"Hon, are you okay? I'm sorry I didn't remember your audition. Didn't mean to make you cry."

Maggie sniffled and wiped her eyes. They were red and starting to swell. "It's not you. I didn't get the part." She brought the tissue to her nose to catch a tear. "Well, I did get a part, but it's an understudy. Which means unless the actress can't perform, I'm not in the play. So, I'm sure you're glad to hear that."

With no reaction to her snippy remark, Dan sat next to her, waving the kids away from the door. "Mom's okay. Let us talk, and we'll be back down in a minute." Dan turned to Maggie. "Baby, I'm sorry you didn't get a part. Maybe another time. You know I wasn't sure how we were going to make this whole thing work anyway with rehearsals and my work and ..."

Maggie looked up. Her disappointment turned to anger. "You didn't let me finish, but now I know how shallow your support was ..."

Standing, she pulled out another tissue and walked away from the bed.

Dan rubbed the back of his neck and sighed. "What are you talking about? I supported you when you wanted to audition. I ..."

"You were hoping I'd fail."

"Not fail. I just didn't know ..." Dan turned away, rubbing the back of his neck again. He mumbled. "I'm sorry. Guess I wasn't as all in as I should've been for you."

Maggie was looking around and trying to decide where to go from there in the conversation. She hadn't told him the entire offer and hadn't had a chance to think it through for herself. One thing was clear—she wasn't going to let Dan's lack of support be her "out." In her heart, she loved the theater and producing a play—telling a story. Dan touched her shoulder.

"I don't want to fight about this. I'm sorry I'm struggling with you committing to something outside the house and the family. I'll work on it." Dan nestled close to Maggie and gave her a kiss on the side of her neck. Maggie didn't flinch. She took a deep breath, sniffed back the last of her tears, turned, and sank into his arms. Dan held her. He couldn't fix it, but he could hold her.

Maggie settled down. His arms were the one place in this world she always felt safe. Even though they were at odds, they loved each other. They would work it out.

Pulling away first, Maggie said, "There is something else you need to know about Jim's call. Before I tell you, I want you to know I'm not sure what my reply will be, so don't react. Okay?"

"Okay. What is it?" Dan took a step back as his expression became more normal.

"He's asked me to be the stage manager."

Dan smiled. "A perfect role for you with your organizational skills. You've kept our lives on track all these years. When do you need to tell him?"

"I told him I had to think about it. He said I could call him tonight or in the morning." Maggie paused to draw a tissue from the box, dabbing her nose and eyes. "I'm tired now. I'll call him after I take the kids to school in the morning. Let's go have dinner with the kids."

Dan stopped her. "What are you going to do?"

With her jaw set, she replied, "I don't know. I haven't decided yet. I'll let you both know in the morning."

# CHAPTER EIGHT

Jen found the best combination of workout attire and what she felt like were manager-type clothes. After considering what her first full day in her new role might look like, she wore her workout clothes in and took another outfit for after she taught. Checking her look in the mirror showed she had brushed her straight hair into the standard workout ponytail—planning to take it down or braid it when she changed. Wearing makeup felt awkward. Most days, Jen capitalized on her natural skin tones and applied a small amount of foundation and some mascara. Today, she might have overdone her look a bit with the blush, eyeshadow, and lipstick. But it was done, and checking her watch showed she needed to leave. Mark had offered to take Brian to school, but Jen wanted to get a feel for what her new normal would look like.

Jen descended the stairs into the living room where Brian was waiting for her, having eaten his toaster pastry while watching television. The six-year-old-old's eyes flashed wide like the cartoon characters he was watching. He scrunched his nose and giggled.

"Mommy, what's on your face?"

"Thanks, buddy, it's called makeup, and a lot of moms wear it." Her self-consciousness grew, even though she knew he was six and had no real understanding of looking appropriate for a work situation. Jen asked her son in a way a first-grader would understand, "Do I look weird or better?"

He shrugged. "You look fine. Just different." Typical boy.

Not knowing what this meant, Jen decided to drop it. "Ok, well, we need to get going. Take your plate and cup into the kitchen and get your backpack."

Pulling into school with minutes to spare, Jen saw Maggie was working carpool. Maggie checked her watch when Jen pulled up to let Brian out. Leaning into the car window as Brian ran into school, Maggie complimented her friend. "Wow, look at you. Are you ready for this new adventure, Ms. Assistant General Manager?"

Jen glanced at herself in the rearview mirror. "I know, the makeup may be a little much. But I need to do something different to establish my new leadership role. Please tell me I don't look like a clown."

"Oh, Jen, you're going to do an excellent job. You love all that healthy living stuff. How many articles have you tried to get me to read on food and exercise? Now you get to set up whole classes about this stuff. You may even entice this old body into the gym more often."

Jen returned the smile. "Thank you. I needed a little pep talk. Mark was out early this morning."

With the carpool line growing, Maggie stepped back from the car. "Go get 'em. Call me later. I want to hear all about it."

Jen took a deep breath and whispered a prayer before stepping out of her car. Her phone buzzed. Seeing it was Mark, she answered.

"Hey there, babe, are you at work yet?"

"I just pulled in."

"Good, I wanted to talk to you before your day began. I love you and will be thinking about you all day. Call me when you can."

Jen almost teared up. With a lump in her throat, she said, "Thank you, sweetheart. Now I know I can take on the day. I just don't know what it's going to be like with my coworkers. And then there is balancing my classes with the new job responsibilities."

"Be your wonderful self. Go in there and take charge without being demanding. You can do it. Call me when you get a minute. I love you."

"Thank you. I love you."

Jen's morning flew by. She had decided to keep her two Golden Yoga classes and wanted to make time for her own workout before hitting the desk job. The ladies in the Golden Yoga class reminded her of her nana growing up. Nana Carol had always been active, walking or playing tennis with her friends.

Daisy came in as Jen was picking up the final mats from her class.

"Jen, I've got a couple of messages for you."

Jen's back was to Daisy as she stepped into the storage closet. "Okay. Just a minute, and I'll be done here." Jen came out of the closet. "What messages do you have?"

Daisy looked at Jen, her eyes wide as free weights. "What happened to your face?"

"What do you mean my face? I'm fine."

"You better look in the mirror."

She turned to look.

"Oh my gosh!" Her hands went to her cheeks where her blush had escaped to her nose and her mascara had run to replace her highlighted cheekbones. "I look like a clown! Why didn't one of the ladies tell me?"

With a slight giggle, Daisy replied, "Probably because your makeup looked like the blue-hairs you were teaching."

"That's not funny. Those ladies are wonderful. During class my back was to the mirror. I never saw my face. I didn't bring any cleanser—what am I going to do?"

"Come on. I keep a full cosmetic emergency kit in my locker. Besides, you don't want Kevin to see you like this. By the way, that was your message. Kevin wants to see you, and you have a delivery. I set it on your desk."

Thankfully, her class was in the studio closest to the locker room. Ducking in behind Daisy, Jen saw herself again. The mortified feelings climbed up from her stomach to the point she almost gagged. So much for looking like a pro today. Daisy opened her locker to reveal what appeared to be a Mary Kay showroom in a twelve-inch-by-twelve-inch locker.

"What on earth?" Jen's jaw dropped.

"Hush now. You know how Kevin is about having second jobs. I needed to make more money to send my son to tennis camp. The coach thinks he's got real talent for the game."

Jen's self-absorbed embarrassment dissolved to consider this coworker's reality. Needing to make a few hundred dollars to send her son to camp? "Oh, Daisy, you are a godsend. Thank you."

"Us girls got to stick together." Daisy's southern drawl showed up. "I'm real excited for you. Not sure what you're going to be doing, but I'm glad for you." Daisy smiled and began to search for the product Jen needed. "Now, you need some cleanser and some moisturizer. I don't know what I have as far as the foundation you will need, but let me look while you get cleaned up." Daisy handed her the items, and Jen humbly turned to the sinks.

In her heart she prayed, *Thank you, Lord, for giving me a connecting point with Daisy. I know she will be a huge help to me in dealing with my other coworkers in this new job. I would have never reached out to her on my own. Thank you.*

As the color mixture was washed away and Jen saw her reflection in the mirror, a different wave of confidence washed over her. What had she been trying to prove wearing all that makeup? It didn't feel natural or comfortable at all.

Daisy brought a small pink basket with makeup for Jen.

"You know what, Daisy, I think I'll stick with my usual eyeliner and mascara. Do you have any soft black?"

Daisy gave Jen a side hug. "Of course I do. When I saw you come in this morning, I was wondering what the fancy look was for. You're pretty just being you." Digging through the basket, she handed Jen the two items she needed and retreated to her locker to replace the rest.

*Just be yourself.* It was the second time today Jen had heard those words. Who was she trying to be with the makeup and the dress clothes? She worked in a gym and happened to be in management.

Daisy closed her locker and squeezed the lock closed. "Well, I'd better get back out front. You okay now?"

Jen turned from the sink, her face showing a moist radiance. "Yes, thank you so much. You have done far more than rescue my face."

Daisy gave Jen another hug. "You're welcome. Let me know what else you need. Don't forget Kevin needs to see you. But I'd stop by your office first." With a wink and a smile, Daisy left Jen to finish.

With her face back in order and feeling fresh, Jen braided her hair but decided to leave her warm-ups and sneakers on. Freed from the mask of makeup, she stepped out of the locker room. Jen walked through the weightlifting area, greeting several of the gym members with encouragement to keep up the good work.

The perfume of the vase that held autumn mums and lilies grabbed Jen's attention before she turned on her office light. She pulled the card from the long plastic holder in the middle of the blooms. "I love you so much. M." It was in his handwriting. Mark must have stopped on his way in to the office to order them. For the third time today, the tears welled up. When she stepped around her desk to call Mark, Kevin poked his head around the door.

"How's my new assistant general manager this morning? Oh, look at the flowers! Nice touch, Mike."

Kevin never remembered Mark's name. Kevin's mindlessness didn't scare away the smile Mark's flowers delivered. "It's *Mark*, and yes, aren't they wonderful?" Jen put the card in her top drawer to focus on her boss. "I was just coming to talk with you. Daisy gave me a message that you wanted to see me. I was headed to your ..."

"Here is fine." Kevin waved Jen to sit behind her desk. She settled into her new chair. "I need you to go ahead and start a list of topics and the structure you think is best for our programs. Let's set up a timetable for when each will be held so we can get them on the upcoming calendars. I'd like the first one to be in a month."

Jen caught herself before her jaw dropped. A month to figure out a topic, locate a speaker, promote the class, and fill the seats. All while mapping out the coming months. Okay, she could do this. Right?

"No problem. I'm done with my classes for the day and was planning on jumping right in." She sounded a little more bouncy than usual. Could Kevin tell it was her jumpy nerves?

With Kevin's departure, Jen exhaled and sat back in her chair. The sight of her lovely flowers reminded her of the confidence Mark had in her success. Picking up the phone to call him gave her a momentary respite from the whirling thoughts about the new job, the makeup debacle, and how on earth she would create a healthy living program. A brief conversation with Mark would make it all good.

# CHAPTER NINE

Nora walked into the office ready to start a new project. Designing a tree for the Festival of the Trees fund raiser was one of the ways Nora had proved her skills to her new boss at Stanton Designs. The fact it was a Christmas tree could have made it a simple assignment, but since the firm was a sponsor, and she was new to the firm, Nora had taken the opportunity to create something special.

Phoebe Hays, a senior designer at the firm, met her with a cupcake and a candle. "What's this?" Nora asked.

"There's something you need to know about the mayor's home and the draft designs you did. His wife called Tony and raved about you."

Phoebe's excitement grew as her words quickened. "She loved your designs for Christmas! I owe you this cupcake because what I didn't tell you when you got the assignment was that we've decorated the mayor's house for Christmas every year, and every year his wife finds something wrong with it, but we don't hear about her disappointment until after. Every time, we think it's our last year, but she keeps calling."

Phoebe set the cupcake on the table and clapped her hands together. "This year we decided to give it to you, our newest talent. We knew you would do well, and we knew she'd probably call to complain. Sure enough, she called, but her comments were far from critical. You did an outstanding job on capturing what she was thinking. Congratulations." Phoebe picked up the cupcake and pushed it toward Nora. "Now, you just need to make it happen. Christmas fantasy and all."

Nora set her satchel on the table in the common area where they stood and pulled out her copy of the proposal. "Are you sure she doesn't have any changes?" Nora fingered through the document. "All I did was review what she didn't like before, gave it a new theme, and get some feedback from a couple of the other designers." She closed the proposal and stared at the cover. "No changes at all?"

"Nora." Phoebe leaned closer to her. "Are you okay? This is good news."

Nora closed and opened her eyes as a smile grew across her face. "Yes. Thank you, Phoebe. I'm looking forward to making it happen. I just ... I just figured there would be changes. I know she's very particular. I thought she would make changes."

Phoebe set the cupcake down. "Nope. You have been successful in wowing our most challenging client. Congratulations!"

Nora shook her head in disbelief. The magnitude of the compliment made her grin as the thought of winning over their toughest client settled in. She missed Seth every day. Taking this job was supposed to be a small step into some kind of normal life. Whatever that was supposed to look like. Maybe she really could rebuild a fulfilling life. She sat down at the table and picked up the cupcake. "I'm ready to dive in."

"I'm glad you're ready for a project, because we don't get this job unless you work on it. The design was your idea, the proposal was your work, and now you get to lead the way on execution," Phoebe said.

Nora listened, but her thoughts wandered to Seth. These were the moments when she missed him the most. He had been the one person she wanted to share her successes with—and to hold her during her saddest moments. His death had come too soon. Would she ever have that kind of love and connection with another man? Was she even ready for it? Nora and Seth had met the summer after she graduated from college. He was finishing at the police academy. They had dated for two years before getting engaged. It took Nora awhile to begin to get comfortable with the idea of being a police officer's wife. Now she was his widow. They had eight wonderful married years together before a stray bullet from a man hopped up on drugs took his life. Their life.

Phoebe began to walk toward her office. "Enjoy your cupcake. I've pulled previous designs out for reference and set up your worktable."

Nora nodded. "Guess we need to get started."

Nora had been in gyms her whole life. As a teenager it was about staying strong for ballet. When she and Seth were dating on a tight budget, they would work out together, go for a walk to cool down, and then have a light dinner. Since his death, she stayed away from big gyms. She had a stationary bike at home, or she'd go for walks by herself. She missed a good sweaty workout. Maybe connecting with Jen would help. Nora opened the glass door, and took another step forward as the door closed behind her, and the familiar clanks of free weights greeted her.

A lady with blonde curly hair and "Daisy" on her name tag was updating the workout flyers on the bulletin board.

"Hello. May I help you?"

Nora adjusted the strap of her large purse. "Yes, I'm looking for Jen Stephens. Is she in?"

With a welcoming smile, she responded, "She sure is. Let me get her for you."

"Thank you."

A few minutes later, Jen turned the corner to the front reception area. "Nora!"

Nora smiled. "I hope I'm not catching you at a bad time. It's my lunch, so I thought I'd pop in."

"No, not at all. Good to see you. What can I do for you?"

"Well, I've been thinking about you and your mention of personal training. What does it entail? How do you schedule? Cost? I need to get moving with something to take better care of myself."

"Good questions. Let's go sit in the smoothie bar and talk about your goals." Jen picked up a notepad and pen from the reception desk and they walked into the smoothie bar.

"Good morning, Jen."

"Good morning, Joe. My treat today."

"No problem. What can I make for you ladies?"

Nora considered her options. The last morning workout guests were finishing up. Another worker was clearing the tables.

"What do you recommend, Jen?" Nora asked as she considered the board with a half-dozen options.

"This early, I like one of the fruity choices, mango or wildberry."

"Oh, mango sounds yummy."

"Make that two." With their orders placed, the two settled at a table to discuss Nora's physical fitness goals.

As the two talked about the benefits of getting into shape, Nora explained her desire to stay good and strong, as well as relieve stress. Jen took notes.

"Tell me what a typical day is for you. Do you work at a desk? A lot of standing? How active do you feel you already are?"

Nora shifted in her seat. "Depends on the day. With interior design, there are desk days, and there are days when I'm on-site checking on progress or taking measurements."

"Okay. How many times a week do you feel you could work out? Realistically."

Nora chuckled, "Realistically? Maybe twice. As much as I hear it needs to be three times to be meaningful, I think I could get over here a couple of days."

"Twice a week can work. I'd rather us develop a plan that works with you without stressing you out. The only way this will work is if it works for you. If it becomes a hassle, then it's not worth it. Tell me about what you've done in the past to stay in shape."

Nora thought for a minute. *Seth and I were always ...* "There's something else I also want to tell you. Not sure if Maggie told you." Nora looked down at her cup and swirled the straw once around. "Five years ago, I lost my husband ... and I'm just now coming out of my grief, trying to put my life back together. I've been riding my stationary bike at home, but I think it's time to take it up a notch. Seth and I were very active, hiking, biking, working out at the gym."

"Oh, Nora, I'm so sorry. No, Maggie didn't tell me."

Nora wiped her nose with the small white napkin from under her smoothie cup. "We were doing life together. As a police officer, he worked crazy hours, and I did volunteer work at the community art center. And when he could get time off, we'd travel or go on mission trips."

Jen reached over and touched her arm.

"He was my soulmate. Then one night, I got the call that we'd supported other couples through. He had been shot and killed. Within a few minutes of hanging up, his commander's wife was at my front door to help me through the longest days of my life. It took the better part of the year for me to grieve and make decisions on what to do next." Nora took a deep breath. "So, I went back to school to finish my degree. That took a couple of years. With my degree complete and four years of healing, I felt like I was ready to work full time."

"Thank you for sharing with me. It probably sounds too cliché at this point, but I mean this—if Maggie or I can do anything for you, please call us."

"You're kind. Thank you. But right now, I just want to begin to move forward."

Nora and Jen finished their smoothies and walked back to Jen's office. Within minutes Jen had printed out a workout plan Nora felt comfortable with and scheduled her first session. Jen offered to work with her personally—at least to get her started.

"I will see you Thursday for your first session."

Jen gave Nora a hug. "Thanks for coming in. It'll be fun to work with you."

"I look forward to it. Take care."

# CHAPTER TEN

The stage was set for the opening scene. The house lights were dim—the two spotlights on the stage. Maggie was alone in the auditorium, sitting on a chair in Auntie Em's living room checking her list. Everything was in good order. Where was everyone? They should be here getting their costumes and makeup on. A heavy thud sounded offstage near the front row. "Maggie, help!" Maggie jumped from her chair to see who was calling. "Maggie, help me!"

"Daddy? Where are you? I can't see you."

"Mag, get ... me ... some ... help ..."

Then nothing.

"Daddy, is that you? I can't see you."

Maggie blinked awake to hear Dan's calm voice. "Maggie. Maggie." Dan wrapped his arms around her. "You're fine. You're safe. You had another dream."

"It was awful. It was the same dream, and I couldn't get to him. Daddy called for me, and I couldn't find him."

Dan's reassuring words washed over Maggie. "Your dad is hanging out with Jesus in heaven. He has no more pain."

Maggie wiped her eyes. "I know. It just feels so real."

Most of the time, when carpool was completed, Maggie would go into the cafeteria and have a cup of coffee with the other moms before they began their food prep for the day.

This morning was different. After tossing, turning, and getting to sleep late, Maggie was ready to make the call to Jim. She hoped he wouldn't be upset with her for not calling last night. In addition to her nightmare, her go-around with Dan had left her feeling weary, and she wanted to sound fresh when she made the call. She needed to let things settle with Dan and in her own heart. Before waking the kids, but after Dan had left for the office, Maggie had taken a few minutes to pray and read the devotion for the day. Those minutes alone with her heavenly Father gave her peace about the whole notion of going back to the theater. It wasn't the way she thought, but maybe God knew it would be better. She wanted to use her God-given talents and open her world up to new people. Making the decision allowed her to look forward to her conversation with Jim.

Forgoing coffee in the cafeteria, Maggie headed for home. She wanted a quiet place, so she could take notes during her conversation.

Her smile stretched across her face as she settled at their kitchen table. With pen and paper ready, she took a deep breath and dialed Jim's cell number.

On the third ring, Jim answered with his tenor voice. "Hello, this is Jim."

Maggie began, "Jim, this is Maggie Nelson. I apologize for not calling last night. Needed to talk all this through with my husband." *Oh, how cheesy did that sound?* "Anyway, I would love the opportunity to understudy and work as stage manager." *That sounded more confident.*

"Great!" Jim sounded thrilled. "It looks like I will be directing on my own, and I will be glad to have you to work with."

Maggie grinned and sat up straighter. He was looking forward to working with her when he didn't even know her or her skills.

Jim continued, "I'd like to meet with you soon to bring you up to speed on everything. Are you available today at all? I know it's short notice."

Not wanting to say no, Maggie offered, "Well, ah, yes, I could come by for a bit. I need to pick up the kids by 2:30, though. Once we talk, and I see the schedule, I can have more flexibility."

"Don't worry about it. This is volunteer work. I know everyone has responsibilities beyond the theater. Come on in about 11:30, and I'll have Sara get us box lunches. Do you like turkey or ham?"

Okay, this could work. "Turkey would be fine. Thank you."

"See you at 11:30, and we should be done by 1:30. That give you enough time to get the kids?"

"Yes. Thank you."

"Thank you, Maggie. See you in a bit."

Maggie hung up and started a list of questions to help her get up to speed on the production. Much of it would come back to her from previous experience. She needed to get dressed for the day. After a few tries, she decided to pull her shoulder-length brown locks up into a messy bun. She settled on jeans with short light-brown suede boots, a white T-shirt, and a navy blazer. Hip yet mature. Her ego was boosted at the sight of how her jeans fit and the outfit came together. Upon final inspection, she added a simple cross necklace, her favorite earrings from Dan, and, of course, her wedding rings. In her many volunteer activities at church and the school, whenever there were men involved, she was careful to leave no doubt about her commitment to her marriage. Maggie dug her soft-sided messenger bag out of the closet to pack a notebook, pens, highlighters, and her tablet. Looking over her shoulder at the clothing disaster in her closet, Maggie grinned and shook her head. *This can't happen every time I dress to go to the theater.* At the stoplight a few blocks from the theater, Maggie checked herself in the mirror.

Arriving right on time, Maggie took a deep breath to calm the butterflies dancing in her stomach. The excitement of something new in her life pumped through her veins.

Sara wasn't at her post when Maggie stepped into the foyer. All was quiet. She wandered into the auditorium. The whoosh of cool air surged with the history of the theater. So many patrons, so many shows enjoyed. Thoughts of her father surprised Maggie. Luke Fenwick had been his daughter's biggest fan. He made a point to be at every one of her opening night performances with a single rose in hand. *He would have been so excited for me.* Just as her thoughts ventured to the night of his tragic death, Maggie started at a heavy thud from behind her. Turning around, she saw Jim. He chuckled.

"Sorry about that. I've been meaning to work on the door. There's no closing it softly." Jim was dressed in khakis, loafers, and a logo T-shirt from one of the last plays. "It helps with the rumors the theater is haunted. Anything to get people to talk about us."

"That's one way." Maggie nodded.

"We're planning a midnight reading of Macbeth on Halloween. I've coordinated with the theater department at the university. This auditorium with its old wood, creaking floors, and mossy scent makes for the perfect setting. You should come."

Maggie gave a noncommittal nod. “Maybe. We’ll have to see what’s going on that night. I have two young goblins, but I’m sure they will be in a candy coma by midnight.”

Jim waved Maggie toward a door off the lobby. “We’ll meet in our conference room.” As they passed through the lobby, they saw Sara was at her desk reading. Looking up, she smiled.

“Good morning, Mrs. Nelson.”

“Please, call me Maggie.”

“No problem. We’re so glad you’re going to help us out with *Wizard*.”

Maggie smiled. It felt good to be wanted and appreciated. “I’m looking forward to it.”

Jim stopped at the desk, “Sara, what time will our lunches be here?”

“They’re on the way now. I’ll bring them in. Maggie, what would you like to drink with your lunch? We have a variety of sodas or water.”

“Water is great. Thank you.”

“And I know Jim always has water.” Sara turned to head to the kitchen.

Maggie and Jim went into the conference room. The room was a long rectangle with tall, frosted windows. The opposite wall had a series of framed play posters. At one end was a mess of costumes and what looked like prop parts—plastic poppy flowers and a bucket of apples. The table ran the length of the room. Maggie set her bag in a chair and began to review the posters.

The posters were framed with matting that had the signatures of all the actors and directors. She noticed Jim’s name on just about all of them. “How long have you worked here?”

“Some days, it feels like forever—especially on mornings like this when I find out through the grapevine my set designer has quit." Jim's fingers went up in air quotes. "She told one of the students last night. When I walked through backstage this morning, all her notes were gone." He shook his head. "It makes me wonder why I left teaching at the university." His dimples made their appearance. "I'm kidding. I left the university about ten years ago after having split my time between teaching and directing. One day, I decided to follow my dream. I was an okay professor, but my soul felt most free here in the theater."

Maggie smiled, understanding the freedom the right role brought. Or just being on stage. "I understand. So, where do we begin?" Maggie sat on the edge of her seat, and leaned in. "Wait. I've got an idea. You're welcome to hate it, because I've been here all of ten minutes, but I recently ran into an old friend who's an interior designer. Do you want me to introduce you? Maybe she can give you some help with set design."

About that time, Sara came in with box lunches and waters for them.

Jim nodded. "Thanks. And if she's interested, it would save me a ton of time. Do you have her number?"

Maggie hesitated. She didn't want to give Nora's number to some guy without Nora knowing. "Why don't we call her together. I'll introduce you, and then, we can see if she's interested." Maggie pulled her phone out of her bag and called the number Nora had given her. After a couple of rings, Nora answered.

"Nora, Maggie Nelson. Did I catch you at a good time?"

"Sure, Maggie. Good to hear from you. What's up?"

"I'm here with Jim Preston from the Oakdale community theater. Can I put you on speaker? We have something to talk with you about."

Nora was quiet for a moment. "Okay."

Maggie set the phone on the table between she and Jim. "Okay, you're on speaker. Nora, meet Jim Preston. Jim, Nora ..."

Jim took the conversation from there. "Nora, Maggie tells me you're an interior designer. Our set designer quit yesterday, and I'm wondering if you might have some time to help us out. We're doing *The Wizard of Oz* in February, so time is running short to not have sets going. In a small theater, everyone wears many hats, but set design is specialized. Unfortunately, I can't pay you, but I do have a budget for the materials you need."

Nora was quiet again. "I don't know ..." More silence. "It sounds fun. How much time do you need?"

"I've got volunteers to help build the sets. Now I need a design for them to build from."

Maggie crinkled her nose. "Nora, I don't want you to feel like we've put you on the spot. It'd be fun to work on something together. Do you want to think about it and call Jim back?"

Nora's voice lightened. "You know Maggie, it *does* sound like fun. Sure, I can help you out. I need to run now. Maggie, give Jim my number. Jim, if you would, give me a call this evening. Sorry for an after-hours call, but I work during the day."

A smile came across Jim's face. "Not a problem at all. I'll call you at about seven tonight. Will that work?"

"Sounds fantastic. Maggie, thanks for thinking of me. Let's have lunch soon."

After the call with Nora, Jim began to share with Maggie his vision for the production and her help as stage manager, which included a few more nontraditional tasks.

Their time flew—as did Maggie's pen, taking pages of notes. Maggie felt like she asked a million questions, but Jim was patient and answered them all. Most everything was familiar to Maggie and reminded her of all the things she loved about acting and production. Jim noticed the clock on the wall. “Oh, my goodness. I’ve gone on and on. It’s one-thirty, and I know you said you needed to get your kids.”

“No problem. I built in a little cushion in my time. But I shouldn’t take any more of yours. Thank you for answering all my questions. I hope they weren’t too elementary.”

Jim stood and leaned on the back of the chair. The hints of gray peeking through his brown wavy hair boasted enough maturity to allowed for his casual professionalism “No, they were all relevant questions. You may have to remind me if we start dominating your time too much. Producing a play has a way of sucking us in. And thank you so much for the introduction to Nora.”

Maggie felt her cheeks grow warm. “Thanks for the warning. I promise not to let the play dominate ...”

“If you figure out how to do that, let me know. Sometimes, I can hardly remember going home at night. But I love this place and want nothing more than to keep it going.”

Maggie reached in her messenger bag to drop her notepad and grab her phone. Four missed calls from Dan, one voice mail. Settling into her car, she pushed the voice mail button. Dan spoke in a tight-jaw, clenched-teeth tone.

“Mag, where are you? I’ve tried to call several times. I spilled soup on my shirt at lunch and have a big meeting this afternoon. I need you to bring me another shirt. Please.” No goodbye, just silence.

With drooping shoulders, Maggie sighed. Like the curtain closing, all her excited energy left. She dialed Dan. He answered, sounding exasperated.

No hello. "Maggie, I've been trying to call you—where have you been?"

"I, I had a meeting at the theater with Jim. Sorry." Maggie's apology was half-hearted. She wasn't sure if she needed to apologize or if he was just being difficult.

"Okay, now that you're done with your little meeting, would you please run home and get me another shirt? Can you manage that in your schedule today?"

This wasn't like Dan. He had needed her to run errands for him in the past, but he had never been this belittling. Maggie agreed, looking at her watch—one forty-five. If she hustled, she could take Dan's shirt and still get to carpool.

Maggie started the van. "First of all, why are you being this way?"

Just as hard sounding, Dan rebutted. "What way? I need a shirt."

Dan went on to ramble about a meeting at three and some incident at lunch. He didn't sound himself. His terse words stung. Maggie got the brunt of his stressful morning. *Lord, I don't understand, but you do. That's most important right now.*

"Okay, okay, I'm on my way home, I'll see you in about forty-five minutes. Dan, I don't know why you are being this terse, but you need to settle down."

A loud exhale. "Please don't tell me what to do. Just get the shirt."

The tears pooled up in her eyes. In the last fifteen minutes Maggie had gone from excited to feeling like dirt. *Guess I'll just do the dutiful wife thing and deliver his shirt.*

Dan's harsh words tumbled nonstop through Maggie's mind as she drove to his office. The conversation—if that's what it could be called—along with the blabbering on the radio, became a confused rumble. She turned off the radio and prayed aloud, "Lord, I have no idea what has gotten into my husband. He is a steady, kind man, but that's not who was on the phone. Something must be wrong. Father, please give him peace, calm his spirit. Help me be the wife he needs, not someone to blow off steam at. Thank you, Lord, for Dan and the life you have given us." At "Amen," Maggie pulled into the parking lot.

Elaine had been Dan's secretary for ten years. At thirty and single, Elaine had a big personality. She drove Maggie nuts. But she seemed to work well with Dan. Elaine looked up as Maggie came through the glass doors.

"Maggie, thank you so much. Dan has been a bear since he got back from lunch with the boss. His shirt had soup all down the front." She leaned in a little. "He's been in his office since with no shirt on, hiding, hoping no one needed to see him."

"Has anyone?"

Elaine flipped her big blonde curls across her shoulder. "Well, a couple of staffers, but I made excuses. The list is growing, so I need to get this shirt on him."

Maggie bristled at Elaine's comment. "I'll take his shirt in."

"Sure, Maggie." Elaine stepped aside. She may have matured, but she still said things that didn't sound right.

A soft knock on Dan's door, and Maggie entered before hearing Dan's answer. His back was to her, and he whipped around. "Elaine, I told you not to disturb me until my shirt got here!"

Maggie took a step back. "Whoa, it's me, your wife. And I happen to have a freshly laundered, light-on-the-starch, dress shirt for you. So, I guess you could say your shirt is here."

Dan closed his eyes and took a deep breath. He reached for the hanger. "Oh, great. They moved our one-thirty meeting to three because of the big soup debacle."

Maggie teased a little to try and lighten the moment and pulled the shirt back, "Wait a minute, don't you think a kiss or a thank you is in order?"

"Maggie, don't mess with me right now. The three highest execs from our bank district are in the conference room waiting on me."

Maggie handed him the shirt, turned, and walked out. Elaine started to jabber something at her. Maggie held up her hand and kept walking. Her quick exit ensured no one saw the tears.

# CHAPTER ELEVEN

Jen looked up from her chart. It was three-seventeen. She had thirteen minutes to get Brian from school. "Oh, *no*!"

Daisy started to ask Jen a question. "Jen, where are ..."

Jen jumped in her car and prayed the lights would be green. They weren't. A deep breath.

*Just relax. Mrs. Fitzpatrick won't leave him.*

Pulling into school, Jen smiled when she saw Mrs. Fitzpatrick was on the swing next to Brian, both laughing. Of course. The seasoned elementary school teacher, recently promoted to principal, was a pro. She loved the kids and supported the parents.

Closing her car door, Jen announced, "I want to play too. Who can swing higher?"

"Oh no, I'm way too old for such contests." Mrs. Fitzpatrick's eyes sparkled from the few minutes of being the "pal" in principal.

"I'm so sorry I'm late. Come on, Brian, let's go so Mrs. Fitzpatrick can finish her day."

"It's not a problem at all. Brian was filling me in on the adventures of fourth grade. He convinced me to come and be their guest reader sometime. I hear you have a new job."

Jen shared the high points of her new job, feeling like Mrs. Fitzpatrick was just being nice and wanted to get home.

"Jen, you'll be so good at that. You live out what you'll be promoting."

"Thank you so much. I hope I won't make this mistake again."

Mrs. Fitzpatrick gave Jen's arm a small squeeze. "Dear, in all my time in education, I've come to quickly figure out parents. I can tell who are dedicated to their families, and whose jobs come in a close second, and others who put their work first. You are so far from the latter."

"Thank you for the encouragement. These have been an exciting few days, and I love it, but I don't want to let it take over." Jen took Brian's hand and headed to the car. "How about we drive through and get you some french fries?" Jen hugged Brian "I'm sorry I was late, buddy."

Brian skipped ahead, "It's okay, especially if it means my favorite, freeeennncccchhh fries."

"I need to go back to work for a little while. Can you sit and color with your snack?"

"Sure, can I ride the bike too?"

Before Jen's new job, when Brian and Mark had come by the gym, Jen would let Brian up on the stationary bike and stand next to it while he reached to pedal.

"It's pretty busy at the gym, and I have work to do, so I can't watch you. I need you to stay in my office with me. Remember, I have a new job now."

"Oh, yeah, I forgot."

"What's wrong? Did you know that one of the first things I put on my desk was a picture of you and your daddy?"

"Really?" Brian happily munched on his french fries. Of course, the lights were green all the way back to the gym.

Walking through the lobby with Brian dragging his backpack, Jen stopped at the front desk.

"Glad I stopped you this time." The smell of Daisy's fresh piece of fruity gum wafted into the air as she held out messages. “Kevin needs to see you right now. That’s what I was tryin’ to tell you when you dashed out of here like your hair was on fire.”

“Mom, your hair was on fire?” Brian’s eyes were as wide as if he had seen an elephant.

Jen’s hand went to his shoulder. “No, I was just in a hurry to get you.”

“’Cause you were late.” Brian twirled around the open lobby area.

Jen caught his shoulder. “Yes, Brian. Now, let me talk with Ms. Daisy.” With an embarrassed grin, Jen turned back to Daisy. “Okay, let me get Brian settled in my office. Tell Kevin I’ll be there in a minute. Come on, sweetie.” Jen hustled Brian to her office.

Jen leaned in Kevin’s half-opened door with a knock. “You wanted to see me?”

He didn’t look up from his papers, “Yes. An hour ago.”

“I’m, I’m, uh, sorry. I ran out to pick up Bri ...”

“Oh, that’s right. Would you let me know when you need to run out?”

Gently sitting on the hard wooden chair, Jen felt her face grow warm. “I’m sorry. What do you need?”

“I got a call from our investors earlier. All of them on a conference line. With the opening of our newest competitor, Workout World, it seems they have decided we need to do better on our financials faster than you and I had discussed. We have to increase memberships and daily average usage by our clients like tomorrow.” Kevin rubbed his forehead. “Look, I don’t like putting this much pressure on you so soon, but I need your draft plan tomorrow.”

Jen hoped her face didn’t look like her stomach felt. “Kevin, are you serious? I’m just getting started. I can’t have the full plan done tomorrow.”

"What can you give me? Part of it? An outline?" Kevin had switched between his pencil and pen three times.

"Well, um, I can get the first few weeks outlined with preliminaries for the monthly sessions."

Kevin shook his head and sighed. "It's a start, but I need the full plan no later than Friday. I'll keep the guys off us until then. But they want to see our plan, and then they're going to ask questions. We'll need to be ready to answer."

"Answer questions? Us?"

"Jen, you're a leader. That's why I promoted you. You have great ideas. You know what we need to do, and I have the experience. You will draft the plan, and then you and I will get it ready to present. I want you with me when I meet with the investors. Please."

With very few choices, Jen stood. "Okay, I better go get started."

Kevin was buried in his papers before she exited his office.

"Mommmeeee, please can we go now." Brian leaned his head on his mother's sagging shoulders.

"Brian, please give me just a few more minutes."

His pout drew larger. "You said that an hour ago. See the clock, the first number has changed from five to six. That's the hour number, isn't it?"

*A fine time to learn to tell time.*

Her eyes adjusted as she looked up from her laptop screen. Six-fifteen. "Oh man, your dad's going to be worried. We need to get home." Jen grabbed her phone to call. Several missed calls from Mark. "Okay, pack up your stuff while I get mine." Jen grappled at the papers that were spread across her desk. She unplugged her laptop as her office phone rang.

"Hello."

"Babe, where are you? Are you okay?"

"Yes, I'm sorry. Kevin called me into his office when I got back from picking up Brian. The timeline for this programming plan has been accelerated by the investors. I needed to get it drafted."

"So much for silent partners."

"Not so much. Brian and I are on our way home. I'll get dinner ready but will have to work on this a little more tonight."

"Oh, babe, jumping in the deep end, huh?"

"Never saw the shallow end."

"It's a warm evening. How about I grill tonight and make salads. You and Brian come home, we eat as a family, and I'll help Brian with his reading and bath."

"You are too good to me."

A smile in Mark's voice. "I know. I love you, and this is a different kind of work for you. Management is a lot different than showing up and teaching."

# CHAPTER TWELVE

Driving home in tears, Maggie spent her pre-carpool hour talking to herself and God about Dan. She picked up around the house praying aloud and trying to decide how to have a conversation with her husband without exploding. *I wasn't wrong to take the position with the play. I shouldn't have to be at his beck and call.*

With the house in better order, Maggie washed her face, grabbed a bottled water, and went to pick up Danny and Emma.

Maggie spied Danny on the playground as she pulled into line. At the sight of her car, Mrs. Fitzpatrick walked up.

"Hi, Maggie. How are you?"

Maggie hoped her face didn't reveal her hurt. "I'm good. Came to take my little monsters off your hands. How were the kids today?"

"They were good ... at least no one ended up in my office, so it must have been a good day."

Danny and Emma came running to the van aglow with sweat as the cool fall morning had turned to a warm afternoon. "Can we stop for ice cream?"

A smile blossomed across Maggie's face. Like most parents, there were times when the kids drove her crazy, but there were far more times when either one—or both when they conspired together—brought her more joy than she could ever imagine. They were a gift from God. An impromptu ice cream stop might be the break her afternoon needed. Not wanting to be such a pushover, Maggie joked with them before agreeing. "I don't know. Have all of you been good today? Mrs. Fitzpatrick was telling me a few things ..."

Eyes wide and jaws dropped, Danny and Emma looked at each other, each accusing the other.

"I never have a problem with your angels." Mrs. Fitzpatrick nudged the kids to get into the car. Maggie winked at her.

"Well, I guess we can stop for *one* scoop each."

The tension hung low over the family dinner table. The kids, oblivious to their parents' silence, dug into the homemade lasagna. In her efforts to organize her time, Maggie had spent the previous Sunday afternoon cooking and freezing or refrigerating meals. Dan's quiet demeanor came in the door with him at six-thirty. A little late, but Maggie said nothing. Silverware clinked, and the kids jabbered on about their day at school.

Everyone fed and off to their respective spots for the evening, Maggie finally felt like she could breathe. It wouldn't last, though. She took her time with dishes, not knowing what she would do with herself next. A normal evening would have included her curling up next to Dan on the couch and talking about their days.

In their fifteen years of marriage, they had had few fights. But when they did, she could never sleep until they were resolved. Knowing sleep would elude her if they didn't talk, Maggie decided to give a conversation a try. Stepping lightly into the dim living room, she sat next to Dan on the couch.

"Dan, what happened today?"

Dropping the paper, his hands caught his forehead. He swiped his hands down his face. "I don't know."

The silence screamed. *Lord, do I get mad and yell or gently offer grace?* Maggie sat quietly, and took his hand. "Honey, what's wrong?"

Both his hands melted into her soft touch. "Maggie, it's work. I try so hard not to bring it home, but I'm afraid it's seeping in. I'm sorry."

"I appreciate your apology, but that doesn't tell me what happened and why you were so awful to me. I didn't deserve that attitude no matter how badly your day was going."

Deep breath. "You're right. I shouldn't have treated you so bad. But ..."

Maggie interrupted, "There is no *but* here."

Letting go of her hands, Dan stood up and shook his head. "I was trying so hard to impress the big bosses today at lunch that I made a fool of myself. I spilled lunch on my shirt and was a mess both inside and out. I was so embarrassed. Then we got back to the office, and they wanted to meet, and I hid in my office making stupid excuses to bide my time. Then, I couldn't get hold of you, and my frustration kept growing."

Maggie sat silent. Taking it in. Trying to listen, process, and decide how to react, her thoughts were like spaghetti. "I don't know what to say. You aren't a prideful man. Why was today so different?"

Dan's piercing eyes targeted Maggie's eyes. "Prideful! I'm not being prideful. I'm trying to keep my job. Those executives are in all week to evaluate the leadership team. And there is talk of accounts not balancing. Something is terribly wrong."

"Dan, you do an outstanding job."

"Maggie, you don't understand." Dan walked into the kitchen.

*What do I do now, Lord?* As she bit her bottom lip, Maggie stood to follow Dan. Maggie turned the corner in time to see Dan's feet going upstairs and hear his muffled "Goodnight."

Clenching her teeth, Maggie called to Dan just a little too loudly. "Dan, no. You are not going to slither upstairs to bed. We are not done here."

Dan froze on the stairs.

Maggie reached the bottom step. "What's going on, Dan?"

Dan sank onto the third step and lowered his head into his hands. "Maggie, one of my team members is suspected of embezzlement. The information became clear after she left today. I had to call her at home to tell her not to come in tomorrow—that we would send her her personal stuff." Dan's eyes softened as if getting this off his chest released the angst. "Maggie, she's a single mom. She put herself through school after the dad took off. Why would she do this?"

Maggie remembered Dan telling her about Stephanie when he hired her. She had outstanding credentials, and he wanted to give her the opportunity for a better life with her son. "What does this have to do with you and your job?"

"You don't get it. She's in my department. My responsibility."

Dan stepped back downstairs into the kitchen, and Maggie made them each a cup of tea. She'd never thought about how Dan felt about his staff. At holidays, he went a little further than the corporate gift and wrote personal notes of gratitude for a job well done. But she never considered how much they meant to Dan personally. He cared about the impact Stephanie's mistake would have on the single mother and her son.

"Oh, Dan, I am so sorry. Are they sure she did it?"

Dan rubbed the back of his neck. "I don't think so. She was beside herself when I called her. I talked Mr. Reid into just a suspension until the auditors come in. There are three other people who have access, but they're upper management, so they don't get suspected until necessary. Public perception and all."

"You mean she could be the fall guy?" Maggie reached for Dan's hand.

"Possibly, but to be honest, I think there was a mistake made somewhere. I don't think she's guilty." Dan took a deep breath and reached for Maggie. "I'm sorry. You didn't deserve to be treated the way I treated you today. Forgive me?"

With a cautious smile, Maggie tightened her hold on his hand. "Please talk to me about these things. I want to know what is going on in your world."

"I'll try. But when I come home, I want to be with you and the kids and leave work at the office."

"Most of the time I'm grateful for you leaving the office behind, but this is big, and I want to be able to support you through it." The spirit between them was warm again. "Do you want to pray about all this before we go to bed?"

In the kitchen, Dan and Maggie took each other's hands, bowed their heads, touching foreheads, and opened their hearts to their heavenly Father. After "amen," Dan's soft kiss sent reassurance through Maggie that they would be fine.

# CHAPTER THIRTEEN

Jen reached in the back of her hybrid to straighten the presentation booklets that slid across the seat. Looking out the rear window, she saw Maggie armed with two steamy cups.

Maggie handed Jen a cup of brew. “Where have you been? Haven’t seen you in carpool and have been drinking two cups of coffee for the last couple of days.” Brian, Danny, and Emma had kissed their moms good-bye and scampered into school. The morning had a preview of autumn with leaves strewed about in a myriad of orange, red, and brown.

Jen accepted the steaming cup of coffee as Maggie took the passenger’s seat. “I’ll be so glad when today is over.”

Maggie furrowed her eyebrows. “That doesn’t sound like my friend who’s all about living a balanced life—being at peace.”

Jen grinned. “It’s not like me, and if I don’t get my butt in a stretch and strength class today, I’m going to implode. I’m sorry we’ve not talked this week. Like my second day on the job, Kevin called me into his office and told me I had to have something for him to present to the investors on Monday on our new programming plan, including costs and return on the investment.” Jen’s inflection tightened, raising her voice a level. “I just started this job last week.”

"Did you get it done?" Maggie's sympathetic tone floated in the space.

"Yes. I did a draft for Kevin to review, and then spent a couple of days refining it." Reaching in the back, Jen handed Maggie a bound color-tabbed booklet.

"Wow, looks impressive."

"I hope Kevin and the investors like what's in it. This was a huge stretch for me to not only outline the healthy living program, give it a working name, work with accounting on how much we will spend, work with Sam in facilities to allocate space, *and* develop a timeline. All in the last seventy-two hours."

"Have you slept?"

"Some. I've taken a break every day to pick up Brian, and Mark has been an angel taking care of our evening routine. I'm not sure, but I think Brian has watched more football than practiced his sight words this week, but it will be fine. I've got a little breathing room now for a bit."

"Why didn't you call me? I would've been glad to pick Brian up. You know that."

"I know. A couple of times, I started to call you. But the hour away from the gym was a good break for me."

Maggie took a sip of her hot coffee. "So, today's the day?"

Jen's face relaxed and she nodded. "The meeting is Monday. But I'm giving the finished presentation to Kevin today. Fingers crossed, and prayers said that they will like it, and Kevin will calm down. For a fitness guy, he gets pretty wound up. Enough about me—tell me about you. How are things going?"

The two friends enjoyed their coffee, connection, and the ups and downs of the week. After stealing half an hour, Jen noticed the time. "Oooh, I've got to run. All this work, probably not a good idea to be there late."

Maggie stepped away from of the car. “Okay, friend, go get ’em today. Call me this weekend. Let’s get something on the calendar for our families to get together.”

Pushing the start button, Jen thanked Maggie for the coffee. “Sounds great—I’ll call you.”

Spending time for a quick visit with Maggie left Jen feeling more centered. With her arms wrapped about the stack of eight bound booklets, Jen stepped into the gym.

Daisy, as always at her post, hair piled on her head and makeup perfect, greeted Jen in her comfortable state of workout pants and zip jacket. The occasional clink of weights rang through the open space. The early-bird workouts were in full gear.

“Good morning, sunshine.”

“You can’t outshine me today. I’m here on time and ready for Kevin Jones and the investors.” Jen plopped the plan booklets on the counter.

Daisy’s perplexed look made Jen chuckle. The two had started a new kind of relationship the last couple of days. Jen learned that beneath the hair, makeup, and bubbly personality, Daisy knew the ins and outs of the gym. She knew who did what and how to get things done. They had done well together, and Jen made a note to do something nice for Daisy to thank her.

“Sounds like you’re ready.” Daisy took the stack of booklets from Jen.

“Is Kevin in?”

“Not yet ... expect him any time.”

“Here, let me have two of those back, and if you wouldn’t mind, please set the rest on his desk. I want him to have them as soon as he gets here. I’m going to jump into Marissa’s class to work out some of this stiffness. How do people sit at desks every day? Come get me if Kevin needs something."

"You got it."

Jen hustled back to the class. Her blonde locks were already in their ponytail. After the earlier debacle with makeup, she had decided less was more. It took a few minutes to calm her mind from overthinking her final draft of the plan. But she was able to find her focus and stretch her body as much as her mind was stretched from the week's work. Blood flowing and muscles relaxed, Jen cleaned up and changed into what she called her "office wear"—khakis, a gym T-shirt, and a light cotton plaid overshirt. A quick stop at the snack shop produced a tropical smoothie.

Jen's morning passed as she kept busy, developing detailed action items and a timeline for the program plan. Too often she checked the clock ... ten thirty, eleven fifteen, eleven forty. At eleven forty-three a knock came on her open door. "Got a minute?"

Kevin's tone and presence were quiet and calm. Unsure what to expect, Jen stood. "Of course. Was hoping we could talk."

Kevin sat down and gestured for Jen to sit as well. "Jen, I know I was like a crazy man last week. I am sorry. I hope I didn't scare you away from your new role on my leadership team."

Under her desk, Jen's twitching knee stopped. Her reply was guarded. "No problem. You didn't scare me away. I did feel like I'd been shoved into the deep end, though. I think I've put something together you can be comfortable with."

Kevin snapped to the edge of his chair. "Oh yes, I love it. You have given me a comprehensive plan for our healthy living and guest retaining needs." He paused, looking down at the booklet. "It's outstanding. I couldn't have done better myself."

A humble Kevin. This was a new sight. Jen didn't know exactly how to react. "Thank you."

With a burst, Kevin stood. "Okay, so now we need to get ready for our presentation on Monday."

Jen shook her head. "Our presentation? I thought you were meeting with them."

"Well, you know what they say—in order to be a success, you have to surround yourself with people who are smarter or something like that." Kevin was always paraphrasing and often messed up famous quotes. "You did an excellent job, Jen. This is your baby, and I want you to be with me to present it. Please."

The butterflies woke up in Jen's stomach. She would need more stretching. "Okay. What time? I'm scheduled to teach."

"They will be here at nine thirty. Can you set up the meeting room? I'd also like you to develop a couple of slides with your bullet points. These stats you found on healthy eating and stress management are wonderful. Let's give them a visual as well. Can you be in early Monday for us to review? Or, I'm glad to meet you this weekend."

Kevin's confidence in her lifted the butterflies from aimless fluttering to smooth sailing.

"Sure, I can be ready for Monday morning. But I'd like to try and get things together today and not work this weekend. Can we talk at the end of the day and see where I am with things? Maybe decide then if we need to meet this weekend?"

Kevin smiled. "That's fine. Anything you need to make this work. Thank you, Jen. I appreciate everything."

As if Mark knew the moment Kevin left Jen's office, her phone rang.

"This is Jen Stephens."

"I hope so, it's your pretty face on my contact screen right now. How did it go with Kevin this morning? I prayed for you on my way to work."

"You're so sweet. Our prayers were answered. Kevin loved it, and he wants me to help present it to the investors on Monday." Jen replied, her voice light and excited.

"Way to go, babe! I'm so proud of you. Do you need to work this weekend?"

A grin swiped across Jen's lips as she teased Mark. "Are you trying to get rid of me? You looking forward to more football time with your son?"

Mark retreated. "Oh no, I just want you to be ready. Whatever you need from us, Brian and I will help. I'd love for us to have some family time this weekend."

"Family time sounds great. How about pizza and game night tonight? I'm going to get all my stuff together for Monday today. I'll get Maggie to pick up Brian. I may run a little late, so I don't have to work this weekend. Does that work?"

"No problem. I'll be home about five twenty if Maggie wants to drop him here. He and I will order the 'za for when you get home."

"Sounds good. Thanks, hon. I love you."

Before she forgot, Jen called Maggie for a favor. As always, Maggie agreed to pick up Brian and congratulated her on the project. Jen hung up, knowing Maggie would make the afternoon a mini-party for the three kids. No doubt there would be ice cream involved. With her family taken care of, Jen set her mind on the presentation. The slide presentation software wasn't one she'd used much. *This could take some time to get rolling.*

After several back and forth conversations with Daisy, setting up the slide presentation template, Jen got the slides set up and had some idea of what she would put on each one. She copied and pasted text to get it on the slide in an easy-to-read format.

Jen was wrapping up the presentation when Kevin came by. They scrolled down, with Jen talking through each slide. Her confidence with the program plan continued to grow with each slide they reviewed.

"That's the last slide, and you can take questions," Jen said.

Kevin sat back and scratched his head. "What if you did the presentation?"

"Excuse me. This time two weeks ago, I was just a yoga instructor. Now you want me to meet with your investors?"

"Jen, you've done all the research, you've written the plan. You know this. You can sell it better than me. Don't worry, I will be right there to fill in the gaps and provide the historical information. Let's present together."

Her head shook slowly with a tilt. "I don't know. All this feels so out of my comfort zone."

"Maybe the writing and presenting part. But you're passionate about healthy living and all the programs you've outlined, right?"

"I guess. I do feel like my head is full of all this information." Taking in a deep breath of renewed confidence, Jen nodded. "Okay, I'm in. But I'd rather us be in front of them together. Why don't you do some kind of intro based on where we've come from as a gym, and introduce the concept. It was your idea to start with." Jen ran her fingers through her loosened hair. Somewhere in the middle of creating the slides, she had pulled the band out of her hair. "What does one wear to a meeting like this?"

"Be comfortable but dress up a little. No one expects you to go from yoga instructor to hardcore corporate. See you early Monday. Have a good weekend." Kevin turned as he headed out her door. "And Jen, don't worry—you will do well. I know you will."

"Thanks, Kevin. Have a good weekend."

The evening gym guests were filtering in as Jen packed her laptop and presentation notes. The morning's stretch and strength class had worn off, but she wanted to get home to Mark and Brian.

The drive home was quiet. Jen didn't have the radio on. Her headset was on, but she wasn't on the phone. She just drove. Her shoulders relaxed as a wave of satisfaction washed over her. A grin crawled across her face as she thought of the events of the last two weeks. A new job outside her self-imposed list of talents, a plan developed to create a new program area for gym guests, and in two days she would stand in front of investors—those who controlled the purse strings—and present her idea. What a ride. The song from her phone caught her attention. Swipe. "Hello."

Maggie was notorious for just starting into a conversation, no "hello, how are you, is this a good time?"

"So, how did it go today? Did you wow your boss like I said you would?"

Jen smiled at her encouraging friend's cheer. "I don't know about wowing. But he liked it and has asked me to help present the plan to the investors on Monday."

Maggie's voice elevated an octave in excitement, "This is huge! Are you excited?"

Jen sighed and shook her head. Maggie had so much more confidence in her than she had in herself. "Let's remember which one of us likes the spotlight and which one trips over her own feet walking. I want to be excited. I think I am. This is all new and cool, but ..."

"But nothing, you've got this."

"Thank you. I have to figure out what to wear. I don't want to be all corporate suit-like. I want to be comfortable but professional."

"What about that pink sheath dress with a blazer and flats?"

"That might work. I'll have to check my blazer situation."

"I'd let you come raid my closet, but my blazers would hang too long on you. But I could call Nora. She's about your size."

"If I had an inch for all the times I've wished to have your five-nine height ..."

As roommates in college, Jen and Maggie always joked about Jen someday having a growing spurt so they could share clothing. Jen was in shape and carried her five-foot-five-inch stature well. Her strong arms and shoulders boasted a confident posture. Maggie had shot up during her senior year in high school to five feet nine-and-a-half inches. Her height was met by most of the boys she would have dated.

Maggie chimed in, "Well, at this point, I'm starting to wish I'd listened to you about all those arm and upper-body core exercises. If I'm not careful, I'm going to get to the point of waving twice when I just want to wave once."

Jen grinned, thinking of all the older women who came in the gym not bothered by the excess skin and loose triceps. "I promise to have a fitness intervention before that happens to you."

"Let me know if you want me to call Nora about an outfit. I need to give her a call anyway. I'm sure she'd help your wardrobe emergency."

"Thanks, I like the dress idea. Let me play with it tonight and I'll call you tomorrow."

"Okay, what are you up to this weekend?"

"Family pizza night tonight. Oh, doody, I forgot to call Mark so he could order." Jen's quirky side always showed with her non-curse words. She'd make up a word in its place. "No biggie, we'll call when I get home. Mark called earlier and offered to have everything ready when I got home. I love that man."

"He's a keeper." Maggie offered.

# CHAPTER FOURTEEN

Maggie's theater schedule was going well. She had designated Sunday afternoons for planning the family's schedule for the week and tried to anticipate when she might need help with picking up the kids. She turned the calendar from the refrigerator to October and added Dan's after-hours meetings along with her theater schedule. This helped with meal planning. With the satisfied feeling of *this is working*, Maggie posted the menu and calendar. Saturday mornings were for menu planning and grocery shopping. Sometimes if they weren't doing anything on Friday night, Dan would be parked with his paper and the kids with video games, so she would sneak out to get a jump on it.

With the week in order and the kids in bed, Maggie joined Dan in the living room. Maggie's orderliness and creativity stopped short when it came to home décor. She kept the house in order and clean, but she had little to offer when it came to decorating. More interested in just being with Dan then watching the football game, Maggie surveyed the room. She liked all the furniture and window treatments. They all matched, but it didn't feel put together.

"You know, Dan, we need to change up this room a little. There is something about it that doesn't feel right."

"Well, whatever you think." Dan didn't look up.

Maggie ran her hand along the smooth black leather couch. "Maybe we need a bigger couch." Her survey continued. "I don't know. I don't have a clue on the decorating front."

"The room is fine, honey."

"Thanksgiving's coming. I want to be sure we have enough seating for everyone."

"Seating for everyone?" Dan closed his paper. "Who's coming? It's not just us?"

"Well, there's my mom and your dad, and whoever they bring. And us ..." Maggie's voice trailed a bit.

"Whoever they bring? Who would they bring? Your mom has sworn off relationships since your dad blew it for all men. And my dad is always by himself."

Dan's reaction was a little surprising. He refused to believe his widowed dad would be serious enough with a woman to bring her to a holiday gathering.

"Sweetheart, you need to be ready for your dad to bring Mabel with him. She's a sweet lady, and they have so much fun together. You can't deny him friends."

Dan continued, "Friends, he can have. But that woman doesn't need to move into my mother's spot." His voice trailed off almost in a pout.

Dan's mother had passed away after a three-year battle with cancer. His father had taken care of her, never leaving her side. She slipped into eternity one evening after Maggie, Dan, and the kids had left the hospice room, all having told her they loved her and the kids having left drawings for her wall. Daniel, Dan's dad, was holding her hand and telling her goodnight when she whispered, "I love you," with her last breath.

Daniel had shared the scene with Maggie and Dan on the first anniversary of her death. Up to that point, he had simply grieved the loss of his best friend and the love of his life. After hearing the story, Dan wept for the first time over the loss of his mother. Since then, Dan and Maggie had visited her grave with his dad each year. Dan always departed the site with a whispered, "Thank you, Mom."

Hesitant, Dan said, "Well, whatever works."

As long as it was on her mind, Maggie reached for the notepad and began the Thanksgiving menu. Her mom would insist on making two kinds of potatoes and some obscure pâté. Maggie wouldn't argue. It wasn't worth the energy. Making her list and menu transported Maggie into a holiday mood. "Maybe I'll go find a pretty Thanksgiving centerpiece for the table and a wreath for the door. Most of the time, I don't decorate for Thanksgiving."

Dan didn't really care about centerpieces or Thanksgiving decorations. But he tried. "I'm sure you will make it wonderful. You're planning way early. And yes, I will try to prepare myself for Mabel to join us. It's so weird to see Dad with someone other than Mom."

With a squeeze of his hand, Maggie cooed, "I know, sweetie. Try to think of her as a family friend. She's a sweet woman. I know it's early. Just want to stay ahead of everything."

"Thanks, hon."

Maggie stood to find something to read. "Oh, can you pick up the kids on Thursday? We're doing a full read-through, and Jim needs to meet with me about the schedule."

His brow furrowed in thought, Dan's reply seemed a little forced. "Yes, yes, I can. I've got a late afternoon conference call, but I can take it here."

Maggie grabbed her glass of water and headed upstairs, "Great. Thanks. There will be a roast ready for dinner. All you have to do is help with homework and serve dinner. I should be home by about seven-thirty."

Monday morning was cool with a touch of fog. The moisture in the air gave the autumn colors a glow. Double-checking backpack contents and kissing the kids good-bye, Maggie tapped on Jen's window. The parking lot was emptying, the final carpool kids running in. Just as she was about to say good morning, a greeting caught her from across the parking lot.

"Hey, Mag!" Nora called as she closed the rear gate of her SUV.

Maggie set her steaming tea on the top of Jen's car and waved. "Hey, girl. What brings you here?"

"Mrs. Fitzpatrick asked me to come by to look at the teachers' lounge for a little rework."

Maggie clapped her hands together. "That's fantastic It could use some TLC."

Nora nodded. "I've dropped off a couple of ideas for her to think about. What are you two doing today?"

Jen chimed in. "Today I've got a presentation with our gym investors. How do I look?"

Maggie and Nora gave her a once-over.

"You look excellent," Nora said.

"I take that as a huge compliment from someone who is always so put together." Jen said, taking a sip of her drink and coming up with a marshmallow mustache.

Maggie agreed and then chuckled. "You may want to take care of the ..." She pointed to her own upper lip and wiped, hoping Jen would mimic. "What, no tea this morning?"

Jen smiled and wiped her mouth. "Mark made me hot chocolate with marshmallows this morning to give me a little oomph for my presentation. I went over and over it this weekend."

Maggie's eyes opened wider. "Of course, you'll do great."

Nora hugged Jen. "Agreed. I've got to run." She touched Maggie's arm. "Maggie, I'll be by the theater tomorrow to look over the stage and to talk with Jim about the set. Looking forward to the work. So good to see you." Nora headed back to her car.

Maggie called over to her. "Wonderful! Thanks for jumping in!"

Jen checked her watch. "I've got to run too. Kevin and I are going to meet before the investors get there."

Maggie stepped forward to hug Jen. "Call me later."

When she arrived at the gym to finalize the setup, the hour and a half Jen had allotted flew by. Daisy complimented Jen on her outfit and the "right application of makeup." The two shared a stress-relieving laugh.

Despite the dance of butterflies in her stomach, Jen presented her plan for the healthy living classes, including study results she found that led to Kevin presenting the attendance goals and how those would translate into revenue for the gym. She'd never been in a meeting with executive-level leadership, but the investors nodded along to the information. They asked a few questions of Kevin that related to cash-flow and staffing needs—all things Kevin had answers for. The meeting wrapped up, and Kevin and the investors were deep in conversation when Jen slipped out. She went to her office, closed the door, and leaned against it with a happy sigh. *Yes*!

Jen busied herself looking over fitness class schedules and anything else she could find while waiting for Kevin to be freed up. She had asked Daisy to let her know when the investors left. He stopped by her office instead.

"Well, they loved your plan and our projected financials. Are you ready to get this new programming going?"

Jen jumped up from her desk. "Kevin, that's outstanding! Congratulations!"

"The congrats are yours too. Thank you for all your hard work. It's going to pay off." Kevin picked up his folder and left.

Jen's face warmed and her smile grew. She closed her office door and in silent enthusiasm did her happy dance. *Maybe I can do this.*

# CHAPTER FIFTEEN

The week's schedule and Maggie's daily plan for the family was rolling along well. Thursday morning, she kissed Dan goodbye and reminded him about picking up the kids.

"Please get there no later than three thirty, or Mrs. Fitzpatrick will have to watch them."

Dan grabbed his keys and briefcase and was out the door. Maggie heard a faint "Got it."

Maggie arrived at the theater early to get her thoughts together for the read-through and to settle her excitement. She gave the heavy, distressed wood door a solid yank. It relented to her confident entrance. Her self-talk was all about focus. It had been fifteen years since she was on stage. Stepping into the auditorium was like putting on her well-worn sweats. She was at home. But what if a lot had changed in the theater since then? The silence echoed as Maggie took an aisle seat midway down. In her heart she took a minute to pray. *Father, thank you for this opportunity. Please let everything work out with managing the house, the kids, and Dan. Lord, I just want to feel like myself again. I love being a mother and wife, but I needed this. I needed to do something just for me. I hope you don't think me selfish. Thank you. Amen.*

Jim cleared his throat, breaking the silence. Maggie looked up. "Oh, I'm sorry, I didn't hear you." Jim took the seat in front of Maggie and looked at her with tender eyes.

"I never get used to it either. There is so much great history here, you can almost hear it screaming from the walls and out of the seats. I love this building."

A slight smile confirmed her agreement. "Yes, it is an enchanting feeling."

Standing, Jim reassured her. "You're going to do well. Thank you for agreeing to come and help us."

That was more than Dan had offered earlier. Maggie gathered her bag and stood. "Ready or not, I'm here and looking forward to the adventure."

Walking to the side door, Jim began to run through the day's schedule. Maggie listened to make sure she missed nothing.

Maggie enjoyed the familiarity of the production routine. She had met all the actors and was navigating her way with them. They were young and already knew each other. Most were in classes together at the university—they went to the same parties. Maggie had no notion of becoming best friends with any of them, but figuring out how to be friends at all was a bit of a challenge. The theater and the production were the thing they had in common. She had no tattoos and no extra piercings. That morning over their parking lot coffee, Jen had continued to encourage her to just be herself. And no matter what she saw or heard, *not* to go into parent mode.

"Thanks for everything, Maggie. Today went well, and things are moving along without a hitch."

Filing her notes in her bag, Maggie reached for her phone. "Thanks, Jim, I'm ..." Her expression tightened.

"What's wrong?"

"Nine missed calls—three from the principal and six from Dan. This isn't good." She pressed the voicemail button. The first message was from Mrs. Fitzpatrick at three-ten.

"Maggie, there's been a fall. I'm so sorry, I turned my head for just a minute with another child." Mrs. Fitzpatrick's voice quivered. "It's Emma, her arm is hurt. I'll try your husband, but I think she needs a doctor."

"Oh my God." Maggie went to the next message from Dan.

"What's wrong, Maggie?" Jim drew a little closer.

Dan's message at 3:20 p.m. was clear and curt. "Maggie, where are you? Emma's hurt. I think her arm's broken. The ambulance is on its way, and we will head to Children's Hospital. *Call me!*"

Maggie's hands trembled as she grabbed her stuff and headed for the door. Over and over, she mumbled, "I knew something would happen. I can't believe I let this happen. Please let my little girl be okay."

Jim caught up to her. "What's happened?"

Maggie turned her tear-stained, contorted face to him. "While I was here playing stage manager, my little girl fell off the swing and broke her arm. I have to go to her."

"Let me drive you. You're upset and shouldn't drive. Where did they take her?" Jim snagged his keys from his pocket, and with his hand on the small of Maggie's back, he led her to the front door. Over his shoulder, he instructed Sara to lock up. She barely had a chance to say yes before they were out the door.

Jim drove a dusty blue SUV with leather interior that was as tidy as if it had just come off the sales lot. On the way to the hospital, despite not having children of his own, Jim tried to reassure Maggie with things he'd probably heard others say, that kids were resilient, and her daughter would be fine.

Maggie listened to Dan's voice mail from an hour before. They were at the hospital waiting for the doctor. In the background, she could hear what she was sure was Emma crying. A mother knew her child's cry. *Lord, please let Emma feel your calm. Please let her be okay. Please give us green lights all the way there.*

The theater was located south of downtown and was a straight shot up Third Street to Chestnut. But every city block had a stop light. Timed right, they wouldn't have to stop and in ten minutes, she would be at Emma's side.

She dialed Dan. He answered on the first ring.

"Where are you? We've been trying to reach you for hours." He was mad. Again.

"We're on our way. With greens, I should be there in about ten minutes. How's Emma?"

In short tones. "Your daughter is fine. She's in pain. We are waiting for a doctor—and you."

Maggie didn't care that Dan was upset. With all her being, she wanted to be with her daughter. Jim dropped her at the emergency room door. Leaving her bag, she practically leaped from the car as it came to a stop.

Maggie ran to the information desk.

"Where's my daughter?"

A familiar voice came from behind her. Mrs. Fitzpatrick stepped to Maggie's side. She reached for Maggie's arm and spoke in a wise and calm voice. "Maggie, she's fine. Emma's in room 4A. I'm so sorry."

Maggie melted into a puddle of tears. After an encouraging hug, Mrs. Fitzpatrick pulled away and handed her a tissue. "Wipe your face, or you'll scare Emma."

The registration nurse handed Maggie a pass to go back. Maggie was headed for the automatic double doors when Jim walked in.

"Jim, you didn't need to come in. I'm going back to see Emma."

"No problem, I'll wait out here. Just let me know if you need anything."

Observing the interaction, Mrs. Fitzpatrick stepped up to introduce herself to Jim.

Maggie took a deep breath, collected herself, and pushed the button to the automatic doors. Room 4A was the second curtained area on the left.

"Mommy!" Emma screamed. The jostle made her flinch. "Oooh, it hurts."

Emma had turned eight earlier in the spring and hadn't called Maggie "Mommy" in about two years. Maggie's shoulders drooped with the burden of her mommy guilt. Gently taking a seat on the side of the bed, she barely looked at Dan.

"Baby, it's going to be fine. I'm here, and the doctor will be in shortly." The bone had not come through the skin but there was swelling and bruising already, and she could see the bone was not right.

Emma started to cry. "It hurts."

Maggie leaned close to her daughter. "I know, sweetheart. I promise we're going to get your arm fixed up."

The pediatrician peeked in before pushing the curtain back fully. Dr. Green was in his mid-thirties. His hospital scrubs featured cartoon characters. His stethoscope had a small monkey clipped on as if it were climbing. Reviewing a chart, he looked into Emma's sad face. "Now which foot did you hurt?" He smiled and winked at Emma, who cautiously smiled.

Observing her arm without touching it, he asked, "What happened? Did big brother get out of line?"

Danny sat up. It was the first time in several minutes he had been acknowledged. Emma slowly smiled. "No, I fell off the monkey bars at school."

Dr. Green logged into the computer to make a few quick notes. "Were the monkeys chasing you?"

Emma went into a full giggle. "No."

"Well, tell me how you fell and how you landed." Dr. Green asked smoothly as he began to examine her head and listen to her chest.

Emma swiped a lingering tear with her good arm, and began to explain. "Well, it was sort of a race to see who could get across the monkey bars the fastest. I was almost to the other side and my fingers slipped loose." She went on to explain how she landed with her arm twisted behind her.

"Sounds rough." Dr. Green stood, making final notes, then he looked up at Maggie and Dan. "She's broken her arm. We need to do X-rays to see the extent of the break and what to do next. The nurse will be in to have you sign a release to treat and ..." A look of fear crept across Emma's face. "I promise it's going to be okay, Emma. My friend Luke, the orderly, will be here to take you for a ride on the gurney you're on to have a photo shoot. Do you know what an X-ray is, Emma?"

Maggie stood back, impressed with Dr. Green's bedside manner. She relaxed again as he explained that the X-rays would hurt some, but the pictures would show her bones and how he could get her all fixed. His final reassuring words were, "and your parents can go with you but will have to wait out in the hall." The doctor leaned in with a bright smile. "I bet if you handle this like the big girl you are, they might find a treat for you on the way home."

Emma's smile had grown back to full size. "Okay, I'll try."

"Mr. and Mrs. Nelson, I don't think this is a bad break, but we will know more with the X-rays. We're pretty busy, as you can see. I'll try to move her along, so we can get her comfortable."

Dan and Maggie both thanked the doctor and turned their attention back to Emma. Danny stepped up to the bed. “Emma, what color do you want your cast to be? Can I sign it?”

Emma’s face shrank again, and the tears pooled. Maggie tried to stop his next words but failed. “You know Sammy in my class broke his arm, and he got a neon-blue cast.”

Emma looked immediately at her mother. “Will I get a cast? Will it hurt more? How long will I have to wear it?”

Maggie pulled Danny away from the bed. “Why don’t you and your dad go get something to drink? This could take a while.”

Dan began to protest, wanting to stay with Emma. Maggie gave him a knowing look.

Dan kissed Emma and motioned to Danny. “Come on, buddy. Let’s go let Mrs. Fitzpatrick know what’s going on.”

“Do you want to go down to the cafeteria and get him something to eat? He’s probably starving.” Maggie didn’t neglect her other child. Her mommy guilt thoughts were pushing to make another appearance. Dan said nothing. He and his son departed.

While they waited, a nurse came in with a dose of pain medication. She left, and just a few minutes later, the orderly, Luke, arrived.

“Emma Nelson? Are you ready to take a ride on the chariot? You stay right where you are. I just need to unlock the wheels.” One side of the gurney already had the side rail up. Luke pulled the other side rail up, made sure it was secure, and unlocked the wheels.

Maggie stayed close by as they navigated the hall to the X-ray area.

Another three hours went by before they got the results and had Emma’s left arm set in a cast. Maggie could have guessed, but Emma chose bright pink for the outside layer.

While there were moments when she was uncomfortable, the pain medicine had worked, and she was looking a little woozy. With pages of instructions and a referral to an orthopedic doctor for follow-up, Dan pushed Emma out in a wheelchair. Mrs. Fitzpatrick had gone after Dan and Danny to explain what was going on. Jim stood when he saw them come from the exam area.

Maggie put her hand to her chest. “Oh, Jim, I’m so sorry. You didn’t need to wait.”

“It’s fine. I wanted to be sure you have what you need.” He smiled at Emma. “This must be the star of the show.”

Emma nodded, and Maggie introduced Dan and Danny. “This is Jim Preston—the director of the play I’m working on. Jim, you didn’t need to wait all this time. Thank you.” Jim handed Maggie her bag and purse. “You left these in my car. Your car is still at the theater. Do you want me to get Sara, and we’ll bring it to you?”

Dan bristled and stepped up. “Thanks, Jim, but we’ll go by on the way home and pick it up. Thanks.”

With a small bow, Jim surrendered. “Maggie, take your time coming in. If you need to stay home tomorrow, not a problem. Just let me know what you need.”

“Thanks, Jim, for everything. Yes, I will probably need to hang with my girl tomorrow.”

“Okay, good night. It was good to finally meet you.” Jim shook Dan’s hesitant hand.

The silence in the car was broken with Danny talking incessantly about Emma’s cast and having it autographed by everyone. Emma rode quietly, in and out of sleep. After a quick stop for her prescription to be filled and Maggie snagging Emma’s favorite treats, the four headed to the theater to pick up Maggie’s car.

At home, Dan mumbled he would get Danny to bed. Maggie, in all her mothering glory, gave Emma her final dose of medication, scurried around getting the right pillows to help keep Emma's arm elevated, and tucked her daughter into bed. She peeked in on Danny, making a small adjustment to his covers. She kissed his forehead and quietly told him she loved him.

Maggie closed his door behind her and hesitated. To the right were the stairs leading down to Dan and what was destined to not be a good conversation. To her left was their bedroom and the thought of a hot relaxing bath. Her little girl was going to be fine. A bath would help drain the remaining mommy guilt. But no doubt the usual sleep that followed would elude her if she didn't make things right with Dan.

*Time to put my big girl panties on.* Maggie headed for the stairs.

# CHAPTER SIXTEEN

Their exchange was short and anger-ridden.

Dan's voice was a little too loud, and his face was red. "Where were you?"

"Where was I? At the theater, where else? My phone was in my bag and on vibrate so it wouldn't interrupt rehearsal."

Dan paced across the living room, shaking his head. "Maggie, this isn't working. That's the second time I've tried to reach you and couldn't because you were at the theater. I don't think you can do this play."

The full weight of Dan's unfair statement pushed through Maggie's soul. Something in her flipped. The gloves came off.

"Are you out of your mind? This didn't happen because I wasn't available to you or the kids. It was an accident. With kids, they fall, they scrape knees, and *sometimes,* they break arms." Maggie was on a roll, her voice was elevated, and she pointed toward the stairs. The guilt transformed to anger and frustration. "Is this about me not being there or because for once, *you* had to be there?"

Her question loomed.

Dan sat on the edge of the couch with both hands on his knees. "What are you saying, *I* had to be there? I've always been there for the kids, and for you, I might add ..."

"Yeah, between business trips and conference calls."

*Ouch.*

"Maggie, we talked about this before Danny was born. You wanted to stay home with the kids, and I would pursue my career. I've done my part. The only thing I see different with what happened today was you were unreachable when your daughter needed you most. Do you know how helpless I felt at the playground when all Emma kept asking for was you? No one else could soothe her."

"You don't think I feel guilty for all of this? I do, Dan. There, are you happy? But I also know in the last few weeks, I've felt more like myself as a whole person than I have in years. I need this, Dan."

"Yeah, yeah, poor Maggie," Dan snapped. "Lonely housewife. It's all about the kids and her demanding husband."

Maggie's voice rose. "Yes, it has been all about you and the kids. And I loved it. But somewhere along the line that's the *only* thing it became about."

The red tinge climbed higher on Dan's cheeks. "Look, Emma needed you today and you weren't there. This can't happen again."

Maggie's hand went to her chest, and she inhaled his declaration.

"Well, maybe if I weren't worried about how starched your dress shirts are and being available to run them over to you after you've been a klutz at lunch, I could be more available for the kids." She couldn't catch the words. They were out there, and she had broken the cardinal rule of arguing. She brought up something they had settled.

Dan got up and immediately and headed for the garage door. "Let me help take something off your plate."

Was he leaving? Dan didn't walk out. They were together and had been since they were teenagers. As he grabbed his keys from the dish by the door, Maggie's heart sank. Where was he going?

Then there was silence. Maggie stood alone in the middle of their living room, the lights as dim as she felt. Her spirit drained away. The day had been too long, and she had nothing left to fight with. Maggie dragged herself upstairs with her cell phone in her hand.

Dan would cool off and come home or call her. They never went to sleep mad. Maggie washed her face and went to check on Emma. With all the yelling and chaos downstairs, her daughter slept soundly. Not wanting to risk jostling her, Maggie knelt beside her bed and rested her forehead on the edge of the mattress.

*Father, help. I've made a mess of things. I thought this would work. I needed it to work. Please, Lord, help me make it right again.*

Maggie's spirit melted into the peace of her big God. He would help her. In the quiet, warmth of a little girl's room, Maggie's eyelids yielded to tiredness, and she fell asleep.

Maggie was working her lines and stage movements. The auditorium was dark except a stage wash of light. The tech guys were in the sound booth working, but the cover of darkness swallowed her and gave her the confidence to rehearse and make mistakes without others paying attention. This was Maggie's time to work out the rough spots on her own. A perfectionist, she hated making unnecessary mistakes in front of others. At the end of a monologue she was certain she had nailed, she heard a thud. And then ...

"Maggie ... please call for help ... I need you to call ..."

"Daddy, where are you? I can't see you. I didn't even know you were here." His voice came from below, just off stage. "Daddy, where are you?"

A feeble voice in the darkness. "I came by to check some props and materials for tomorrow. Mag, call for help."

Pushing through the dreamy fog, down the three steps from the stage, Maggie found herself with her father at her feet. His arm flopped to his chest with his last breath.

"Daddy, nooo!"

Maggie jerked awake, her stomach gnawing and her face feeling tight from dried tears. The silence roared through the room. She had fallen asleep while praying. She tiptoed out of her injured daughter's room. Alone. Where was Dan? What time was it? Only ten thirty.

*He's probably just driving around, settling down.* She slumped on her bed as the fight and the exchange of harsh frustrated words rushed through her mind. *Dan's never done this before. What have I done?*

# CHAPTER SEVENTEEN

Mark answered the door to find Dan leaning on the doorframe, head down.

"Hey, man, are you okay? Come in."

Dan didn't say a word. He walked into his best friend's house. Mark followed him into the living room. "What's going on?"

Dan paced around their living room, rambling in frustration about some argument with Maggie. He stopped with one hand on his hip, raking the other through his hair. "What should I do?"

A smile crossed Mark's lips. "Let's start with you sitting down and telling me what happened."

Jen came down to see who was at their door so late. "Dan, are you okay?" Mark turned to look at his wife and shrugged in question.

Jen looked over at Dan sitting on the couch with his head in his hands. Something big was wrong. She started to slowly turn to slip back upstairs and give the guys some privacy.

As if he hadn't thought about disturbing them, Dan stood. "Oh Jen, I'm sorry. I didn't think. I was driving and ended up here. It's late, I'm sorry, I should go." Dan rose to leave. "I needed to blow off some steam, and I didn't know where to go."

Mark reached for his shoulder. “Just stop. You don’t need to be driving around.” Mark’s sympathetic look at Jen was her signal to give them a minute.

“No, Dan, don’t go.” She waved at Dan. “You and Mark hang out and talk. Do you mind if I call Maggie to let her know you’re okay?”

Dan smirked. “Call if you want. She probably doesn’t care right now where I am.”

“I doubt that, but I will leave you guys to talk.” Jen headed upstairs.

Mark handed Dan a glass of water and sat across from his college roommate and best friend. The silence hung between them long enough for Dan to take a couple of gulps of water and settle down a little.

Mark looked at Dan. “So, what’s going on?”

Dan dropped his head back to his hands and sat silent. His anger had been melted away by his own guilt for walking out on Maggie. He shook his head, drawing his hands over his face.

“This afternoon Emma fell and broke her arm. It was awful. She was in pain, and I couldn’t make it better.” Dan stood and walked around the room. “You know, when Maggie started this talk of a role in a play, I saw a glimpse of young Maggie. Remember when we were all in college, running hard, having fun.” He turned to look at Mark. “I fell in love with her spirit and passion for the things she was interested in. That’s the Mag I fell in love with. Even in our early years of being married, life felt ... lighter. But then kids, and the job ... looking back, it feels like the years have been a slow boil, with all the fun being lifted away in the steam, leaving a hot mess. I wanted her to do something for herself. God knows she’s spent the last decade taking care of me and our family. But ...”

Mark didn’t react. He listened.

Dan hesitated, wiping his left hand over his mouth. "It's hard to not rely on her to just run things. I don't know how to handle her having something outside our family that I'm not a part of. And today, with Emma falling and breaking her arm ... I felt so helpless."

Mark nodded. "You felt helpless. Is this about you or Maggie?"

Dan shook his head. He continued to pace, not answering Mark. "Who are these people she's spending all this time with? Some Jim fella brought her to the hospital. I don't know him." Waving his arms, he said, "If you ask me, he seemed a little too interested and concerned for her." He settled back on the couch. "She's got everything at the house on a schedule and organized, but she's still asking me to pick up the kids, and I know she's asked Jen to help. Why does she have to do this now?"

Mark asked in a knowing tone, "How's work right now?"

Dan blew out a puff of air. "You don't want to know. I've got auditors crawling all over my department either because of an accounting error or some serious embezzling by someone on my team."

"Ugh. Lots of pressure." Mark's career was in IT. He worked for an accounting software company. He didn't jump in with a solution. He sat and let the situation hang between them.

Dan's footsteps on the hardwood floor stopped. He sat back down. The room was silent again.

Mark was the one to speak first. "What exactly did you argue about? Was it about her doing this stage manager thing or not being available when Emma got hurt? Or was it because you felt so helpless with Emma?" A little sting to the ego, but their friendship was based on honesty.

Dan shook his head and sighed. "I don't know. Now's not a good time for her to be doing this. I mean, yes, she's always been there to take care of the kids. But I had no idea what to do, and Emma was inconsolable."

"What is it, Dan? Are you mad because she wasn't there? Or is this just not a good time for you for her not to be there? Or was it Emma wanting her mom when she was hurt, and you couldn't fix it? That's only natural and you know it." Marked nudged Dan's knee. "Look, I understand what it's like when your wife decides she wants something different and more out of life."

Dan looked up. "That's right, Jen got a full-time job. I thought you two agreed she would only work part time until Brian is older."

Mark smiled. "We did. But then this opportunity came along, not falling in our timeline. She was excited about it, and I knew she could do the job well."

"But how do you two manage everything?"

Mark exhaled. "Good grief, Dan. We just do it. We work together. I want her to be happy with her life more than I care if I'm inconvenienced or have to take up the slack with Brian. In fact, he and I have had a good time hanging out together. Time we wouldn't have had otherwise."

"You think I'm being selfish."

"I think you're being more foolish than selfish. You're under pressure at work, and now Maggie has changed your wonderfully organized and scheduled life."

Dan nodded. "That about sums it up. It, it just ... it scared me today when Emma got hurt and Maggie wasn't there to hold us all together. She is our family's glue."

Mark agreed. "Yes, she is. Remember our wives are more precious than rubies." A half-grin snuck across Mark's lips. "Jen and I are always amazed at how much Maggie gets done and has time for. And with such a fun spirit." Mark chuckled. "She's always been like that. Remember her senior year in college? She had the lead in some Shakespeare play. Learned all her lines in old English and finished all her final five classes with straight As. Oh, and planned your wedding. You do remember the wonder woman you married?"

"Yes, I do. She had more energy than me then and still does."

"Yeah, I'm convinced if she and Jen hadn't married us, they would have taken over the world." Mark paused and let it sink in. "Dan, you and Maggie have gotten a little crossways. But you'll find your way back. She needs you to love her. Support her. Is it convenient? No. But becoming one as we did with our wives the day we married them isn't about convenience. It's about loving sacrificially."

The two men talked about finishing college and all the fun times the four had had, Maggie being the one who always had the plan and details for their adventures.

"Got to love the woman with the plan," Dan mused.

"Seriously, Dan, I know you well enough to know change isn't your favorite. But Maggie's great. She's not abandoning you. She's reaching to do something she loved and gave up for a long time because of her love for you and the kids. Let her do this. Quit being a jerk."

Dan perked up at Mark's directness. "Ouch, man. That stung. I thought I was the one who knew how to handle women. When did you get so smart? You certainly weren't in college."

Mark stood. "Yeah, yeah. Believe me, I've screwed up with Jen more times than I care to count. Somehow by the grace of God, we've survived, and our love continues to grow."

Mark and Dan walked to the door. "Hey, don't forget the guys' night at church is this weekend. Haven't seen you at any of them lately. They've got food coming, and there's a speaker. Why don't you come? Might help you re-center."

Noncommittal, Dan said maybe, then he checked his watch and grabbed his jacket. "I'll let you know. Right now, I need to make things right with my bride. Thank you, brother."

"No problem. You would've done the same for me."

Dan drove home lost in thought. No radio, just quiet. Mark had reminded him of some terrific times the four of them had had in college. A smile crawled across his face as he thought of the camping trips, canoeing, and young Maggie. She was full of life and going to take on the world. No doubt she would be victorious.

The curvy back road was dark. Dan jerked alert with the fleeting flash of movement from the side of the road. He swerved to miss whatever was coming at him. The thud echoed as the car bounced off the guardrail on one side of the road and slammed into the tree on the other. The last thing Dan heard was the horn blaring and the airbags detonating. And the last thing he felt was the warm stream of blood rolling down his face.

# CHAPTER EIGHTEEN

Maggie wandered into the bathroom to wash her face. The phone rang hard and broke the silence. She practically leaped over the bed to grab it. "Dan?"

"It's Jen. You okay?"

"Well, it's late and I'm wondering where my husband is."

Jen quickly interrupted her. "He's here and fine. He and Mark are downstairs talking. How are you?"

Maggie relived the argument and guilt-ridden feelings, short of explaining the nightmares that had invaded her sleep. Not knowing exactly what to do about them, she wasn't ready to share them.

"Maggie, Dan looked pretty upset when he got here. He's working it out. He loves you—that's not going to change."

After Jen's reassuring words, Maggie crawled into bed to watch the news. She had paced and prayed. Her emotions were mixed—worried about Dan, but confident Mark would talk some sense into him, and he'd come home.

The clock read one o'clock in the morning. Something was wrong. Dan wouldn't have talked to Mark this long without calling. She hit the name at the top of her recent call list—Dan. Straight to voice mail. His phone was either dead or off. Why would he turn it off? As much as Maggie hated to disrupt Jen and Mark again, she called.

A sleepy hello from Mark.

"Mark, it's Maggie. Is Dan still there?"

Mark in a breathy whisper: "No, Mag. He left an hour ago. He's not home?"

"Oh my God, Mark, where is he?"

Jen took the phone.

"Maggie, I'm sure he's fine. Maybe his car broke down."

Maggie began to panic. "An hour ago! Why didn't he call?"

Jen's soothing voice continued. "I'm sure he's fine. Did you try his phone?"

"Yes, and it went straight to voice mail." Maggie heard the covers rustling and Jen murmuring to Mark.

"Mark's going to head your way to see if he's broken down along the road. Do you know if he goes the parkway or back roads?"

Maggie ran her hand through her hair, "I don't know, he's always going different routes. I guess try the back road."

"Mark's leaving now."

From the background, Mark called back, "Don't worry, Maggie, I'll find him."

"Maggie, I want you to take a deep breath," Jen said. "Dan will be fine. How about I talk to you until he calls or comes home?"

"Jen, this is my fault. Something's happened, and it's my fault. I ran him out of here. I made him mad. I don't even know what the big deal was. I shouldn't have upset our life."

"Listen to you. While you're at it, is world hunger your fault too? Breathe and try to relax. Dan is fine and will be home with you in no time." Jen stayed on the phone, encouraging and talking to Maggie. They prayed for Dan and for their marriage. Then they chatted about random things. Anything to keep Maggie's mind from pure worry.

Jen's house phone rang in the background. "Hang on, Maggie, my other phone is ringing."

Maggie could hear Jen talking on the other phone to Mark. Pressing her cell phone closer to her ear, she leaned forward a little to see if she could hear better.

She couldn't.

Mark was taking too long to be telling Jen that Dan's car had broken down. Something had happened.

Jen came back to the cell phone.

"Maggie?" Jen's voice cracked.

"What, what happened? Where's Dan?"

Jen's voice calmed down for the sake of her friend. "Mag, there's been a wreck. It appears Dan hit a deer. An ambulance took him to Baptist Hospital, and the police are having his car towed."

"Oh no!" Maggie melted down in full sobs. "No, please no."

Jen gave her a minute. Then she went on, her voice calm and quiet, but authoritative, "Maggie, listen. I'm going to call your mother to come stay with the kids. You need to get dressed. I'm going to bring Brian over there, and you and I will meet the guys at the hospital."

Maggie sat on her bed, not saying a word.

"Maggie, are you there?"

"Yes, yes, I'm here. What did you say?"

"Maggie, I am going to call your mother to come stay with the kids. I'm headed that way. Sweetie, go wash your face and put some clothes on. You and I will head to the hospital."

"No, I'll call my mother. If you call at this hour, she may not answer."

"Okay, I'll see you shortly." More silence. "Maggie, are you there?"

Maggie hesitated, lost in her worry. "Yes, I'm here. Oh, Jen." The tears came back quickly. "What if ..."

Jen interrupted, like a big sister, "Maggie, honey, he's going to be fine. Just call your mom and get dressed. I'm on my way."

Maggie hung up and dropped to the floor by her bed. With her face in her hands, she let the tears go. It was all too much. She let the stress and heartache of it all flow out with every tear. As she caught her breath, she reached for her phone to dial her mother, who answered on the third ring.

"Mom." She sniffed while dragging her sleeve across her cheek.

"Maggie, what's wrong? Are the kids all right? Why are you calling me at this hour?"

Too many rapid-fire questions. "Mom, Dan has been in a wreck, and I need to go to the hospital. I need you to come stay with the kids." To say she *needed* her mother crashed through her like the deer crashed into their car.

"What happened? Why was he out so late?"

Frustrated to even have to ask this favor, Maggie raised her voice. "Mom, I need you to just come now. I've got to get to the hospital. Jen's on her way over to go with me. Please, put a coat on and come over here. The kids are asleep. You can get the bed in the guest room."

"Well, I hope the kids aren't up at this hour. Good grief, Maggie. I'll be there in about fifteen minutes."

Not a good night for her mom. She was in a mood.

Maggie managed a pair of jeans and sweater. Glasses, not contacts. Her eyes were tired and puffy. Running a brush through her hair, she grabbed a washcloth, trying to wipe away the disbelief of visiting the hospital twice in one day.

Joanna Fenwick blew in sounding like she had started talking before Maggie opened the door. She was wearing her fur coat over her designer silk pajamas. Her hair was askew, and her face was shiny with night cream. The fur coat was a little much for the situation. No doubt her pajamas cost more than Maggie's winter coat.

"Hi, Mom. Thanks for coming." Maggie left the door open, looking for Jen to follow any minute.

Maggie's mother grabbed her, jerking Maggie into a hug. "Oh, baby, are you okay? You sounded so distraught on the phone."

Distracted again, looking for Jen, Maggie mumbled, "I'm fine, just need to get to the hospital." She turned her attention to the medicine from Emma's earlier trip to the emergency room. Maggie took a deep breath. "Mom, Emma took a small fall this afternoon and ... um, broke her arm." She braced herself for her mother's dramatic reaction.

"What? She broke her arm! Why didn't you call me? I love my grandkids, Mag. You should have called me."

"Mom, it happened after school. Dan got her to the hospital. I met him there." She took another deep breath. Breathing deeply wasn't helping. Her head hurt. "It's been a long day, Mom. Look, she's fine. I've got her arm propped up. Please look in on her. If she wakes up hurting, give her one of these."

"Okay, but ..." Before she set in on the second stanza of her lecture, Jen slipped in the front door with a very sleepy son.

She whispered, "Hey, you two. Maggie, where can I settle Brian?"

"Come on, he can sleep in the other twin bed in Danny's room. Mom, come up. You can settle into the guest room. I pulled out towels for you."

"Maggie, how on earth can I sleep with all this going on? Emma's broken arm and Dan's been in a wreck?" Babbling on about how much all the news was affecting her, Joanna followed Jen and Maggie up the stairs.

In the middle of her mother's harangue, Maggie kissed her on the cheek. "Mom, thanks for coming."

After her mother's drama, Maggie welcomed the silent ride with a trusted friend.

# CHAPTER NINETEEN

Maggie opened the door before Jen had a chance to fully stop in the ambulance bay. Grabbing her purse, she rushed through the automatic doors and got her bearings.

Mark jumped up from the waiting area. "I'm glad you're here. Let's get you back to Dan."

With the sight of the machines, the oxygen tube in Dan's nose, and bloodied bandages, Maggie's hand drew to her mouth. "Dan." The tears came again, and Maggie immediately found his hand.

At her touch, his swollen eyes opened. "I'm okay. You should see the deer I mounted on the hood."

His attempt at humor was lost on Maggie.

The doctor stepped back in the room. "I'm Doctor Hart. You must be the amazing Maggie I've been hearing about. Your husband assured me you would have all the information we need for his medical history."

Glad she had grabbed her planner from the counter on the way out the door, Maggie pulled it out of her bag. "Doctor, is he going to be all right?"

Dr. Hart nodded. "It looks worse than it is. He is going to be fine, but I want to run an MRI on his head. He bumped it pretty good. I'm guessing on the driver's door. But the airbags saved us the big problems. One of my residents will come stitch the cut on his head. Fortunately, it wasn't too deep. He was awake when they found him but wasn't clear on his name and the day. Your friend Mark helped me with the time frame, so he probably wasn't out for long. He seems with it now. We're probably looking at a mild concussion, but I want to be sure. And he's got a broken rib or two. So, we need to get some pictures to be sure his chest is clear."

Maggie felt the room begin to sway. It was too much—his head, concussions, broken ribs. *It was all my fault.* Jen stepped up behind Maggie and took her arm, steadying her. "Mag, you want to sit down?"

Maggie pulled herself together. "Doctor, will he have to stay the night?"

Dr. Hart looked at his watch. "Given the hour, I probably won't admit him, unless his chest X-ray gives me reason to. I need time to run the tests and observe him. So, you need to get comfortable."

The doctor's tender eyes were a comfort. "What questions do you have for me?"

Maggie's mind went blank. She was sure she should have questions, but nothing came. She looked at Dan, the red scratches and bruises on his face. "I, I, I don't think I have any questions right now."

"Okay then, let me go get all these orders in. You are going to see nurses in and out of here taking his blood pressure and watching his vitals. That is all routine. It's pretty quiet around here tonight, so they should be able to come get him for his scan soon."

"Thank you, Doctor," Dan whispered, and Maggie said aloud.

Jen and Mark followed the doctor out of the curtained area. Maggie pulled the chair up to the bedside and rested her forehead on his hand. "Dan, I am so sorry."

"Look at me." Dan's voice was strained, his swollen black eyes fixed on her. "My wreck is not your fault. It was an accident."

"I know, but it feels like I'm the one who has shaken up our home and relationship. You wouldn't have been out late driving if I hadn't ..." Her words were replaced by tears.

"We aren't having this conversation right now." Dan spoke a little stronger. "Please, let's get through this debacle." He winced as he attempted to roll the other direction.

"Mr. Nelson?" The resident came through the curtain. "I'm Mary, and I'm gonna get you stitched up."

Maggie pulled the chair away from the bed to make room. She sat staring at the brown fake-wood cabinets.

Jen's singsong "knock, knock" brought Maggie out of her most recent daze. People had been in and out for the last hour taking care of Dan.

"I brought you a soda, full-bodied, no diet."

"Thank you. They've taken Dan for an MRI. Not sure how they tell if he's sore from the wreck or from all the poking they do. Where's Mark?"

"He went home to shower and change and pick up Brian and Danny for school."

Maggie had called her mom to let her know Dan was going to be all right and give her instructions for the morning routine with Emma's arm needs. Her mom must have been tired. She didn't give her the fifth degree and agreed with the instructions.

Maggie took a long draw from her soda. It was a refreshing break from her concern for Dan. "Jen, why do I feel like all of this is my fault? My family is falling apart. Literally!"

The voice of calm, Jen said, "Your family isn't falling apart. A few bumps and bruises in the last twenty-four hours, but not falling apart. Let's take a walk while Dan's gone."

"A little walk might help."

Their stroll out to the parking lot and back served for Maggie to talk and Jen to listen. Jen didn't say anything. Didn't even try to fix the problem. Both being problem solvers, this was how the two friends helped each other during crises. Jen joined Maggie in a few tears. They walked, Maggie talked out all her feelings, thoughts, and concerns. By the time they got back to the curtained area, Dan was back, and Maggie was exhausted.

"There you are. The doctor's on his way with the results." Dan seemed a little more alert.

Jen said her goodbyes. Mark was coming to pick her up so Maggie could drive Dan home.

Doctor Hart stepped through the curtain. "Well, Dan, given the accident you were in, you were lucky. No internal bleeding, just a cracked rib, which will be more of a nuisance than anything. No hard coughing or laughing. Your MRI doesn't show any problems with your skull or brain. But with the injury, you have a small concussion. You're going to have a pretty good headache for a few days. Don't be surprised if you feel a little foggy."

Maggie swallowed. *Foggy. Dan's the sharpest guy I know. He's never been foggy in his life.*

"You said you're a banker, right?" the doctor asked.

"Yes. When can I go back to work?"

Back to work? Maggie grimaced. He needed to take it easy for a while. The doctor continued with the instructions.

"You're not going to work for at least a couple of days. You need to rest this weekend, and let your head heal. Besides, you are going to be sore tomorrow and the next day. Moving around a little will help any stiffness. I've got two prescriptions for you that have been sent to the in-house pharmacy. You rest here while they're being filled, then we'll get you discharged."

Dan rested his head back and closed his eyes. "What time is it? I need to call the office and let them know."

"It's a little after two in the morning. I've already left Elaine a voicemail." Maggie told him. Impulsively, she added, "Dan, I'm quitting the play. This is all too much for our family right now."

Dan attempted to shift in the bed. His eyes were heavy as the pain medication began to work. "If that's what you want to do, Mag. I'm all for it. But I love you and want you to be happy." Dan drifted off to sleep.

Maggie sat feeling like she had a brick in her stomach. *What have I done?*

Maggie assisted Dan through the door a little after seven a.m. Mark had picked Danny and Brian up early to take them to breakfast before school. Joanna greeted Maggie at the door and doted over Dan as they both helped him upstairs. With each step, Joanna added unneeded advice for Dan's care. "You need to make sure he has everything he needs. He shouldn't want for anything or have to wait for you to fix food. Just have it ready."

Her mother's words loaded more guilt into Maggie's heart. Now she wasn't a good enough wife to know how to take care of her husband.

"You know, Mom, I think I can take care of Dan. We've been married long enough for me to know ..."

"Clearly you don't know everything, or he wouldn't have been out so late. Why was he out driving at all hours of the night?" Joanna shifted into a new diatribe. "Oh, honey, he wasn't out drinking or carrying on, was he? You know, Maggie, you can make life so comfortable at home that sometimes men need a little adventure."

"Mom. Stop. Stop talking. He wasn't out on some middle-aged escapade. We had an argument, and he went over to Mark's to talk to his best friend."

"An argument, what about? Are you two okay? Is your marriage in trouble?"

With Maggie at one elbow, and Joanna the other, Dan sat gingerly on the bed. "Joanna, Maggie and I are fine. We're working through some stuff. She'll take great care of me, I promise." He winked at his overbearing mother-in-law. "If she doesn't, you'll be my first call."

Maggie reached for Dan's hand and smiled at him. His defense gave her a little relief from her mother's denunciation. "Let's give him a few minutes to get settled."

Maggie tugged at her mother's arm to leave. "I'll walk Mom out and be back up."

Joanna followed Maggie out of the room and downstairs with continued tips for taking care of Dan. Maggie sighed and picked up her mother's coat, holding it out to her. "Mom, we're fine. Just a normal couple who disagreed on some things. I promise to take good care of him."

Joanna cupped Maggie's chin. "Oh, sweetie, you have a lot on your plate. Why don't I go home and make you a pot of chili?"

"Sure, Mom, that would be great." *Just please go home.*

Maggie climbed the stairs, checked on Emma—who was still sleeping well—and slid softly into bed with Dan.

"Mommy!"

Maggie jerked awake. She had made it into a deep sleep. Emma was calling for her. Maggie forgot to get up slowly. Dan moved and groaned.

"Coming." Maggie hustled into sweats and into Emma's room.

"It hurts."

"Okay, let's get you some medicine. Are you comfortable in bed, or do you want to come downstairs to the couch? We'll take your favorite fluffy blanket."

Maggie's eight-year-old, full-of-life little girl was hurting and needed her mom. In full mom mode, Maggie would make it better. "Careful getting up."

"Do I have to get dressed?" Emma leaned into her mom.

"No, sweetie, today is a pajama day."

Trailing behind Maggie, Emma poked her head in her parents' room. "Why's Daddy still home?"

It hadn't occurred to Maggie she would need to tell the kids about the car wreck. Danny had left early for school with few questions. He was excited to have gotten to ride to school with his friend Brian.

Maggie paused, "Well, last night your dad went over to visit with Mr. Mark for a while, and on his way home, a deer ran in front of the car, and Daddy had a wreck."

"A deer! Did it get hurt?"

Maggie smiled. The innocence of a child.

"Both the deer and your dad were injured."

"Daddy? Is he going to be okay?"

"Yes, sweetie. He needs rest." Tucking the blanket up around her legs and propping her arm on a pillow. "Just like you."

Emma was settled with a stack of Disney princess movies and her coloring books. The pain medication drew her into a nap. Maggie took Dan the morning dose of pain medication and then retreated to the kitchen for tea and time for a devotion.

With the last peaceful word, the doorbell rang. A glance at the clock made her wonder who could be there.

Opening the door for the second time that day, Joanna marched in, chili pot encased with potholders. She started in with instructions. "This is ready to serve for lunch. So put it on the stove until Dan's ready to eat."

Emma, groggy, awakened. Joanna handed Maggie the warm pot and headed straight for the couch.

"Oh, my baby girl, how are you feeling? Are you in pain?"

Maggie quietly closed the front door and took the chili to the kitchen.

"Oh, wait, I've got more," Joanna called. "I got to cookin', cooked all morning, went ahead and fried a chicken and made a meatloaf. You have meals for the next several days."

Cooking—her mother's love language. "Give me your keys, and I'll carry it in while you visit with Emma."

"Oh, and I stopped by the grocery to get Popsicles for this cutie and a treat for Danny. Don't want him to feel left out. Bring in all the bags."

*All the bags? Shouldn't Popsicles and one other treat be one bag?*

Three trips to the car later, Maggie began to unload the groceries that included fruit, a loaf of bread, sandwich meat, orange and apple juices, and fresh vegetables. "Mom, why did you buy all this? You know I go to the grocery once a week."

"Maggie, it's fine. I just wanted to help. Now you've got plenty of food in the house for easy meals and you can focus on taking care of your husband and daughter."

*Because I wouldn't otherwise ...?*

# CHAPTER TWENTY

The next couple of days Maggie worked out her guilt by doing things around the house and serving the food her mother had brought. All crazy aside, the woman could cook.

Everything with Dan felt too formal and polite. He wasn't demanding, and he said "please" and "thank you" with every request. To enlist Danny's help, Maggie tried to make a game of going and fetching. Dan slept, read, made lists of his work priorities, and wandered around the house to work out the soreness. He stayed quiet. Maggie felt like she was walking on eggshells, not knowing what he was thinking. Neither of them spoke about the argument or the play.

Maggie and Jim spoke several times a day as she answered questions for him and Sara, so they could take care of things for a few days. She said nothing to Jim about quitting. Nothing in Maggie wanted to quit the play. The scene in the hospital played over and over in her head. Why had she blurted out that she would quit?

Emma was doing well. On Monday, she went to school for a half day and came home with autographs on her cast. She was her energetic self, chatty and happy. If only Dan would chat some.

The dishes done from dinner and the kids watching a video, Maggie couldn't stand it anymore. Three days of interactions as sterile as his bandages! She had to try and talk to Dan again. He had gone back to bed and was watching something on the History Channel. Giving the bedroom door a gentle nudge with her hip, Maggie brought them both a cup of tea.

"How are you feeling?"

"I'm fine. My head hurts if I read too much, though, so I'm not getting any work done."

"It'll wait for you."

"Maggie, you don't seem to understand what is going on at my office right now. My team is being audited, and I'm not there!" He muted the TV. "And we need to find another car. Wasn't in the mood to spend the money this year." He wiped his fingers across his face. "I thought I heard you on the phone with someone from the theater. Didn't you say you were quitting the play?"

*Whoa*, Maggie thought, *here it all comes. This is what has been bouncing around his head for the last three days.* "Honey, I said something about that in the hospital, but I ..." Dan interrupted, placing his hand on Maggie's arm.

"Maggie, I'm sorry, but I don't feel well. Need to be sharp for a couple of conference calls I'm going to do tomorrow." He settled his tone a little. "The night of the wreck, Mark and I had a talk about marriage and the things you want. He helped me remember that part of my being a godly husband is allowing you to do the things you love too. But now, I feel the weight of everything on me, and I'm not exactly a hundred percent. I was struggling before. Now I don't know how to do all this. I want to support you in this. I'm just not sure how well I'll do."

Maggie looked down at his hand and grazed it with hers. "I'm not sure either. But can we keep trying? Let's work together. I want to support you in all you have going on as well. I don't want to quit the play."

The next seven weeks brought a smooth routine—rehearsals, school events, Dan's work meetings, and trying to get in the holiday spirit. Peace pushed into Maggie's heart as her spirit turned toward Thanksgiving with her family. Although they had never completely resolved the disagreement, Maggie continued with the play. She worked things around Dan, rarely asking him to help or step in with the kids. She avoided the conflict, and the constant guilt of the wreck, and Emma's arm.

Rehearsals were dismissed for the week of Thanksgiving, allowing Maggie time to get her house decorated and groceries purchased. Everything was under control. At times, Maggie ached to have the full support from Dan. She felt more separated from him than when he went off to college the year before she did.

The bright song of her phone brought a smile. It was Jen.

"Maggie, I'm so glad I caught you." Jen spoke in an unlikely panic.

"I'm here, what's wrong?" Maggie pulled up a stool from their breakfast bar.

"Our washing machine hose burst, and there's water all over the kitchen. I turned it on and then ran to the grocery. By the time I got back, there must have been two inches of water everywhere. The plumber can't come. The wallpaper has started to peel from the moisture. The bottom cabinets have flooded. The insurance adjuster won't be here until tomorrow, and I've got Thanksgiving to get ready for. Help!" Jen wasn't usually one to panic, but entertaining wasn't her forte.

Maggie was slow and calm. “How many are coming? Isn’t it only you, Mark, Brian and Mark’s dad?”

“Mark’s dad and his girlfriend, who Mark is not thrilled about.” Jen paused. “There’s a little tension between them. I just want it to go well for Mark and the kids.”

“I understand. Dan’s not thrilled with his dad’s lady friend either. What if you join us? Bring whatever food and ingredients that didn’t get wet, come over, and let’s do the holiday together.”

“That’s a lot on you, Mag. Are you sure?”

“I’m positive. Besides, it will take a little pressure off me and my mother.”

“You’re an angel. Thank you. We would love it. Let me get my act together here, and I’ll be over in a while. You should see me—I’m a mess from sopping up water.”

Maggie and Jen spent the next two days talking like a couple of old hens. It was a fun time catching up all they both had going on. They had dumpling broth simmering on the stove and the ingredients for potato casserole, cranberry salad, dressing, and two huge turkeys ready to go. Maggie had the oven items scheduled. One turkey and the ham could cook together, then the other turkey would go in. Jen had her family recipe book and Maggie hers. Both knew there would be way too much food, but that’s the way it worked for both their families. Thanksgiving meant more than eating for the one day. It was an eating fest for four days—turkey, ham, dumplings, and all the fixings to go with them. Maggie’s perfect kitchen was organized chaos, but the air was filled with warmth and the aroma of dumplings, turkey, dressing and desserts.

Maggie was chopping vegetables for Jen’s dressing. This was the first time the two friends had extended time with no one else around to talk. Jen brought up the night of the wreck. “I’ve never seen him that upset.”

"You! He's never walked out on me. I didn't know what to think or to do."

"I let him and Mark talk. Mark told me later about the fight, at least from Dan's point of view." Jen stopped cutting the dough for dumplings and brushed the flour off her hands. "Sounded like you two have gotten sideways with this theater thing. Is it worth it?"

Maggie's eyebrows came together. Was she going to have to defend her time at the theater with Jen too? "Is it worth what? Asking him to kick in a little so I can do this one thing, this one thing I love that only lasts for a few months? Yes." Maggie's neck tightened and her flour-coated hands slung a white puff as she gestured.

Jen's hands came up in surrender. "Okay, just checking. I didn't mean to question you. I've supported this from day one, remember? I'm sorry."

Maggie's shoulders dropped. "It's okay. I don't mean to be hypersensitive. The fight rattled me. Somewhere deep inside, I've always been afraid he would get tired of me and leave. But we get along so well, and our marriage has been more than I could have asked for or imagined." Shaking her head. "God really delivered me a loving husband, and all these years later I still struggle with feeling like I don't deserve it." She swiped her bangs from her forehead leaving a swipe of flour. "Maybe I'm being stubborn. Dan is trying to be supportive of the play, but we barely talk about it. And when I ask him to do a pickup, there's always a sigh."

Jen hugged Maggie. "Oh, Dan loves you and the kids like crazy. You threw him a curve ball when he wasn't expecting it. On top of Emma's arm and his wreck, and buying a new car, Dan's orderly, unchanging life has changed a lot."

"I know. I'm in a constant state of guilt. Did you just get flour all down my back?" Maggie swatted a wisp of flour in Jen's direction.

The two smiled with Jen's sheepish reply. "Well, sort of."

At the same moment, both moms looked at the clock on the stove. "Oh, it's time to get the kids," Maggie declared.

"You want to go get all three and I'll finish cutting and adding these dumplings to the broth?"

Wiping her hands on her grandmother's daisy-patterned apron—only worn for holiday cooking—Maggie agreed to the carpool plan. "You're pretty close on those. Why not finish up and head for your house, and I'll meet you there with Brian."

"But don't you want me to stay and clean up?"

Maggie was the master of her kitchen and making it sparkle. Maggie called as she headed out the door, "No, thanks. I got it."

Jen smiled, knowing her friend's obsession with a particular order. "Okay. And, Maggie, I'm sorry for what I said earlier. I wasn't trying to take sides."

"Forgotten. Looking forward to doing Thanksgiving together."

Thanksgiving morning started early. Maggie was up and enjoying the quiet with a cup of tea. The sun pushed through the dining room sheers warming the perfectly set table. Strolling along the chairs, she made minor adjustments to each place setting of her grandmother's silverware and china. All set. The adults would sit at the antique table she had rescued from her great-aunt's estate sale. The kids would eat in the kitchen at the table that had a tissue paper turkey centerpiece. The parade would be on in an hour, giving her time to get the turkeys started. Fortunately, Jen's turkey was the same size, so cooking times would be easily managed.

Maggie slid back into bed with her tea and the remote in hand. Danny and Emma came bouncing in, waking their dad and snuggling in with their mom in time for Tom Turkey to start the parade. Dan rolled over and propped a pillow up to protect Emma's arm from the movement on the bed.

As Santa and Mrs. Claus closed out the parade, Maggie was up and shooing the kids to get dressed. Dan pulled Maggie back into bed. "Dan, I need to get to work."

"You've got a minute. I miss you, Mag." The warmth of Dan melted Maggie's need to get busy. The two cuddled for a few minutes until Emma and Danny invaded again. Danny bounced into the room while dragging his shirt over his head. "I thought it was time to get up."

"Yoohoo, anyone home?" Jen had let herself in. "I'm here ready for basting, cooking, and more importantly eating. Who's with me?"

In unison, with "Aunt Jen!" Emma and Danny raced downstairs. Maggie got up and rooted for a sweatshirt to wear while she finished cooking. Pulling it on in Danny's ten-year-old fashion, she went to the side of the bed where Dan was sitting. "I love you and am so thankful for you and the kids. The play will be over in a couple of months, and I promise life will go back to normal. Please give me this time."

Dan encircled Maggie in a secure hug. "I love you. I'm trying. But you couldn't have chosen a worse time for me to do this."

Maggie sighed. *All about him. Again.*

## CHAPTER TWENTY-ONE

The day was crisp, the leaves were past the scenic colors, and the smell of their demise was in the air. Throughout the Nelson home, the air was thick with the salty, meaty aroma of a traditional Thanksgiving meal. Maggie had all the goodies cooking in the kitchen when the doorbell rang. She and Jen had put the final touches on the meal, and she left to get cleaned up for dinner.

The Stephens clan paraded in. Mark introduced his dad's friend, Gladys. Dan offered to take her coat. The sounds of simmering and cooking were washed over by the chatter and excitement of the kids. Danny, Emma, and Brian disappeared into the finished basement for ping-pong and video games.

Tying her apron, Jen rejoined Maggie in the kitchen. "Didn't mean to leave you with the turkeys."

The kids were playing well downstairs as usual. Mark's dad and Gladys seemed to hit it off with Dan. Jen gave Maggie the scoop on Gladys and Mark's dad. "Gladys seems pretty nice. She's a little too doting for me, but Dad doesn't seem to mind."

The doorbell broke through their conversation. Dan went to greet his dad and his dad's friend, Mabel, as Maggie's mom pulled into the driveway. "Your mom's here too," Dan called toward the kitchen.

"The gang's all here." Maggie replied with an anxious smile.

Joanna immediately joined them in the kitchen. "Oh, everything smells delicious. Did you make dressing or stuffing?"

"I made the dressing, Mrs. Fenwick. It's my grandmother's recipe," Jen volunteered.

"Really? I would have thought a woman of your grandmother's generation would have made stuffing." Joanna sounded snide.

Jen added a serving spoon to the dressing. "Since my grandmother had a family of six to feed, the turkey wasn't always large enough for stuffing. For us, it was more about everyone being together and sharing family stories."

Maggie cut in. "Mom, Jen and I attempted your dumplings. Hope you'll like them." Why did she care? But like most daughters, Maggie wanted her mother's approval on *something*.

The Thanksgiving meal was ready, and everyone gathered in the living room, clasped hands, and Dan said the blessing. With "amen," Maggie gave brief instructions for how the buffet was laid out. "Let's get the kids taken care of first."

Danny followed Maggie and Emma. Emma had been doing well with only one arm, but meals were still a time when she needed assistance.

Mark and Dan were lingering in the living room as the quarter ran out on the football game. Mark took advantage of being alone with Dan to ask how things with Maggie were. Dan rubbed the back of his neck. "I'm wrestling with all this. Won't lie to you. I've prayed about my pridefulness. You were right, I'm being selfish. The woman is amazing, and I should love and support her in what she wants to do."

Mark agreed with a nod. "Jen told me she read an article about this. It's not uncommon for women to lose themselves in their relationships and roles in life. Balance. They need to create space for themselves and their interests. Us lug heads need to figure out how to embrace that."

"I know you're right. It's time for me to lay it down, love, and support her."

Everyone had taken their seats, and plates were filled to the edges. Dan sat at one end of the table and Maggie at the other. There was only the sound of silverware clinking and the cheerful chatter of the kids in the kitchen. Mouths were full. Dan looked down at Maggie as he raised his glass of tea and winked at her.

He broke the silence. "Well done, chefs Jen and Maggie. For a couple of working ladies, you did an outstanding job of pulling all of this together."

Mark raised his glass. "Here, here. Outstanding job on everything."

Maggie's mom raised her glass with a nod. "I didn't know you had gone to work, Maggie. What are you doing outside the home?"

Outside the home. Maggie knew that tone—her mother wasn't pleased. When Dan had started getting promoted into executive positions, Maggie's mother was constantly sharing morsels of wisdom on how to be an "executive's wife." It all sounded very 1950s to Maggie. Most of what Maggie remembered about those wise words were laundry always done, dinner on the table, and being available for the social outings and client dinners.

With a quick glance at Dan, Maggie began, "Yes, Mom, I've been asked to stage manage the spring production at the community theater."

Her mother's brows furrowed. "I thought you'd given up all that nonsense to raise the kids and take care of Dan and the house."

Maggie wasn't going to ruin Thanksgiving with this conversation. "Mom, I'm doing both. The kids are in school all day, and Dan's at work. The house is running fine. We're making it work, and I'm loving the opportunity to be back in the theater."

A curt rebuttal. "You got all the ridiculous theater stuff from your father."

Mark saved the conversation. "Jen's doing great in her new job at the gym. She already has her first healthy living program dates set for January."

Dan helped carry the ball. "What's your first topic?"

Jen explained the progressive subjects scheduled for once every two weeks, beginning with what New Year's diet success looked like. Grateful for the change of conversation focus, Maggie relaxed into her chair and finished her dinner. But it didn't die completely with the next lull. Gladys decided to agree with Joanna's opinion.

"I don't know how you girls do it all. Back when I was raising my kids, it was all I could do to get to the market and have dinner on the table by six o'clock every night."

Jen gave a nudge to Mark, who wasn't sure how to change the conversation again. It was his dad's guest who had stirred the pot.

He stammered awkwardly, "You know, Gladys, Jen and Maggie are both outstanding women who have more energy than Dan and I put together."

Dan backed up Mark this time. "Yes, our wives do so much for us, why not support them in something they want to do?"

Maggie couldn't look over at Dan fast enough. *That's the Dan I fell in love with.*

Mr. Stephens tackled the next conversation change with football talk as they all finished their dinner. Jen and Maggie were taken out of the spotlight. Both silently ate while the men talked sports, and the older ladies talked about the grand old days of housekeeping and bridge night. Each of the kids paraded in with their plates, asking if they had eaten enough to warrant dessert. After a discerning inspection by both moms, the kids were granted a reprieve on finishing the little that was left.

"Now there's something we would have never done," Mabel, Daniel's lady friend, chimed in. "If every speck wasn't eaten off our plates, we didn't dare ask to be excused."

Through gritted teeth, Daniel politely quieted Mabel. "Dear, we've already addressed twenty-first-century child-rearing habits. The kids ate plenty." Mabel shot him a look and hushed up.

There wasn't anywhere else to go with the conversation. Working moms, child-rearing, and supportive husbands had all been covered. The guys were finishing up their seconds and itching to get in front of the TV for more football games. As everyone adjourned from the table, Dan caught Maggie, leaned in, and gave her a peck on the cheek. "Everything was wonderful. Thank you."

Maggie's cheeks flushed with the warmth of his words.

Dan had always supported Maggie in navigating the challenging relationship she had with her mother. Joanna Fenwick loved her husband and family, but she was demanding. Maggie often wondered if her strict requirements of perfection were a mask. Was Joanna deflecting her own lack of self-confidence? Her own unfulfilled desires? Whatever the reason, she set lofty expectations for Maggie. She pushed Maggie to have the life she had wanted and had never had—the executive's wife life. That was never what had Maggie wanted. It wasn't what she had married Dan for. After all these years and hundreds of hours of listening to Maggie and holding her in disappointing moments, Dan knew exactly what his wife needed in that moment—his total love and support.

A warm smile lit Maggie's face. "Thank you. We'll bring desserts in after we stack the dishes."

Dan patted his belly. "Please give us a little eating timeout."

Maggie served the elder women coffee in the dining room while she and Jen cleaned up the kitchen. The two friends talked softly, encouraging one another from the dinner comments. Gladys, Joanna, and Mabel were chattering on about their days of going to "the Club" every Friday night, bridge on Wednesdays, and their weekly trips to the hairdresser. What was just a community pool, Joanna made sound like a country club. The masking continued.

In contrast, Jen and Maggie spent their Friday nights at home with kids, husbands, and a G-rated movie. They had their hair cut and styled once every couple of months. It was the swim club in summer, chatting and watching the kids play. Jen looked at Maggie. "I wouldn't trade it for all the weeks of going to the beauty shop and shopping our moms did."

"Me neither." The two hugged and finished wrapping up the leftover food. "So, what about that husband of yours defending you at dinner?"

Maggie smiled and shook her head. "I know. It surprised me, while reminding me of how supportive he can be when he wants to. When it comes to my mom, he's always been protective."

"Maybe a little Thanksgiving spirit."

"Maybe." Maggie hoped so. Dan's lack of enthusiasm had put a shadow on her work at the theater. She was so excited about how the production was coming together. The only thing that would make it better would be Dan's endorsement.

Dessert was served, and the turkey had been sliced and packaged for leftovers to be taken by all the guests. With hugs and kisses, the parents left early.

Joanna whirled her fake fur around her shoulders. Everything with her was a production. "Call me, ladies—let's go to lunch." Mabel and Gladys both agreed. Jen and Mark called Brian in from shooting basketballs with Danny. Emma had tried—unsuccessfully—to shoot one-handed, so she'd decided chalk art was a better activity.

"Thank you for rescuing us for Thanksgiving." Jen hugged Maggie.

"Not a problem. It was fun to have you. Let me know how things progress on your kitchen."

"I will." Jen handed Mark his coat. Dan and Mark shook hands.

With the last of the guests gone, the house was immediately quiet and settled. Maggie took a deep breath. Dan pulled her close for a solid hug. "You okay?"

Maggie pulled away, "Yeah, I guess. I wish Mom hadn't mentioned Daddy. I'm trying to not to relive his death."

"Your dad was so proud of you. And he would be proud of what you're doing now." More encouraging words from Dan, but again, not specifically his support. Maggie dipped her toe in.

"Thank you, honey. What about you? Any chance you're proud of my good work too?" Maggie looked up at Dan with childlike eyes seeking his.

Their foreheads touched. "Oh, Maggie. I'm sorry I've been such an ass." Maggie leaned back in his arms, not having heard such strong language from Dan before.

"I've gotten all out of whack with work and you and the kids," he went on. "Sitting at dinner with our crazy parents and hearing them put down your work made me realize what I sounded like." Dan pulled her in for a warm hug. "I am so selfish. I am sorry."

Maggie started, but stopped herself from letting him off the hook before he was done. "Mags, forgive me. I need to man up and be supportive." Dan stepped back. "Which is what Mark told me to do, but I ignored him. I am so, so sorry."

Could she believe him? Trust him? It was Dan, humbly asking for her to forgive him. The love of her life. How could she say no when what he was offering was what she wanted most of all?

"Forgiven. I love you and need your support. I know we can work all this out with the schedule. Will you do one more thing for me?"

Dan tilted his head and raised an eyebrow. He had humbly apologized and offered his support, and now she was asking for something more. He smiled bravely. "Sure, name it."

"Will you be there front and center on opening night?"

Dan's head went back as he laughed. "Of course. I'm your number one fan. I love you." Dan wrapped Maggie in his arms as they shared a reuniting moment.

"Where are the kids? Usually they show up about now."

"They're in front of the TV with the newspaper ads and the big toy catalog, starting their Christmas lists."

Both parents smiled and shook their heads. Their home had peace and love. That was all Maggie wanted for Christmas.

# CHAPTER TWENTY-TWO

The kids were getting their shoes and jackets on for school. Their weekend had been filled with getting out Christmas decorations and launching the holiday spirit in the house. Maggie used the day's activities to fight off the dreams that attacked at night.

Her dreams took her back to the theater near the house where she grew up and the night her father was found dead. He had been helping with props for a play Maggie was starring in. He was so proud of her and spent many evenings helping paint and assemble backdrops. That evening it had snowed, and no one could get there. "The show must go on" was the last thing he said to her on the phone when she begged him not to go out on the blustery night.

The director found him the next morning at the foot of the red-carpeted steps to the stage, still wearing his tool belt. He was gone. By the time Maggie got there with her mother, the paramedics had the fifty-five-year-old-old man strapped to the gurney, his face covered with a starched white sheet. Maggie would never forget that moment. Her dramatic mother almost fainted. The box office manager took care of Joanna, and about the time Maggie didn't think she could take another minute, Dan came in and held her close. Maggie had melted into tears. "Not Daddy. Why did he have to come over here last night?"

Maggie's cell phone rang. She had a hundred ring tones available, but still chose the traditional phone bell tone.

Reaching for her phone, she said, "Danny, help your sister, please ... Hello?"

Jim Preston was usually calm and friendly. Something wasn't right in his voice. "Maggie, glad I caught you. What time do you think you'll be in today?"

"I was planning to be there this morning. Emma's doctor appointment is this afternoon." Despite her nightmares and dreams, she had told Dan she was okay to go to the theater. Gentle as he could be, he reassured her if it bothered her, to please come home or call him.

"Perfect. I didn't want to bother you this weekend, but Friday I got a letter from the Planning and Zoning Commissioner. They may take the theater and bulldoze it for new housing. Something about eminent domain laws. Our lawyer is coming in this morning, and I'd like you to be there too."

The theater ... torn down? "Sure, sure Jim, I'll be there. Don't know what I can do to help, but I'll be there."

"I need someone else to hear what the lawyer has to say. I'm afraid Sara would go drama on me. So, I'm not saying anything to any of the cast or crew. Let's just see what this means and go from there."

Maggie had planned to go straight to the theater for rehearsal after dropping the kids off. Looking down at her jeans, T-shirt, and blue-jean jacket, she decided to make a quick change. Danny and Emma were headed to the car.

"Hang on, guys, I need to change real quick. Mr. Jim has a meeting for me to be in, and this isn't the best outfit."

It was shortly after nine when Maggie arrived at the theater.

"Boy, you and Jim are sure dressed up today. What's the occasion?" Sara demanded.

Of all the days for Sara to not be lost in a textbook, today was the day. Maggie had chosen navy, mid-waist poly-blend pants that accented her five-nine height. Her white cotton blouse buttoned up the front and the navy and yellow scarf brought out her striking brown hair. Typically, she would wear her hair in a ponytail and less makeup.

"Just thought I'd clean up a bit today. Have you seen Jim yet?"

"Yep, he's down in the meeting room with some guy in a suit."

"A suit?"

"Some guy wearing a suit and carrying a briefcase."

Maggie smiled at Sara's description and headed into the meeting, but not without noticing Sara's baggy shirt looked bigger. Was she gaining weight?

"Sara, when Cindy gets in to start working on costumes, would you let her know a friend of mine, Jen Stephens, has volunteered to help her? All she has to do is give her a call when she's ready for help." Maggie jotted the number down and gave Sara the paper.

"Will do."

Jim had grabbed all the costumes that had been askew on the table the week before and piled them in the corner, freeing the table for the meeting. Sara was right. Carl Stiles, Jim's lawyer, wore a brown tweed suit and was seated with his black leather, hard-shell briefcase open. The tweed jacket worked, but the tweed pants were a little much.

Jim introduced Maggie. He opened the conversation by asking Mr. Stiles to tell them what he had learned.

"Well, it's not all bad news," Stiles said. "I called one of our first-year guys this weekend and got him on researching what this land deal is about and some history on your little theater. You know, I did some summer stock back in college." With a faraway look, Mr. Stiles leaned back in his chair as if in his mind he was reliving his theater glory days.

"Mr. Stiles, please continue." Jim brought him back to the moment.

"Yes, well that was a long time ago. Now your letter, here, indicates the demolition isn't for certain. You are among fifty building owners to receive this letter. Depending on which direction they decide to develop, your theater may or may not be in the way. We should know something in a few months." As if that were the end of the issue, Mr. Stiles leaned back in his chair.

Maggie remained silent but felt her heart drop. *Oh no, not the theater.*

Jim remained on the edge of his chair. "That's it? There's nothing we can do to influence their decision or have the theater removed from the list?"

As if he hadn't considered that Jim would fight this, Mr. Stilts quizzically looked at Jim. "Well, I guess you could try a few things, but fighting Planning and Zoning isn't going to be easy. Rarely do individuals win."

Jim shifted in his chair. "You don't think we can win? Easy or not, we are going to try. What are our options?"

Mr. Stiles shook his head. "I'm not saying you can't win. I'm saying it could be difficult." Mr. Stiles stood and shoved his pad of paper back into his briefcase. "I could draft a rebuttal letter stating the importance of keeping the theater intact. Are you a historic site?"

Jim smacked the table with his hand. "Yes, we've been here since the late nineteenth century."

"Well, great. Be sure to include your historic landmark papers in your letter."

Jim deflated. "I don't have an official historic landmark designation. Is that hard to get? Could we get it in time?"

Mr. Stiles continued, "There's a Planning and Zoning meeting in two weeks. It's open to the public. If you get the process started, you might be able to show your intent. That might get them looking elsewhere, if they're even considering this site seriously at all. I told you there are several on the list."

"I know, but I can't risk them choosing this one. By that time, it will be too late."

"Okay, call the landmark commissioner. His name is Larry Turner. Tell him you're working with me. Tell him about the letter and that you want to start the historic preservation process. He'll help you get in touch with the local historical societies." He paused and looked across the table at Jim and Maggie with stern eyes. "This is going to take a lot of work to succeed. Be ready for a fight if you want to protect the theater."

Jim and Maggie looked at each other, then at Mr. Stiles. They nodded.

"I'm up for a good fight." Jim said as he stood to walk Mr. Stiles out.

Maggie sat rethinking the conversation as she read the letter for the first time. Jim returned, and they spent the next hour building a strategy to keep the production moving forward while fighting this issue. Who should they tell? It had to be either no one or everyone. In the theater, there was no keeping a secret. Everyone worked too closely for too many hours.

"This is the nature of theater. There are seasons of challenge in fundraising, getting audience attendance increased, working on sponsorships, and protecting the building." Jim paced the length of room and paused to look out one of the tall, slender windows. "We have to save and preserve this building. Let's pull the cast and crew together tonight and tell them what's going on. With all those young, creative minds, maybe we'll come up with some ideas."

Maggie agreed. "Let me get Emma taken care of this afternoon, and I'll be back for the meeting. Do you want me to have Sara send an email or text to get everyone here?"

Jim remembered this wasn't going to be a full crew rehearsal night. "Oh, yeah, um, yes, let's not tell her before others, though. I don't want her trying to explain when they ask why the meeting."

"Good plan. I'll give Nora a call as well. She may have some ideas."

"Thanks. She's doing a great job with the set." Jim headed to his office.

Maggie called Dan on her way out of the theater. After explaining the events of the morning, she asked if he would take care of the kids for dinner and homework so she could run back over for the meeting.

Dan hesitated. Maggie sat waiting for the sigh. And there it was. "I guess. I was planning to go to Emma's appointment, but if you can do that, I'll stay here and finish up some things I was going to do tonight and then meet you at home and take the kids for pizza."

"Sweetie, she's getting her cast off. It's a pretty important appointment. I put a roast in this morning. It's Emma's favorite. I wanted this to be a special day."

Dan's frustration was thick in the silence. But Maggie didn't relent. She let the silence hang until he answered. "Maggie, I'm trying. Work with me here a little. If I can have the time to work instead of the appointment, then I can focus on the kids tonight."

He was right. To work together there needed to be a little give and take. "Okay. You're right. You take care of work, and I'll take her to get her cast off."

"Oh, I've got a late meeting with the auditors tomorrow night. Remember?"

*Give and take, Maggie.* "I didn't, but thanks for reminding me."

On her way to pick up the kids and take Emma to her appointment, Maggie called Jen. There was something nagging at her about her conversation with Dan. After one ring, Jen picked up.

"Hey, girl, how you doin'?"

"Okay, I think." Maggie's voice trailed off.

"You don't sound convincing. Something happen?"

"I don't know." Maggie shook her head. *I don't know how I feel. Am I frustrated? Bored? Can I trust Dan's intentions?* "I just got off the phone with Dan. We had to work out our schedules for this evening."

"That sounds good. He's working with you."

"I guess, but tomorrow night, he's got a meeting. We won't be able to have our family dinner then either."

"Maggie, I'm your best friend, so hear what I'm about to say with all the love in my heart. What do you want? He's helping with the kids tonight. Tomorrow night, you'll be with the kids so he can do his work meeting. That's how this works."

"You're right. I'm being selfish and wanting him to do all the sacrificing."

# CHAPTER TWENTY-THREE

Maggie sat on the front row of the auditorium. Jim had his notes together. The actors, crew, and a few key volunteers wandered in and peppered themselves through the first four rows of seats. Jim began to speak, telling his audience about the letter and the meeting with the attorney. Maggie listened, but she was distracted by the four wooden steps leading to the stage.

The stairs were dark wood, the stain worn in the middle from the hundreds of entrances and exits they had supported. She'd never paid much attention to them but had certainly used them. The red carpet at the base was frayed. Why did the steps capture her attention?

As Jim continued to explain, he said there were several sites being considered and that he would be contacting the historic preservation society. He concluded with asking everyone to be ready for petitions and whatever needed to be done. Maggie realized what the steps reminded her of. She gasped and slapped her hand to her mouth. Jim completed his comments and thanked everyone for coming, sharing any ideas were welcome. The cast and crew dispersed and stood around talking about the announcement and chattering about ideas for saving the theater. Maggie sat there.

"Maggie, are you okay?" Jim took the seat next to her.

Maggie looked at Jim. "My ... my father," she stammered. "I've been having dreams about the night he died. Really horrible nightmares."

Jim looked puzzled. "Was this recently?"

Of course, he didn't know the history. Maggie shook her head with a small smile. "No. You're going to think I'm crazy. My father died from a massive heart attack in the last theater I acted in. He was alone, working on props, and they found him the next morning. It's been fifteen—no—seventeen years ago. Recently, I've been having nightmares about it." Jim sat down with a seat between them and listened.

"For some reason tonight, sitting in this seat, I became acutely aware of those steps. They kept distracting me, and I didn't know why. Then it came to me. They reminded me of the stairs to the stage in that other theater."

Jim sat quietly for a moment, then shook his head. "Maggie, I'm so sorry. What can I do to help?"

Tears gathered in her eyes, "He was such a sweet man. And he loved me and was always supportive of my acting."

"And no doubt he will be proud of you when you help me save this theater." Jim gave a shameless grin.

Maggie smiled, wiping the tears. "Yes, he would be, and he would be in the thick of the fight with you. I'm sorry for the tears and emotion. I feel like a crazy person with these dreams and memories resurfacing."

"I wish I had answers for you. I can assure you your help and dedication have already made an enormous difference." Jim touched Maggie's arm, and then stood.

Maggie smiled. "Thank you for your kind words."

"Please, I should be thanking you. Having you here is a constant encouragement to me. I am sorry for your nightmares and sad memories. Please let me know if I can do anything."

"Thank you. I'm sure there's nothing right now."

They finished up a few details for the week. As Jim was going to fight the good fight, he asked Maggie to do a few extra things. Maggie called Dan from her car on the way home. No one answered.

When Maggie got home, she noticed Dan's car was gone. Instantly, she thought of Emma. Having recently gotten her cast off, had she done something to her weakened arm?

Maggie stepped into the kitchen. The stench of burnt popcorn stopped her at the door. At the sight of her kitchen, she was quite sure Dan and the kids had run away. Her pristine kitchen that looked clean even when she was in the middle of cooking looked like a bomb had gone off. She covered her nose to ward off the offensive smell while she looked around.

She called Dan's cell phone. No answer. She checked the other rooms of the house. The tornado of food and stink was isolated to the kitchen. She felt like someone had punched her. Notes from the front of the refrigerator were strewn all over the floor. On the stove, spaghetti noodles had apparently boiled over the side of the pot. Why were they fixing spaghetti? The roast was half eaten. She opened the microwave to find a bag of burnt popcorn. *What happened here*?

She heard Dan's car pull in.

Dan and the kids walked in, chattering and laughing. Maggie stood in the middle of the kitchen with her hands on her hips and her brow furrowed. Dan stopped short. She stepped carefully toward Emma. "Are you all okay?"

Emma saw her look and stepped behind her father. Dan began to explain. "Yes, honey, sorry about the mess. We're planning to clean it up. We were hoping you wouldn't get home until we had a chance at it."

"Where have you been?" Maggie controlled her voice.

"We ran out for a quick ice cream. Thought we'd get back in time to ..." Dan's shoulders slumped.

Maggie's arms were crossed, and her voice rose. "How did you manage to make this mess? I don't understand what went on here!"

"Danny, Emma, you should go hit the homework. Let me talk to your mom," Dan said.

"No! You kids are going to stay right here. The three of you took my perfect kitchen and, in a matter of hours, turned it into shambles. I'm glad no one is hurt. Based on seeing this room, I thought maybe a tornado hit. I'm going upstairs and take a hot bath. When I come back and this room is as clean as you can get it, then I will listen to what happened. Should you need a power washer, it's in the garage!" Maggie stomped upstairs.

Dan and the kids looked at each other. Danny and Emma had never seen their mother so mad. Dan knew he had some making up to do. The three of them went to work picking up and scrubbing. Forty-five minutes later, the three looked around and decided it was as good as it was going to get.

"But is it *Mom-good*? She's so particular, I'm not sure we can ever get it clean enough," Danny said.

Dan looked around. "I think she will appreciate our effort. Your mom has her own way of doing things. Her way keeps our house clean and in order and helps each of us with what we need—me with work and you with school." Dan heard himself and realized he hadn't appreciated Maggie. She had spent her adult life supporting him in his career efforts and keeping the house in order. She did an outstanding job with the kids. Never once had he come home to this kind of debacle.

"Go work on your homework. Danny, help Emma with her spelling words. I'm going to talk to your mom. Also, you may want to practice your apology. Not to worry—I am too." Grabbing their backpacks, the kids headed for the den.

Dan went upstairs to find Maggie out of the bath and sitting in a chair in their room. Dan slowly sat down on the edge of the bed. "Honey, I am so sorry. We thought we could get it cleaned up before you got home."

"What happened? Dinner was ready. All you had to do was put it on plates and eat. I don't ask much. When the play's over, I'll go back to being the wife and mother. All I wanted was to be able to do something for me—and everything here falls apart. You don't understand what it feels like to want to crawl out of your skin. To look in the mirror and not recognize the person looking back." She buried her face in her hands.

Dan hung his head. He had blown it. "Maggie, God made you wonderfully unique and perfect for me and the kids. All this time, you've given and given, and I have failed to take time to recognize it. No, I don't want you to give up the play, and even when it's done, we're going to work together to find a better balance in our lives." Dan stood and walked around as he gave an account for the evening.

"Emma was excited about having roast for dinner, but Danny wasn't. He mentioned he'd rather have spaghetti, and then Emma changed her mind about the roast." Dan smiled at Maggie. "How do you manage all the different opinions about the menu? Anyway, I made spaghetti. But I got distracted on the phone, and the water boiled over and down the side. Danny tried to save it and managed to move it off the stove to pour the water in the sink, but he missed." He raised his hands to stop Maggie before she asked. "He didn't get hurt. He tried to save things and did save enough for Emma to eat. That's how the spaghetti and sauce got all over the floor. Emma came dancing through and slipped on the floor and ran into the refrigerator while Danny was making microwave popcorn."

Maggie looked up. "She didn't hurt her arm again, did she? Why was Danny making microwave popcorn?"

"No, I promise, she's fine, but Danny got distracted, and the popcorn burned. I have no idea why he was making popcorn. Maybe because it's the only thing he knows how to make. Hard to say. It was all a comedy of errors. I made more spaghetti, and we ate dinner and then ran out for some ice cream, thinking there was time to get back and clean it all up. Time got away from us."

Dan fell silent. He had no idea what Maggie would think, but he couldn't stand the silence. "We are so sorry about the mess and losing track of time."

Maggie looked up at Dan and was about to speak when Danny and Emma peeked in the door. "Can we come in?" Big brother Danny led the way.

"Mom, we are soooo sorry we messed up your kitchen. Dinner wasn't the same without you," Emma said as she climbed up in the chair with Maggie.

Danny stood back like a young man. "Mom, I am sorry too. We didn't mean to make a mess of things. I think you'll like how it looks now."

Maggie's heart melted. Her babies were getting bigger and able to make a huge mess and clean it up. "I love you all. Thank you for cleaning up your mess. I'm sure it's wonderful. Sorry I got so upset. You three are the most important people in the world to me. You have your favorite things to do, right? Danny, you love to play ball or ride your bike. Emma, you love to swing. Daddy enjoys watching a ballgame. Well, I'm now doing something I love to do. Does that make sense?" The kids nodded. "I want you to be my fans at the play."

Maggie looked at Dan. "Please hang on just a little longer. In fact, I would love you to come with me on Saturday for our volunteer day at the theater."

Emma jumped up, saying, "Can we put on the costumes and the big hats?"

Maggie smiled cupping her daughter's chin, "Sure. Jen, Mark, and Brian are planning to help." She looked at Dan. "Can you come too?"

Dan smiled. "Yes. I haven't spent much time in that theater in a long time. It will be fun to clean the old girl up."

Maggie hugged Danny and Emma. Dan came over and kissed her. "You relax. I'm going to get the kids settled. I think I can do it without flooding the bathroom." Maggie laughed lightly and snuggled into her chair.

Dan came back a half hour later with a cup of tea. Maggie put down the book she was reading. "Thank you. You know you don't have to suck up much more. I may have overreacted a little."

Dan joined her playful tone. "Ya think?"

"Tonight at the theater, I kinda melted down on Jim about these dreams I've been having."

Dan sat cross-legged on the floor in front of the chair and listened as Maggie recounted the meeting and the stairs.

"Sweetheart, we need to figure out a way to get your mind to settle down. You know how much your father loved you."

"I do. But Mom's comment on Thanksgiving bothered me."

Dan reached up and took Maggie's hand. "I know. Please don't let her have that much control."

Maggie's tired shoulders sagged. She scooted out of the chair, onto the floor next to Dan. He pulled her into his arms. As they embraced, he whispered a prayer.

"Lord, please calm Maggie's spirit and mind. Give her your peace. Allow her dreams to be inspired by you and the fact she is your child. Your daughter. Thank you for such a wonderful wife. Allow me to be the husband she needs me to be. Amen."

The hours Dan and Maggie had spent over the course of their relationship discussing her mother, her mother's attitude, and expectations, were too numerous to count. But by the end of their conversations, Maggie always felt better.

She leaned back. "Thank you, honey." She kissed her husband. "It's been quite the day."

# CHAPTER TWENTY-FOUR

Christmas and the spirit of giving were not lost on Maggie. After Thanksgiving, Maggie spent time planning for December, the holidays, and making sure she could manage her theater schedule along with all she wanted to do for her family. With her planner, a note pad, and a cup of tea, she sat at the kitchen table making lists and notes. Her month-at-a-glance calendar allowed her to do the high-level planning, to mark out the full days she would be at the theater. She added dots to the days she might need to go in for part of the day. She mapped out three shopping days, including the one she hoped she and Dan would do together. Their tradition had been an evening out for dinner and shopping for the kids. Dan would shop on his own for Maggie. There was also an afternoon planned for Maggie to take the kids shopping for their dad. She always tried to steer them away from the ugly ties, sometimes more successfully than others. The endearing part was to see their excitement when Dan came down to breakfast wearing the specially chosen tie.

"Dad, that's the tie we got you!"

Dan would kiss Emma on the head. "Of course, it's my favorite."

Maggie knew he wore the tie when he had no important meetings.

Leaning back to examine the calendar, Maggie took a deep breath. Sipping on her orange spice tea, she shook her head. The month was going to be full. Looking at it all at once was admittedly a little overwhelming. She put it aside to work on her list.

She underlined the heading "People to Shop for." She listed everyone they would give gifts to—eighteen. Stars were placed next the names of those whose gifts needed to be shipped. Those gifts would need to be purchased first to get them mailed by the fifteenth. She and Dan would discuss gift ideas for his dad. And what about Mabel? Would she be coming to Christmas?

Next heading—"Cookies and Food for the Holidays." Maggie listed the three cookies they made every year. There were a couple of homemade candies, but she would leave room for the kids to choose either another cookie or candy. To the side, she listed cookie containers as an item needed for giveaway cookies and treats.

Next heading—"Menu Ideas." December could be a big grocery month between the kids being home on break and the holiday meals. Maggie tried to buy nonperishables throughout November, so her budget wasn't completely blown in December.

Maggie watched for gift ideas, things people had mentioned, or things she saw that would make unique and perfect gifts. Halfway through her list, the phone rang.

"Maggie, it's Jim. Are you busy?"

"Not really, working on my December list of to-dos. What's up?"

"I just heard that Planning and Zoning will consider my appeal to take the theater off the list, but we need to have the petition routed and at least two hundred signatures. What do you think about our recruiting other volunteers for Saturday? They could scour the neighborhood to ask the neighbors to sign it. I spoke to the president of the historic neighborhood association. He will support us and is letting me come to their meeting this week. That'll give me the opportunity to let them know our folks will be coming around."

"We could also contact folks in our database. Send an email to let them know we need help. They could come by Saturday to sign the petition or help walk the neighborhood."

"I'll get Sara working on a draft email this morning. Can you work with her to make sure it sounds compelling?"

Maggie chuckled. "Sure, but are you sure you don't want to see it before it goes?"

"We need to get this out. I've got to run over to the preservation society office. Mag, you understand the importance of this. I trust you to make sure that is conveyed in the email."

"Okay, get her started, and I'll come by on my way to pick up the kids."

Maggie finished her big list and then looked at the week ahead. With her plan in hand, she updated the calendar on the refrigerator. Stepping back and crossing her arms, she saw Dan would need to help one evening with the kids. She circled it in blue marker to help her remember to ask him about it.

Having everything for December outlined or listed helped Maggie relax and take on the month ahead. She finished her tea and decided a little prayer would go a long way with the month and the significance of the holiday. Christmas and the wonder of the Christ child always gave Maggie pause. A miracle. A child who would change the course of human history, whether or not someone believed in who he was.

The whoosh of the heavy walnut theater doors never got old to Maggie. Sara was at her post.

"I'm so glad you're here. I have no idea what to put in this email. Are we staying? Are we being bulldozed?"

The drama in Sara's voice made Maggie chuckle. "Well, good morning to you too. And I like the holiday hair color."

Sara touched her long red and green hair. "I was feeling festive."

Maggie dropped her stuff on the table and pulled a chair out of the meeting room to sit next to Sara. "Maybe we shouldn't start with the word 'bulldoze.'" The two settled in to craft a message to those who had purchased tickets and to the parents of child actors. "How many email addresses do you have?"

Sara clicked on a spreadsheet and began scrolling to the bottom, "Not a lot. We started collecting them last year when I started working here. Previously it was hit or miss." Landing at the bottom of the list she said, "Only two hundred and seventy-one emails."

Now Maggie was feeling dramatic. "Eek, not very many."

"Like I said, not a lot."

"We need two hundred signatures to even have a chance with Planning and Zoning. And they have to be people who live in the area."

Both were quiet for a minute. Sara sat up suddenly. "What if we not only contact these people, but we also have an event? We could invite the neighbors and these folks we're emailing. And all the faculty from the fine arts department at the university. They could come see the theater, and maybe Jim could give tours and ask them to sign the petition."

Maggie was considering the idea as Jim came racing in.

Maggie looked up. "Didn't think we'd see you today."

Jim combed his wind-blown hair with his fingers and laid his bulging folder on the counter. “I got a call that Planning and Zoning wants to hold their executive committee meeting here next Monday. So, on top of having two hundred signatures to hand them, we need to have this place in shape to show off.”

Maggie lit up with a big smile.

Jim looked perplexed. “Are you glad about this?”

“Well, Sara and I were brainstorming ways to get the support we need. She had the idea of holding an event of some kind for people to come see the theater and offer support. What if Saturday we have our work day as planned, get additional volunteers to go door-to-door, then on Sunday, we invite the neighborhood and anyone else we can to come by for cider and the hanging of the greens?” Maggie opened her notebook to start a list.

Jim scratched his head. “Let me catch up here. So—in the next seven days—we’re going to clean this place up, get two hundred signatures, decorate for Christmas, and invite a bunch of people in. Pretty ambitious.”

“Yep, but we have something worth putting out some extra effort for.”

“We don’t have a budget for this shindig.”

Sara sat quietly as Maggie started a list. “What if we could get the decorations donated? Dan and I will buy a tree for the lobby here. Part of the fun will be to have people stop by to help us decorate, and they can bring an ornament to add to the tree. We can bake cookies and have cider. Can you spring for cider? Sara, can you bake some cookies?”

Jim and Sara both had dropped jaws as they listened to Maggie reel off ideas.

Beginning to catch the spirit, Jim nodded. “Yeah, we could get cider. Sara, go look in the storage closet to see if we have cups, napkins, and plates left over from our last cast party. I think there's an artificial tree and ornaments at the prop warehouse."

Maggie looked up from her list. "Sure, we get everything cleaned up Saturday. And get the tree set up." Shyly she asked, "Do you mind if we get a real tree? It would look and smell so holiday-ish!"

Jim laughed at the made-up word. "Remind me not to put you in charge of script edits—you'll be making up words. Thank you, I love the idea of a real tree."

Back to her list. Maggie asked about lights and other decorations.

Sara came back to the lobby juggling an armful of plastic cups and plates. "Here you go. What do you think about me designing a flyer inviting the neighbors when they're out getting signatures?"

"I love that idea, Sara." Jim reached for a piece of paper off the desk to make his own notes. "I'll have to check. Maggie, do you want to meet me at the warehouse on your way over in the morning?"

"Sure. So, we will change our email to an invitation to stop by for a cup of holiday cheer and to show support for the theater."

Sara jumped into the planning. "I'll take a few fliers and put them up around the faculty offices at school."

Jim looked at the two women. "Sounds like we have a plan. Let's get after it."

Maggie helped Sara finish the email and headed out to get the kids.

Maggie was a few minutes early to pick up the kids and decided to walk into the school. Mrs. Fitzpatrick finished talking with the after-school care staff and walked over to greet Maggie.

"How are you? We haven't had a chance to talk much since Emma got her cast off."

Maggie gave her a side hug with a deep sigh. "Life continues to be exciting."

"Yes, I hear you're involved with a play at the community theater. Sounds like fun. When my husband and I were dating, he took me to several plays at that theater. It was so close to campus we could walk to the drugstore for a burger and then over for the play." She smiled.

Mrs. Fitzpatrick's remembrance gave Maggie an idea. She told her about the hanging of the greens event, the petition, and the Planning and Zoning meeting. "Would you like to come Sunday?"

"I'll do one better. Let me make some of the cookies you need. I've been itchin' to try a couple of new holiday cookie recipes from *Southern Living*."

"Thank you, that would be a big help. I was wondering how we were going to get enough cookies baked. Didn't think store-bought would do."

"Consider it done."

Emma and Danny jumped and skipped through the cafeteria and hugged their mom. Maggie thanked Mrs. Fitzpatrick again, and they headed for the door. Maggie had a few more things to add to her list.

# CHAPTER TWENTY-FIVE

Nora hauled the extra fabrics, bows, tools, and silk flowers from her car into the office. Sparkles clung to her argyle sweater. Her hands were dry and tired from stapling and adjusting, staging every little candle and Christmas fixture in the mayor's house. Did the result match the design? The mayor's wife wasn't home when Nora left. She did that by design too. She wanted her to come in and experience it on her own. No doubt she would call if there was a problem. Nora had worked on the decorating for two weeks. Together, Cheryl and Norman Watson were kind people. Separately, there were times when Mrs. Watson got a little snooty with others in her service.

As with everything about her, Mrs. Watson wanted her decorations to be perfect. She needed them done by December first. It was November 30, and at dusk the lights on the exterior of the early century home would automatically come on. Before the housekeeper left each day, she would walk around and plug in the five Dickens-themed trees and eight strands of lights that had been carefully integrated with greenery and bows among the antique casework and stairwells. It would be lovely. Hopefully, Mrs. Watson would agree.

As Nora dropped her boxes and headed to the ladies' room, Phoebe came rushing at her in a flurry. "You did it! I should get you another cupcake!" She was talking so fast, Nora wasn't sure what to think, but the mention of cupcakes was always good. "She loves it! The mayor's wife called and said everything looks great. She even used the word 'breathtaking.' You did it! Tony wants to talk to you himself."

Nora's head was swimming. She needed something to eat. "Mr. Stanton wants to talk to me?"

"You have to act surprised, but the word is after Christmas, the mayor's wife would like us to come in and redecorate their upstairs. They have four bedrooms *and* two bathrooms *and* a sitting area," Phoebe practically skipped as they headed toward the common work area. Tony stepped out of his office as they reached the end of the hall.

"Sounds like Phoebe spilled the good news. Congratulations on winning over our most difficult return customer." He maintained his refined stance, but his eyes sparkled. "The way that woman always finds something to complain about, I always think it's the last we'll hear from her. But she continues to call. And we try our best. Not only did you give her nothing to complain about, but she loves your style and offered a bonus to you specifically for your efforts." He grimaced at Phoebe. "As you've already heard, she would like us to give her a proposal for her second floor."

Overwhelmed, Nora stood in silence, then looked at Phoebe, who nodded, and then back at Mr. Stanton. Nora said, "Thank you so much. Please, let's use the bonus to have a celebration here. Mrs. Watson knows me, but we all know it was a team effort."

After all the congratulations were said, the three sat down and settled into planning the options for Mrs. Watson. Nora felt like she was taking on the biggest challenge. She wowed Mrs. Watson once—could she do it again?

She and Phoebe spent the afternoon with pattern books and fabric samples, developing two presentation boards for Mrs. Watson. They had three weeks to finalize their presentation, but their initial thoughts were a good start.

Nora drove home that night, thinking of the day. The accolades. The bonus. Why wasn't Seth here? His death brought a silence to her world. With his passing, she'd shut herself off from their friends. She didn't have many friends now. She was becoming reacquainted with Jen and Maggie ... she couldn't just call and share with them ... could she? She had chosen to go back to work to keep her mind busy. The money from their insurance and his trust fund was invested to ensure her financial future. And now she was designing for the mayor's wife and getting a bonus.

The afternoon had been filled with plans and draft sketches. Her thoughts had been focused on the mayor's house. There had been no thought of the theater or the set design. Her apartment was still. Her keys jingled as she hung them by the door. They echoed through her heart. So many good things happening in her life and no one to share them with. How could life be so wonderful and so empty all at once? After changing into some comfy clothes and fixing a cup of tea, Nora pulled out her calendar and notes. Again, she would bury herself in her work. Emptying her satchel, Nora pulled her theater set design notes out to look over. The play. How would she manage designing the set, helping build it, and decorating the mayor's house?

She enjoyed the people she was meeting at the theater. And exercise was helping to rebuild her energy. Five years of mourning was tiresome.

Merely wanting to connect with someone, she dialed Maggie. Two rings and then an answer. Nora hesitated. Why had she called? Maggie wasn't going to care about her project and bonus.

"Hello? Nora?" Maggie asked.

Coming back to the moment, "Yes, hi, Maggie, it's Nora, I ..."

"Hey, Nora, how are you?"

She took a deep breath and smiled. "I'm good, very good."

"That sounds like more than just ideas for the set and props. What's going on?"

"Well, today I finished the Christmas decor for Mayor Watson's house."

"The mayor's house—that's a big deal!"

Nora relaxed and decided to share her news with her rediscovered friend. She dove into sharing about presenting the ideas, Mrs. Watson loving them, and then later finding out how difficult she had been in the past.

"I'm so excited for you. Congrats! We should grab Jen for a celebratory coffee."

"That'd be great."

In a moment of silence on the phone, Nora didn't know where to take the conversation. Maggie sounded excited for her. Was she just being nice? It had been years since she had had a close friend. The friends she and Seth had were a huge support for a long time. But then they got on with their lives and growing families. Maggie and Jen were so close. Would Nora always feel like an outsider?

# CHAPTER TWENTY-SIX

Jen checked and double-checked the seating, chairs, projector, and her note cards. Everything was in order for the healthy living preview class. Daisy wheeled a cart in with fruit, whole grain bagels, coffee, tea, and juice. Kevin had given Jen permission to ask Daisy to help. Jen had asked Daisy to dress up a little but not too much. She made the attempt. But Jen quickly realized the term *dressing up* could be subjective. Daisy's dressing up meant additional makeup and wearing high-heeled, glittery shoes with her workout leggings. Jen closed her eyes and shook her head as Daisy went to work setting up the glasses and food.

"It all looks grand, Jen. You'll do great today."

Daisy's heart was in the right place. "Thank you, Daisy. And thanks for your help. Hope it hasn't put you too far behind with the front desk."

"Nah, I'm good. Once you get started, I'm going to head back up there until the break. If that works for you."

"Perfect." Jen was again adjusting her laptop and testing the slides. She had chosen to wear khaki pants with a knit sweater. It was sporty casual, but different than workout clothes. Her goal with this first class was to get folks engaged and talking about what healthy lifestyles could look like. Knowing that during a holiday time no one wanted to hear about working out or diets, she chose an overview, high-level approach. She and Kevin discussed how this topic would make a good starting point. She saved goal setting, dieting, and getting into shape for the start of the new year.

"Did we have any last-minute registrations?" Jen's goal was to have twenty attendees. For the last three days, they had been at sixteen.

"I checked the email this morning. There was one more registration that came in last night. We're up to seventeen. Do you want me to let last-minute folks in? Everything we sent out said they had to register in advance." Daisy's Tennessee twang came out sharply in her short *a* sounds and tended to hang on.

"I know, but at this point we need to fill the seats and get our members involved. Go ahead and let last-minute folks come in."

Kevin popped in the small meeting room. "How's it going? You look like you're all set up. How many are coming?"

Jen grimaced inside, but replied with a positive, "Daisy said we had one more come in overnight."

"How many is that now?" Kevin wanted numbers. It was always about the numbers.

"Seventeen." Jen continued adjusting her handouts at each place.

"We were working for more."

Before Jen had a chance to respond, four guys came to the door of the room. A tall twenty-something with jeans and a T-shirt and brown shaggy hair spoke for the group.

"Excuse me. No one up front." Daisy huffed out of the room mumbling about good help. Jen smiled at the young man.

"Can we help you?"

"Yeah, we're looking for Ms. Stephens's healthy living class?" The way he said the words *healthy living* made Jen think he had never used those two words together in a sentence in his life.

"This is it. Have you registered?"

"Oh, man. Mark, I mean Mr. Baker said to just come over." Jen caught the code. Kevin had busied himself reading her handouts. Mark had come to her rescue. When Jen had told him that she was shy of her twenty-person goal by four, he had offered to send some of his guys over, calling it "continuing education hours." Jen told him it wouldn't work because they wouldn't be talking technology. "You'll be using technology, won't you? Besides, a healthy staff is a productive staff." She snickered and told him it wasn't necessary. True to his character, he sent guys anyway. Not knowing about the overnight registrant, he sent four to be sure she made her twenty. Baker was their code and her maiden name. Thankful for the rescue, Jen welcomed the goal-saving group.

"No problem. Come on in and find a spot. I'll have Daisy give you some registration forms." Other attendees began to file in. "Come on in, folks, and find a seat. Don't be afraid of the front row."

Intuitively, Daisy returned with registration cards for the four young men, whom she promptly attempted to flirt with. Their faded jeans, T-shirts, and shaggy haircuts clearly made them stand out from the rest. One of them carried his morning can of Red Bull. Jen saved the guys from Daisy's flirtatious assault.

"Daisy, would you please check the refreshments and make sure we have enough?" Jen had already planned for one or two additions, so there were enough handouts.

Jen presented her information, and surprisingly, the guys Mark sent asked insightful questions and seemed interested. One of the gym members, a nutritionist, challenged some of Jen's research on proteins for a balanced diet. Jen had solid answers, and the question became a smart discussion point.

With the class over, and the room transformed back into a yoga suite, Jen headed to the locker room to change clothes. Checking her mailbox on the way, Daisy informed her that Kevin wanted to see her. “Sure. Is he in?”

“Yep. Can’t read his mood, though. He might be a little grumpy.”

“Thanks for the warning.” Jen’s step was light, coming off the high of a successful first presentation. She gently knocked on his opened door. “Kevin, you wanted to see me?”

Kevin looked up from some papers, took his reading glasses off, and gestured for his manager to take a seat. Daisy was right. His mood was hard to read today. Jen had worked closely with Kevin as she developed a plan and schedule for the member retention program the funders were supporting. Kevin agreed doing the first one between Thanksgiving and Christmas would make for good timing. Further, he had agreed starting with a class of twenty would be a good benchmark. As she took her seat, Jen noticed Kevin was reading her handout.

“Jen, this is good material. You did solid research.” Kevin flipped through the pages nodding.

“Thank you.” Jen shifted in her chair. *Where was he going with this?*

“You chose an appropriate topic and had a room full ... Congratulations.” Kevin added flatly.

Jen hesitated. “Thank you.”

“But you didn’t hit your attendance goal, and we absolutely have to have those numbers.”

Jen’s jaw dropped, “What do you mean? There were twenty-one people in the room. We were one over.”

Kevin smiled. “Yes, but four of them were plants.”

"Plants?"

"Am I to believe the four young men who came in with their torn jeans and caffeine energy drinks were looking for tips on healthy living? Seems more likely they were here to make sure you had your numbers and flirt with Daisy ... special delivery from Mark."

*Busted.*

Jen sat up straight. "Well, Kevin, uh, well they were, but ..."

Kevin held up his hand. "Don't, Jen. I appreciate the support Mark has shown you over the last couple of months. Except for today. It doesn't help us to have a false sense of interest."

Jen interrupted. "I would agree with you normally, and yes, at first they were sent to be seat fillers, but believe it or not, they actually got into it and asked some great questions."

"Really?"

"Yes, I know it wasn't right for Mark to send the guys over, and I will talk to him about it, but it did turn out pretty well. One of them asked me if I was going to do other programs."

Kevin backed down. "I guess it didn't hurt anything today. But no more. You need to get your numbers right. And remember, these programs are for members or potential members."

Jen stood up to go. "I promise, and I'll take a couple of membership brochures home for Mark to give to the guys. I think at least the one would consider joining."

The stress of the morning and the whirl of emotions almost had Jen's thoughts spinning. Was she successful or not? She hustled past Daisy and headed for the yoga room. She needed to breathe. She was a personal trainer, not a businesswoman.

Closing the door and dimming the lights, she pulled out a mat. The CD player needed to be plugged in to add some light music. A reaching stretch and deep breath gave release of the stress. Thirty minutes later, feeling somewhat better, Jen reached for her phone to see three missed calls from Mark.

*My number one fan.*

She dialed him back.

"Hey. Sorry I missed your calls."

"No problem. I heard you were amazing. One of the guys is even talking about joining."

"That's great." The stress in Jen's body was gone, but her spirit was still heavy and confused.

"What's wrong? I thought you'd be thrilled."

"Mark, I am." She hesitated. "But I don't think I can do this job."

# CHAPTER TWENTY-SEVEN

Jen, Mark and Brian were out early Saturday morning on their way to Maggie's for breakfast before they volunteered at the theater. Mark reached over and took Jen's hand. "You haven't said much more about your first class. Did Kevin say anything else?"

Jen took a deep breath. "Not specifically about that one. We've talked about the schedule for January, and some of those details."

"How are you feeling now that you've had a couple of days to let things settle down? You sounded a little overwhelmed the other day. And haven't seemed to want to talk about it."

"Yeah, I know. I'm sorry. Wasn't trying to not talk about it. Just needed to do the job for a few days. It's different from being a personal trainer. But the more I get into it, the better I like it."

"You're going to wow Kevin and have all the gym members lined up for the classes." Mark squeezed her hand and winked.

The doorbell rang at eight o'clock Saturday morning. Maggie opened the door. "C'mon in! Good morning! Breakfast is served." Nora, Jen, Mark, and Brian headed for the kitchen. Maggie had made a sausage and egg breakfast casserole, fruit bowl, and cinnamon rolls. Danny, Brian and Emma skipped the casserole and went straight for the cinnamon rolls.

"Everything smells great! Brian, you need to at least have some fruit too." Jen reviewed the counter full of food.

"Danny and Emma, you both too. Add some fruit to your plates." Maggie gave Nora a quick hug. "I'm glad you joined us today." Maggie looked at the whole crew as they filled their plates. "I appreciate your help. All of you, thank you. Enjoy the breakfast. We need to be at the theater in an hour."

Nora wiped the corners of her mouth in true ladylike form, "Maggie, I was telling Phoebe at work about today, and she asked if she could join us. I said yes. Hope that's okay."

"The more the merrier," Maggie chimed in. "We're glad for all the help. There's a ton to do."

"I'm sure you've planned the decorations, but I had a few odds and ends left from the mayor's house I thought we could fit in here and there." Putting a finger to her lips, Nora indicated not to tell.

"Thanks, and your secret is safe." Maggie whispered.

While everyone finished up, Maggie put the dishes in the dishwasher. Dan retrieved their coats from the closet. The kids got their shoes on, and everyone headed out the door.

When the eight of them walked in with Maggie in the lead, Jim and Adam, the lighting guy, stopped mid-sentence and looked up.

Adam said, "Looks like Maggie brought a small army."

Maggie pulled her gloves and hat off, and her paper from her bag. "The fellas are pretty handy with tools, and the kids will be helpers anywhere. Nora has some decoration ideas in addition to some set ideas she wanted to have ready for tomorrow, and Jen is your seamstress. I think someone named Phoebe from Nora's office is meeting us. And I'm going to get my nails done. See ya." Maggie giggled.

"Very funny," Jim shook hands with Dan and Mark. He looked at Maggie. "You're not going anywhere. Phoebe is already here. I think she stepped into the restroom. You brought this army, now you've got to get them working."

Sara showed everyone where they could hang their coats. The group dispersed, chattering and following Maggie's direction.

Jim showed Nora the updated stage sketches. She pulled out her laptop to compare notes. She would need to shoot more pictures of the stage from a variety of angles. From there she could add walls or backdrops to develop the look and how they might move the set around. Impressed, Jim nodded, looking directly into her deep hazel eyes. His gaze lasted just a little longer than usual.

Jim took a small step back to break his gaze. "I'll let you ladies get started with your fancy software. When you get to the point of designing the space, I can walk you through how we need it all to work." Jim explained.

Jen and the seamstress, Cindy, headed for the costume room. Emma was close behind.

"Don't get in their way," Maggie called to Emma.

Dan was assigned some painting in the lobby. But first, he and Mark headed to the attic to get the rest of the decorations. Maggie would clean them first. The men undid the tree from the top of the van and set it on the porch for after the painting was done. Adam and Mark were running wires, and the other kids went to help wipe down the counters and clean the concession area. Maggie and Sara went to work cleaning the brass door pulls and knobs. Everything would need to sparkle. Throughout the theater, there were friendly conversations, laughter, and a spirit of community.

Sara's friends came early to get going with canvasing the neighborhoods, knocking on doors, and getting signatures. The cast and crew all signed the petition to get things going. And they set up an online petition option for actors who had performed there in the past. Maggie's army buddied up with a production member and busied themselves on their assigned task for several hours. The kids finished their tasks and got a little restless.

Mark and Dan volunteered to take the kids to get some lunch and bring something back for everyone else. Throughout the day, Dan and Jim would have side conversations, pointing and problem solving. When Jim shared some of their financial challenges, Dan offered a few questions for Jim to ask his accountant.

Dan and Jim finished up their list. Jim wiped off his hands. "Thanks for the ideas, Dan. You've given me plenty to think about. You know, I have to tell you. Your Maggie is some lady. I don't know what I would do without her. Thank you for sharing her with us."

Dan shifted back and forth. "Well, uh, thanks. I think I'll go check on the kids." Dan stepped away in any direction Jim wasn't headed.

Nora and Phoebe had all their photos. With Jim and Adam looking over their shoulder, they began to design the set and movements. After several adjustments, they had captured the set for each act. Nora saved the files.

"We can print these and make a set for the stagehands." Phoebe offered.

"We need to find a thronelike chair with a table next to it. Maggie, have you or Sara seen anything we can use in the prop room?"

"No, but we will go check again." Maggie offered. She and Sara stood up to go.

Sara grabbed her protruding belly. "Ouch!" she yelped.

"Are you okay?" Maggie asked.

Sara slowly stood up and took a deep breath. "I'm fine. Probably the baby."

"Excuse me, the baby?" Maggie had noticed Sara's weight gain over the weeks, put hadn't wanted to assume or pry.

Sheepishly, Sara took Maggie aside to explain.

"Six months ago, I found out I was pregnant."

Maggie reached over and squeezed her arm. "I'm so sor ..."

Sara stood up straight. "Don't feel sorry for me. I made a mistake with a guy I thought loved me. But his family has 'expectations' for him." Sara's fingers did air quotes.

Maggie leaned against the wall in the tiny hall and listened. Sara sounded so matter-of-fact.

"Mom took me to the doctor and then to the attorney to get the parental rights of the father terminated." Sara looked at the floor and shifted her feet.

"But my frame is so small, the doctor said I might feel more muscle adjustments in the second trimester." Maggie listened and prayed in her heart about how to react.

"Oh, how I remember those pains. Are you okay?" Maggie said.

"I'm fine. I wasn't at first. But mom's been great. I've wanted to tell you but wasn't sure what you'd think. You seem kinda religious. Mom and I are talking about how all this will work with me trying to finish college."

"My faith doesn't ask me to judge others. It teaches me to have grace." The two slowly walked back to the prop room.

Phoebe wrapped up her measurements and notes for the design. "What else do we need to do today?"

"You have done so much. Thank you," Jim said.

"Phoebe, why don't we go by the office to print these out while we're waiting for the guys to come back?" Nora and Phoebe grabbed their coats and headed for the door.

Maggie went to see how Jen and Cindy were doing.

"We're rockin'. We have a system to get all these costumes organized and ready to be altered. How are the others doing?"

"They're doing well. The guys took the kids to get some lunch and bring pizza and salads back. Nora and Phoebe went to print some stage designs."

"Nora looks like she's having fun." Jen observed.

"I walked out there a little while ago," Maggie said. "She and Phoebe were shooting photos and talking about space and design ideas. They must have measured the stage four times. She looked happy. You should have heard her explain all this to Jim and Adam. She knows her stuff."

The guys got back with lunch for everyone. During the break, everyone sat around eating and talking about their work. After they ate, the kids got brooms and dust cloths to go up and down every row sweeping the floor and wiping down all the seats. This accomplished a needed task and kept them away from the wet paint. Late in the afternoon, all the volunteers wrapped up their work, cleaned up their workspaces, and put their tools away. Jim gathered everyone in the auditorium.

As Jim got started, someone stuck her head in the door to the auditorium. "Hello?"

Jim shielded his eyes from the spotlights to see who it was. "Yes, ma'am, can we help you?" Everyone turned to see who came in.

Maggie immediately greeted her. "Mrs. Fitzpatrick! Come in."

Jim asked, "How many people did you invite to help today?"

Maggie got up to help Mrs. Fitzpatrick, who was juggling three containers of cookies, trays, and an envelope. "Here, let me help you. Jim, this is the principal from the kids' school, Mrs. Fitzpatrick. She volunteered to make cookies for tomorrow."

Jim smiled and shook his head. "Wow. Thank you."

"Glad to help. This ole theater means a lot to my sister and me. Our beaus brought us here. I was telling Maggie about it the other day." Mrs. Fitzpatrick looked around at the aged walls. "Those were special days. Oh, and my sister came over to help me bake. She brought these." She picked the envelope off the top of the pile Maggie was balancing. Out of the envelope came two photos from the 1950s. "We took turns with the Brownie, taking pictures of each other on the porch of the theater. Just out front there."

Jim gently handled the photos. "These are outstanding."

"My sister and her fella only dated a short time after. But she carried a torch for him for years. And that's Harry and me. Little did I know he was going to propose later that night."

"Mrs. Fitzpatrick, these photos are wonderful, and your story is touching. Thank you for sharing. And thank you for the cookies. Do you have a minute to join us? I was just about to talk about tomorrow." Jim lightly directed her to an open seat on the front row. "It's no secret how much I love this theater. We've managed to open productions at least once a year, sometimes twice depending on our resources. Every year, we have a volunteer day to do clean-up and odd jobs." Jim paused as if remembering each time the doors opened for the season. "This ole theater comes alive—not just from being cleaned up, but also from the energy each of you brings. Thank you for being the breath of life to these walls."

Everyone clapped.

Jim held up his hands. "A couple of things. First, I hope you will all join us tomorrow for what I know will be more fun than you had today. The reception starts at three. We will finish decorating the tree out front and meet our neighbors. Most importantly, we'll gain their support and signatures on the petition." The doors to the auditorium swung open again. This time a brigade of college students marched down the aisle. Startled, Jim looked up from his notes. "Can I help you?"

One of the young men with mittens and a knit hat on spoke up, "Yes. Yes, sir, we're friends of Sara's." Hearing her name, Sara jerked around.

"Oh yeah, Jim, these are my friends who volunteered to walk the neighborhood. How'd you do?"

"Not too bad. It got pretty cold though."

Shuffling in his shoes, Jim asked, "The number—how many signatures?"

"Oh, uh ..." the young man stammered.

"One hundred and fourteen, sir. And we handed out all of the flyers for tomorrow." A girl in a long toboggan hat from the back of the pack spoke up as she carried the ragged-edge pages to Jim.

"Wow!" A smile radiated from Jim's face. "Way to go, you all. Thank you." Jim looked at the hundred varied signatures with addresses and phone numbers. "This is an outstanding start. Thank you."

Not fully understanding the impact, the young man shrugged. "No problem, sir. Glad we could help. We all hope to act in this theater someday. We'd like it to be here for us."

Jim looked down for a second, and then stopped the students from leaving. "Wait a minute. Can you all join us? I'd like to talk to you."

The students took their seats to wait.

"Quickly—I know everyone is ready to go, but I want to invite you to be our guests at opening night in February. Our treat—made possible by a sponsor. Even with the risk of this being our last season, we have been fortunate to have two significant sponsors this year. One will remain anonymous. The other one is Mark Stephens's company, IT Specialists, Inc." More clapping from the group and the young people chattering about free tickets. "Thank you, Jen and Mark. Nora, I can't wait to see the set designs. And thank you, Maggie, for bringing your talented and willing volunteers. Be safe going home, and I look forward to seeing you tomorrow."

Maggie nodded and looked over at Jen with a smile. *Little sneak.* Maggie had no idea of Mark's generosity.

Everyone started to disperse when Jim reminded the cast members they needed to stay to run through lines. Maggie looked at Dan. "Can you take the kids home, have some dinner, maybe stop and get burgers, and have them get ready for bed?"

"No problem." Dan said as he kissed Maggie on the forehead. "We'll eat out, so we won't even have to go into your kitchen."

Maggie swatted at his arm. "You're allowed to go in the kitchen." They both laughed and kissed good-bye.

Jim asked the students to come to the front with Mrs. Fitzpatrick. "You've given me an idea."

Before Mrs. Fitzpatrick settled in a seat, she touched Maggie's arm. "Maggie, do you mind if I make a guess about something?"

Maggie turned to her elderly friend. “Sure.”

“I’m guessing your participating with this play has been a bit of a challenge for Dan and the kids.”

Maggie’s heart sank. Did it show? Had the kids said something at school? “Why, what do you mean?”

“Maggie, I’m not trying to overstep here, please. But I’ve noticed a few things lately that make me wonder.”

Maggie fidgeted with the script she was holding. “Like what? Are the kids okay at school?”

“Your kids are fine. I just know that when a wife and mother decides to take on something unrelated to the family, sometimes it mixes up an otherwise tidy routine.”

She nailed it. That was exactly what Maggie had done. Her shoulders slumped. “Oh, Mrs. Fitzpatrick, you have no idea.”

The creases on her face climbed as the older woman patted Maggie’s arm. “Oh, I do. About a month after the last of our three boys went to school, I was climbing out of my skin. The house chores were in order, the meals were planned, and I still had time on my hands. So, I decided to go back to teaching. My husband was fine with the idea, because I was on the same schedule as the kids. The problem came when I was placed at a school across town from them and had all the after-school duties teachers have.”

Maggie stepped a little closer to listen to her story.

“It was a rough first semester of trying to find rides for the kids and getting home to meet them. The kids were my responsibility. It’s just how it was back then.” Mrs. Fitzpatrick nodded.

“How did you resolve it?”

“Well, we talked and argued and kept talking until he understood my need for something to do, and I understood this was different than how our friends were raising their families. Understanding each other made a huge difference in how we handled things."

Maggie listened intently, and shared. "We've had a few hard conversations, but I think he's coming around. It's hard. And my nightmares about my dad aren't helping."

"Nightmares?" Mrs. Fitzpatrick sat on the edge of her seat turning toward Maggie.

"Yeah, you see, my dad died of a heart attack while helping with one of my productions. Going back to the theater seems to have dredged up those memories. And along with fighting with Dan, I just feel so guilty sometimes."

"Maggie, I'm sure your dad loved you very much. He was probably helping with the production out of love and support for you, right?"

Maggie voice broke. "Yes."

"Honey, I don't know why your dad's last day happened while doing something for you. But I do know our God is the great comforter. Maybe coming back to the theater is your way of doing it for yourself, and not as a connecting point for you and your dad. Try praying the comforting Scriptures. Seek God in this sadness, and he will bless it."

Maggie lightly touched Mrs. Fitzpatrick's arm. "Thank you for listening."

Mrs. Fitzpatrick took her seat. Maggie left to meet the cast for rehearsal. As she exited through the stage curtain, she heard Jim say, "You two have given me an idea that could really help."

*He is determined.*

# CHAPTER TWENTY-EIGHT

The aroma of cider wafted and mixed well with the old wood of the theater. Maggie and Mrs. Fitzpatrick busied themselves getting cookies on trays, lights plugged in, and candles lit. The lobby had been given a clean coat of paint and a strong dose of Christmas decor. Nora's little extras brought the decorations together.

Maggie arranged the last of the three batches of cookies on the tray. "Thank you for helping me set up—and a big thank you for all these cookies. I don't know how we would have managed to get everything baked."

"I'm glad to help. It's given me the opportunity to relive my memories of my sweet Harry ..." Mrs. Fitzpatrick's voice trailed off into the memory.

Jim and Sara arrived. Jim stood with his hands on his hips. He nodded and smiled at the result of everyone's hard work. Sara went straight for the compliment.

"Wow! This place looks great."

"It does look amazing—fresh and like Christmas. I hope we have a good turnout." Jim busied himself with the one-page information sheet he and Sara had developed.

About half an hour later, the cast and crew sprinkled in, followed by the first of the guests. Jim and Sara gave tours and shared the history of the theater.

Mrs. Fitzpatrick had found a frame for her picture and displayed it on the desk next to the petition. She and one of the drama students stayed close to invite guests to sign the petition. About an hour into the reception, Jim finished a tour and called for everyone to join him in the auditorium. There were well over a hundred guests. They all turned and filed through the doors to find seats. Jim's voice cracked as he began.

"Thank you for coming this afternoon. The tree looks great with the colorful ornaments you brought—in some cases, an ornament you made. Each of you has added something to what was a plain tree. Now the tree is bright and colorful and bears a little part of all of us. That tree is not unlike our theater. When it's empty and quiet, it's a lovely building, but when the actors are on stage, and the audience is coming and going, the theater comes alive." Jim's hands waved with emphasis.

"As many of you know, the Planning and Zoning folks have put the theater on a list of fifty buildings considered for demolition to develop the area. That would be an atrocity. This theater has been a part of our community for a hundred years. It's been a part of each of our lives and we'd like ... no ... we need it to remain for the generations to come." Jim gestured to the student group. "If you haven't already, please sign the petition on the desk before you go. If we don't save the theater, this spring may be our last production. Thank you in advance, and thank you for coming." Jim paused to gather his closing thoughts. "Stay as long as you like, look around and feel free to ask questions. Our next production opens February tenth. I hope to see everyone there."

Sara turned the Christmas music back on, and the guests continued to mingle and chat. Maggie found Dan, and they had a quiet moment to watch the guests and talk. Dan gently reached for Maggie's hand. "I'm sure there will be enough signatures."

Monday morning dawned cold and rainy. Maggie prayed the weather wasn't foreshadowing the result of the meeting with the Planning and Zoning Committee. She didn't have to go to the theater today but wanted to be around to support Jim in his presentation. Dressed in slacks, sweater and blazer, she looked a little more professional than her typical attire for rehearsals.

Sara was at her post. "Good morning, Maggie. I didn't know you were coming in today."

"I don't need to be here, but wanted to offer a little moral support." Maggie shimmied out of her coat and hung it in the coat room. "How's he doin'?"

Sara tilted her head. "He's a ... a little short-tempered, but I think he's nervous."

"Probably. Is there something I can help you with as long as I'm here?"

Sara reviewed her desktop. "Yeah, you want to make coffee? I've got the room ready."

Maggie busied herself in the kitchen. Sara turned on the tree lights to try and push back the darkness of the day. Instantly, they warmed the lobby. Jim came out of the conference room, wringing his hands.

"Are they here yet?" Without waiting for Sara to answer, he paced across the lobby to look out the window. "Now, when they get here, be your friendly self and show them to our meeting room."

"Coffee's ready." Maggie announced as she joined the two.

Jim ran his hand over his fresh haircut. "Great. Thank you, Maggie. As long as you're here, I'd like to introduce you to them. You know, to give them a little ..." he hesitated "... a little of our mature factor."

Maggie smiled. She hadn't known Jim long and had never seen him this nervous. "Thanks, I think." Her teasing was lost to his anxiety. "Jim, it's going to be fine. Just be yourself and show your passion for your theater and what it means to our community."

"Oh, I've got a plan for that." As if perfectly on cue, Mrs. Fitzpatrick and Matt, the student they had met Saturday, walked in.

Maggie perked up. "Mrs. Fitzpatrick, what are you doing here?"

Jim shook Matt's hand and helped Mrs. Fitzpatrick with her coat. "These two have offered to help me with my presentation this morning. They're, for lack of a better term, the theatergoer of the past and the actor of the future."

The five of them had a stress-relieving laugh, then Jim explained how the presentation would work. Mrs. Fitzpatrick and Matt only needed to give a couple of minutes on what the theater meant to them. Jim would present status of the theater.

Maggie clapped her hands. "That's a great idea. I know it will work."

The executive committee from Planning and Zoning peppered in. Sara greeted them and offered coffee. Jim introduced Maggie as his stage manager and right hand of the current production. With everyone in and seated, the door closed. Maggie and Sara were left on the outside. The quiet hung like the forty-foot, red-velvet stage curtains.

The two looked at each other. Sara peeked through the silence. "Well, I'm going to go check a shipment of costume fabric that came in this morning. Want to come with me?"

"I'm going to have to. Standing on this side of the door will drive me crazy."

"That's why I saved this shipment for now. Staring at the closed door is more than this pregnant woman can take."

Maggie smiled at the thought of the young mother and her baby. "Let's go. We'll talk baby stuff. Maybe that will help pass the time."

The two headed backstage to inventory the contents of three large boxes. Maggie checked the packing slip as Sara pulled fabric and sewing materials out. Sara shared a little more about her mother's support and having the baby. Maggie tried to be more big sisterlike than mothering, encouraging Sara to take good care of herself and get rest.

"If our production schedule gets too much for you, please let me know. We don't have to make a big deal of it, but if you need to slip out early or have extra time for snacks, just let me know."

"Ugh, snacks. I'm starting to get hungry again. Lost my appetite during all the morning sickness time. Now, it feels like I want to eat all the food I missed plus what I should be eating."

Maggie laughed, "Yep, sounds 'bout right."

"There you two are." Jim rushed over to them. "I've been looking for you. You will not believe what happened."

"Hope it's good news." Maggie set the packing slip on the box.

Sara set aside the material. "All this talk of food has me pretty hungry. Can we go up front so I can get my granola bar?"

Jim nodded, heading to the front meeting room. "Yeah, yeah, let's go sit in the meeting room. This news is going to affect you both."

The three filed into the room. Maggie stopped for a bottled water. Although her stomach was rumbling for lunch as well, she could wait. Eating for two was another matter. Sara needed to keep her hunger at bay.

Jim paced around. His earlier anxiousness had transformed to an excited energy. “This is good, ladies. It’s going to take some work, but it’s good.”

Amused, Maggie couldn’t resist. “Are you going to tell us or have the conversation with yourself?”

Jim snapped to focus on them. “Dr. Crosby, the head of the graduate fine arts department at the university, showed up after the meeting started.” Jim’s speech got faster and more intense. “I can’t believe this happened. As Matt and Mrs. Fitzpatrick finished their part, which, by the way, was outstanding, Dr. Crosby walked into the meeting. He apologized for being late, as if he’d planned to be here. He also apologized for missing yesterday and wanted to be sure and sign the petition. At this point, I just sat down.”

Dr. Crosby was in his early sixties, had built his career at the university, and was heavily involved in the performing arts community. Jim went on. “Dr. Crosby presented to the committee a plan moving forward where each semester, the university would support an internship program within the theater. Three positions—acting, lighting, and set design. Then he asked me for the petition and signed it in front of the committee, taking us over the two hundred signatures we needed.” Jim’s excitement was bouncing off the walls and boosting the spirits of both Maggie and Sara.

“The university has pledged ten thousand dollars a semester to underwrite the productions these interns will be working on.” His hands reached out. “This is great! With the commitment from the university and their support for the theater staying, the committee immediately agreed to recommend taking us off the list!” Jim was practically dancing.

The three cheered in excitement.

"We've got work to do. I'm going over to Dr. Crosby's office this afternoon to work out the details. He did say he wanted to get things going immediately. Since we don't have a formal intern program this semester, he handed me a personal donation of twenty-five hundred."

Each of the three did their own happy dance. Jim and Maggie walked out together. Jim's demeanor was settling into his normal tone and energy. "Thank you for coming in today. It meant a lot to have your support. You know, I could use you and your organizational skills beyond our spring production. If you've got a little more time ..." Jim's request trailed toward Maggie.

Excited about the news and the opportunity, Maggie's eyes sparkled. But reality settled her heart before she could say yes. "Let me talk to Dan. You find out exactly how this will work, and we can talk later."

Maggie and Dan had finally found peace. Things were working for now. She didn't want to stir things up again until she had more information.

# CHAPTER TWENTY-NINE

Maggie caught up to Jen right before she opened the door to school. Both were running close to on time for pickup. "Hey, girl, how's it goin'?"

Jen stopped short of the door to greet her friend. "Doing great. Did you get all the signatures you needed to save the theater?"

"More than enough, and the last name was a doozy."

The two working moms stood near the door basking in the unseasonably warm December sunshine. Maggie told Jen the details of the meeting and Dr. Cosby's offer.

"Wow, that sounds great!" Jen cheered. But Maggie's expression deflated enough for Jen to ask the next question. "What's wrong?"

Maggie fidgeted. "Well, Jim has asked me to commit to helping around the theater a little longer than the play in February. I'm not sure about it ... or if I even want to bring it up to Dan."

"I thought you said he was doing better with all of it. He seemed good this weekend."

"He is ..." Maggie's voice trailed off. "But I think that's just because he thinks it's short-term. Jim's talking about something longer now."

Jen looked around. "You know, Jim seems pretty nice. And he admires you like crazy." Something in the way

Jen's inflection changed sounded more inquisitive than definitive.

Without thinking, Maggie replied, "Yeah ... Wait a minute, what do you mean saying 'admires me' like that?"

Jen laughed at her friend's defense. "Just checking on things. Making sure you aren't going down that slippery slope from work colleagues to friends to ..."

"How long have you known me? I would never let something like that happen."

"I know you wouldn't go there intentionally. Be careful, friend. He's good-looking, he admires you, and right now, Dan's on the verge of not being fully encouraging."

Maggie and Jen had kept each other accountable on several things over the years. In college, it was study time versus having fun time, how late to stay out with a guy, even maintaining relationships with challenging parents. So, for Jen to offer this caution, Maggie wasn't even close to being offended.

"I'm too old and tired for such shenanigans. I am fully committed to marriage. Dan's stuck with me," Maggie teased. "Now, let's go get our kids so we can be good working wives and have dinner on the table when the guys get home."

"Sounds good. But listen—On the other thing, if you want to pursue this theater thing further, talk to Dan about it. Speak from your heart. You seemed so alive on Saturday. I remember *that* Maggie. The one with a spring in her step and a long list."

"I do feel more like myself these days than I've felt in a long time. Thank you for your encouragement." The two moms caught up on the news with their kids as they walked in to pick them up from the cafeteria.

Maggie was in and out of listening to Danny and Emma chatter. They were doing homework at the kitchen table. Lost in her thoughts, Maggie tried to distract herself with dinner preparations. The quandary of talking to Dan nagged at her like an itch that couldn't be scratched. The prospect of staying with the theater beyond February was exciting. If it was only up to her, she'd do it in a heartbeat. But she had Dan and the kids to consider. The guilt gnawed at her heart. Her mother had driven into her that she was supposed to be available for her family and to take care of her husband. At least that's what her mother always said.

Lost in her dilemma, she didn't hear Danny ask for help.

"Mom!" Danny yelled.

Maggie turned sharply on her heel. "Daniel, you do not yell at me."

Danny sank back in his seat. "I'm sorry, Mom. But you weren't listening to my question."

A guilt pang struck. She didn't hear her son's need. What was she thinking? Maggie sighed and walked over to look at his worksheet.

"I'm sorry, sweetie. What's your question?"

Danny asked his question, and Maggie asked him another question that helped him figure out the answer for himself. "See, you knew the answer all along."

She was taking the chicken out of the oven as Dan came in from work.

"Hello, family."

Maybe she would wait to talk to him.

"Hi, honey." Wiping her hands on the kitchen towel, Maggie walked a little too quickly to kiss her husband.

Dan kissed her and pulled back. "What's wrong?"

Feeling like the script was all over her face, Maggie played her role. "Nothing. Just finishing dinner. It will be ready shortly."

"Okay."

Maggie bit her bottom lip. "If you want to change clothes before dinner, now's your chance."

Dan headed upstairs to change. Maggie stirred the vegetables, lost again in her thoughts. *What will I do after the play closes? Do I want to continue to work at the theater?*

The evening was quiet. Maggie stayed busy with nebulous tasks. She could hardly look at Dan. He knew her too well. With the kids settled, she was running out of tasks, and it was too early for bed. Dan's work cell phone broke the silence. With a questioning furrowed brow, he answered the call. He grabbed his notepad and headed for the kitchen. All Maggie could hear was Dan telling the caller that it wasn't a problem to call him at home. Then all she heard was a lot of "ahas" and "sures."

# CHAPTER THIRTY

Dan was on the phone for about ten minutes before he came bounding back into the living room. "Great news!"

Maggie lit up. "What is it?"

"That was my boss. He just went through the summary of the auditor report, and there was no evidence of any wrongdoing on the part of my staff, including Stephanie!" He pulled Maggie up to dance around with him.

"That is great news!" she exclaimed, celebrating with Dan.

"There are still a few questions to be answered. The discrepancy was in some data that didn't get moved to this year's ledger. But my staff has been cleared. And Stephanie can come back to work with no ding to her HR record."

"I am so happy for you. This has been such a burden for you. And all those auditors in the office every day."

Dan whirled Maggie around into a dance dip. He pulled her upright again. "We need to go dancing. It's been too long."

The temperature plunged overnight, and a freezing rain began. Maggie dropped the kids at school and headed for the theater. She was scheduled to be there all day, watching and taking notes while the director ran the rehearsal. Jim was walking out of the kitchen with steaming coffee. He was wearing a turtleneck. Not something Maggie usually liked on men, but with his physique it worked. Maggie dropped her bag by the desk to say good morning to Sara. She rubbed her hands and blew into them. Jim handed Maggie his cup. "Here, this will get you warmed up. I'll go grab another."

"Thank you. Do you have a minute?"

"What's up?"

"You wanted an answer today about this extra help you need."

"You don't sound like you've got one."

Maggie walked around hugging her cup in her palms. "It's not a simple answer. My deal with Dan was that my venture back to the theater was short-term. He thinks our lives are going back to the way they were in two more months."

"What do you want to do?"

"What do I want? Good question. This all started because I was feeling restless. It was just a brief break from the routine." She was trying to convince herself.

Jim put his hands on his hips. "You're like a duck who has found its way back to water. I've watched you run lines, work with blocking, manage people, figure out how to stretch our already-stretched budget. You are in your zone. This is where you belong. Our little theater has a chance to do some good work with students ... to make a difference. We need you."

Another man who needed her.

"You don't understand. I'm struggling with some guilt. Shouldn't I be focused on my family and husband?"

Jim tilted his head and squinted. "Who are you? Betty Crocker, homemaker?"

Maggie heard her question and Jim's together and how insane it all sounded. She laughed. "Maybe. I can cook, and my house is well kept."

"I have no doubt your home is in perfect order." Jim took a step back. "Would it help to have some more time to think about it? What did Dan say?"

"I haven't talked to him."

"Why not?"

"It's complicated."

"Oh." Jim wrapped his hands around the steamy coffee cup. "He didn't strike me as an unsupportive husband. We had an enjoyable conversation on Saturday. And he's handy. He got through most of my list of little projects that I don't seem to ever have time for."

"I'll talk to him. And I need to pray this through. I want to, or at least I think I do. Please give me some time." Maggie's stomach rolled around in her confusion. More restlessness.

"No problem. I've got you until February at least. Mind if I add a few things to your list?"

Jim gave her a few extra things to begin to organize the intern program but didn't mention their conversation again. This gave her the opportunity to relax and enjoy her day. Then Jen called and asked Maggie to pick up Brian too. It was raining again, so Maggie treated the kids to ice cream and time in the indoor play area.

Dan pulled in the garage as Maggie and the kids stepped into the house. Why was he home?

Dan jerked his coat off. "Is there a reason your Jim guy called me at work to ask permission for you to take on more at the theater? Something about an internship program he wants you to coordinate. Why is he calling me, Maggie?" His keys hit the key bowl a little too hard. Brian, Danny, and Emma stopped in mid-chatter.

"Kids, take Brian and go downstairs to watch TV. Dad and I need to talk."

Emma picked up her backpack, and Brian and Danny followed.

Maggie turned back to Dan. "Now, if you wouldn't mind settling down, we can talk about this."

"No, Maggie." Dan glared at her. "I felt like an idiot, not having a clue what he was talking about. What are you doing?"

She shook her head and grimaced. "I don't know. Things had finally settled down with you and me. And you got good news from work. I didn't mention it because I didn't want to stir things up again." Her voice softened. "I didn't think you would understand."

"Understand what? This thing you needed to do to get theater out of your system is now more than just a part in the play."

*Get the theater out of my system?*

"What if I don't want to get it out of my system? Maybe being in the theater is a part of me. This isn't about getting something *out of my system*, Dan. I am lost here!" Maggie's frustration moved to anger. Her hands were waving, and her voice got louder. "You want to know what this is about? It's about me being *me*. I'm tired of only taking care of the kids and making sure your shirts are ironed. I'm tired of being known as *Mom* or *Dan's wife*. I want to be *Maggie*!"

She took a deep breath and held it a moment, stretching the silence. "You want to keep me in my place. To be honest, I'm not sure what I want to do. I've prayed about this and the way I'm feeling. I need God to show up with his peace."

"Mag, settle down." Dan reached for her arm.

Maggie jerked away. “Don’t tell me what to do, Dan.”

Taking a step back, Dan shook his head. “I can’t win.” He loosened his tie.

The doorbell rang. Dan took his exit upstairs. Maggie completely forgot that Jen was picking up Brian. There was no hiding from Jen. When Maggie opened the door with a quick yank. Jen’s smile dropped.

“Something wrong?”

Maggie nodded and led Jen into the kitchen. Jen’s perceptiveness was keen. “You were arguing again about all this theater stuff.”

The floodgate of tears opened. She fell into her friend’s hug and cried harder.

“Did Dan say no?” Jen asked.

Maggie backed away to reach for a tissue. Wiping her nose and eyes, she choked out a feeble, “No ... we didn’t get that far.” She blew her nose and Jen started to shimmy out of her coat. But Maggie shook her head.

She lowered her voice. “I still need to decide. But I need to be able to talk to Dan without it turning into a fight.” Maggie threw the tissue away. “Jim must have thought he and Dan hit it off on Saturday, so why not call and talk to him. You can imagine from looks of things here and that Dan is home before five it didn’t go so well. Jim’s good intentions blew up in my face.”

All Jen could respond was, “Oh.” Both stood in the kitchen quietly—Maggie, tired from the whole thing, Jen fidgeting with her keys.

Maggie sighed. “I’ve made this mess. Guess I’ve got to clean it up.”

“Life’s messy sometimes. It’s not all calendars and lists. It’s people trying to live together. It gets messy when all our selfish willfulness gets in the way.”

Maggie frowned. “Are you saying I’m being selfish?”

Jen smiled. "Settle down there. You feel like everyone is against you right now. We aren't. We love you and want you to be happy. You've thrown this wrench and now those around you need some time to adjust."

"I guess. This restlessness has been nagging at me a while. A lot longer than I've shared." Maggie confessed. "Probably since Easter."

"So, you've felt this way for six or seven months and you think the last two months were sufficient time for everyone to catch on?"

Maggie saw Jen's point. "You're right. I kept this to myself and let it fester for a long time before I decided to act on it. Now I've rocked my husband's world." Maggie sniffled and raked the back of her hand across her cheek. "What do I do to clean up this mess? I really don't want to give it all up."

The air was calm, and Jen shrugged her shoulders. "Dinner."

"Dinner?"

"We need to feed the kids. Why don't I take the three kids and call Mark to meet us for burgers? You and Dan can have some space to talk this out."

"You don't have to take mine. I've got dinner about ready."

Jen raised her voice a little. "Maggie, quit it. You don't have to do everything per the schedule. You don't have to do everything perfectly. Let someone give you a little help. You and Dan eat your dinner. Take a time-out from perfection to clean up this mess. Let me take the kids, give them something else to think about this evening besides y'all's fight."

Maggie conceded. "Okay. Can I go with you?" She smiled.

Motherly, Jen pointed her finger in jest. "You may not, young lady. Stay here, go tell your husband you love him, and talk all this through. Just don't burn the house down."

The two friends hugged. Maggie called the kids down while Jen called Mark. "Thank you, Jen." The kids came barreling down the steps. "How's burgers and fries sound?" The cheers went up as they scrambled for coats and hats. As they walked out the door, Emma turned and ran back to Maggie and gave her a tight hug. "Thank you, Mom. Wow, eating out on a school night."

The kids left with Jen. Maggie stood in her kitchen. The peace and quiet was overshadowed by the conversation waiting to be had at the top of the stairs. With each step, she prayed for the right words, the right attitude, the right spirit. It was time to stop fighting.

*Lord, please open Dan's heart to me. Let him not just hear me, but understand me. And let me hear and understand him.*

# CHAPTER THIRTY-ONE

Burgers on a school night. Such a simple pleasure for an eight-year-old. When did life get so complicated? Dan was on his knees at the bedside. *Lord, I've been a prideful fool. Forgive me. I pray Maggie will forgive me. Please help me be the husband you want me to be, and the father my children need as an example. You have blessed me with such a great life. Open my heart to live it better for your glory.*

Dan heard Maggie's light tap on the door. As she came in, he turned and sat cross-legged. Maggie joined him on the floor. He took her hands and looked deep into the eyes of the woman he had loved since he was twenty. Dan's shoulders slumped, and he looked down at their intertwined fingers, not letting go.

"Maggie, I'm so sorry. I've been so prideful and even a little jealous. Please forgive me. I love you and want to support you in doing the things you love. Jim caught me off guard today with something totally different than we've talked about. He was so over-the-top complimentary of your work ..." Dan shook his head. "I know you deserve every word of it, but it ... it made me jealous to hear another man sing your praises. I'm sorry I got so upset."

Maggie squeezed his hands, and softly spoke. "You're forgiven. I love you."

Dan raised his head to look again into her deep blue eyes. His heart thumped. She offered forgiveness he knew he didn't deserve. He drew her hands to his lips and kissed them. "Thank you."

The two sat holding each other in the quiet of their bedroom. They sat like they had in college, back when they'd talked about life, sitting face-to-face on the floor in his apartment.

Dan broke the silence. "Now, please tell me about this internship program, and what they're wanting you to do."

Maggie sat back and took a deep breath. "The university is going to fund an internship program each semester at the theater. Jim has asked me to take care of the administrative part of it. I don't know what all it entails, but I'm sure there will be requirements we'll need to have students meet, etcetera." Maggie shifted her legs around. "To be honest, I haven't made any decision about taking it." She looked down at their hands. "Right now, I just want to talk about the option. I've realized that maybe I don't want to go back to acting. I do love stage managing and even helping with some of the administrative stuff around the theater. But any decision I need to make, I want us to decide together."

Peaceful silence lingered. Dan nodded. "Okay. When you have all the details and are ready, let's talk about it."

She slouched with her head in her hands resting her elbows on her knees. "I'm not sure I want to commit to all that. I do love being back in the theater ... and I do desperately need something of my own to do." She caressed his hand. "This has been a rough adjustment for us. And my mother thinks I'm failing as a wife and mother. No doubt she thinks my kids are going to be juvenile delinquents. I'm wrestling with all that too." Maggie looked into his eyes. "Sweetheart, I don't want to be crossways with you. You know I love being a mom and your wife. This has been nagging at me for several months, like since last spring. I kept pushing it back. Then when the auditions came along it sparked something in me ..." Maggie's voice trailed off.

Dan's soft voice picked up where hers had landed. "The kids aren't going to be juvenile delinquents. I had no idea you were feeling so lost. You are so much more than just a wife and mother. I guess I forgot that because you're so good at both."

Maggie's dimples were deep in her smile. "Thank you ... and thank you for listening."

Dan brushed a curl from her forehead. "I'm going to work on being better at the listening part. The position sounds like all the things you're good at ... administration, organizing ... But what about being around the theater? Any more thoughts of your dad? Any dreams?"

"I still think of Daddy when I'm in the auditorium. But it's more of the good stuff like when he would help build sets." Her smile grew. "He was always the first to buy tickets to my plays."

Dan softly said, "I'm glad your memories have settled down. He loved seeing you on stage and would be so proud of you. How can we make this work? We've got Christmas to get ready for."

"Yeah, it's going to be busy, and I don't want to be so harried that I miss the joy of Christmas. It is one of my favorite holidays." Maggie smiled for the first time. "Besides my birthday."

"One national holiday at a time." Dan returned the tease.

"Dan, let's slow down a little. There's a lot going on right now, wanting Christmas to be special, your work, and my play. What if we don't make the full decision right now? What if I do everything I've committed to, and some of the other things Jim needs done in the next couple of months? Then after the play has closed in February, we make the longer-term decision."

Dan smiled gently and squeezed her hand. "You're so wise. Great idea to at least slow down on this transition. Will Jim be okay waiting on a full decision?"

"I'm a volunteer. What's he going to do, fire me?" They shared a laugh. Dan settled into a more serious posture. "Are you sure *you're* okay waiting to make the full decision?"

"I'm sure." Maggie nodded.

Dan stood up and helped Maggie up. Took her in his arms and held her tight. Whispering in her ear, "I love you, Maggie Nelson. Just hold onto me, and we'll figure it all out together. You have my full support to do the play and my open mind to discuss the next commitment after that."

"I love you too, Dan Nelson." Maggie held on a little tighter, for a long quiet embrace. "Let's go eat something. I made chili for dinner. Do you want a sandwich with it?"

"Sounds yummy. How about I heat up the chili, you make cheese sandwiches, like we did when we were childless and poor."

Maggie led the way. "Those were the glory days, weren't they—in our first studio apartment?"

The two went down to the kitchen sharing more stories of the early days. The lawn furniture Dan and Mark had in their living room. They had quite the touch for decorating.

While Maggie was finishing up the sandwiches, Dan slipped into the dining room to get a couple of candles. Halfway through dinner, Jen poked her head in the front door and came around to see them laughing over their chili and sandwich candlelit dinner.

"Okay, thought I'd check before Mark and the kids came in. Everyone still standing?"

# CHAPTER THIRTY-TWO

The sun was a welcome change after several days of rain. Cold winter rain always cut to the core both physically and emotionally. Day after day of no sun made everyone fussy. But the morning brought sun and glistening frost. "You had me worried last night." Jen stepped out of her hybrid with her coffee in hand. Maggie was getting into her van after volunteering for carpool duty, helping the kids out of cars with school bags.

"Hop in, it's too cold to stand out there." The final tardy bell had rung, and the two moms stole a minute in the parking lot to chat. "We were bound to hit a wall like that. I'm the one who rocked the boat."

"You didn't rock the boat. If anything, it was a little tilted all along." Jen cupped her tea and took a slow sip.

"I don't know, but thank you for making us talk last night. Enough about my drama. How's your new job? How's it going?"

"It's great. We have plans for January and all the New Year's resolutions. Kevin seems pleased so far. We did a little preview class that went well, but Mark, in his attempt to help me, sent a few guys from his office over. It made my numbers, but Kevin was less than pleased with the gesture."

"I'm sure Kevin will get over it when you launch in January and have hundreds screaming for your classes." Maggie waved her hands as if to show the mass of people who would come. "You know, I'm not the only one rocking the boat on a smooth family life. You've made a pretty big change from part time to full time."

"Mark and Brian are doing well with it. Brian gets a little tired sometimes when we go back to the gym after I pick him up. I signed him up for the after-school program a couple of days a week to break it up a little."

"After school care—does he like it?"

"He loves it. It's like a big recess time. He only goes for about an hour in the afternoon."

Maggie's phone sang out. Looking at the screen, she saw it was Dan. Noticing the time, she saw he was just getting to the office. "I'd better get this. He's probably forgotten something."

"Hello."

"Hey, babe, did I catch you at a good time?"

"I'm sitting in the van talking with Jen. What do you need?" Dan rarely called this early in the day.

"You."

Maggie giggled. "Excuse me?"

"Elaine and I were going over my schedule this week, and I'm wondering if you'd like to spend Wednesday afternoon Christmas shopping. You know, like we used to do when the kids were babies."

Maggie remembered. "We'd have a date night and go to the toy store. That sounds great. Are you sure you have time?"

"I was thinking about it last night when you said something about taking a few days to go shopping, but I didn't want to say anything until I was sure I could sneak out. Will Wednesday at noon work? We'll start with lunch."

Maggie's smile took over her face. Jen looked at her with a curious head tilt.. "Sounds like a blast. I'd love it. Thank you."

"It's a date. I'll have Elaine mark me in a meeting all afternoon."

"Sounds great. I love you."

"I love you. Got to run."

Maggie hung up, her cheeks warm from the call.

Jen was all over her with questions. "What was that about?"

Maggie told her about Dan's invitation. She felt like her face would pop from smiling so hard.

Jen shared in the happy moment. "He's a good one. I've been telling you that since college."

Maggie swatted at Jen. "You thought he was a nerd in college because he studied all the time. The only reason you wanted to hang out with us was to flirt with Mark."

"Guilty. And it worked out for both of us, didn't it?"

"It did."

They talked for another few minutes about Christmas plans and what the kids wanted. Jen said she was going to call Nora about her kitchen and the final color scheme.

Maggie headed to the theater. Warm thoughts of her call from Dan swirled through the stage of her mind. Things were starting to feel peaceful again.

Mother nature cooperated that afternoon with snow flurries swirling but not seeming to land. It put them in the Christmas spirit. The list was marked off but, more importantly, Dan and Maggie spent two hours playing and teasing each other through the toy store. After shopping, they shared a pizza and a couple of sodas. IIolding hands in the car on the way home, Maggie leaned her head back against the leather headrest. Dan's hand felt familiar, warm, and strong. A few hours and a simple touch settled her heart. Was this what she had been missing? Maybe it wasn't the theater. Maybe she and Dan had become too complacent. Maybe she missed being courted. Had she forgotten to flirt with her husband?

Sitting at a stop light, Dan reached over and brushed a stray curl from Maggie's cheek. She opened her eyes and rolled her head to look at Dan. He leaned over with a gentle kiss.

"Mmmm, that's sweet. I love your kisses."

"Thank you for going out with me." Dan's expression was light.

"Thank you for asking." Maggie sat up as the light turned green. "Dan, I miss this. Thank you for remembering our Christmas shopping date."

"Yeah, I should ask you out more often. I'm sorry if I don't pay closer attention to you. I need to remember to take my best girl out every now and then." Dan's familiar, playful tone soothed the frosty air.

Maggie smiled. Such a simple thing. An afternoon out, just the two of them, had reminded her how deeply she loved her husband. The time together seemed to melt the corporate pressures Dan was carrying, and they had escaped to the core of their relationship—their love and respect for each other.

Maggie and Dan both tucked the kids in bed that night. There were bedtime stories, laughter, and hugs. After praying with the kids, they resigned to the living room. As Maggie settled in to read, her phone sounded off..

"Maggie, it's your mother."

*Nine o'clock. Ugh, this can't be good.*

"Hi, Mom, what' up?" Maggie's attempt to not sound cautious was lacking.

"Well, I was just thinking about Christmas. Would you mind hosting? I'm not feeling up to it."

Maggie sat up straight. "Are you okay?"

"Oh, I'm fine, dear. I'd like you to take this Christmas. You'll make it wonderful, I'm sure. I'll make a few dishes for the meal."

"Okay, Mom. Do you want to come over Christmas Eve and spend the night? We could get up and open presents with the kids."

"Oh, no. I'll just come over on Christmas day."

Maggie rolled her eyes. Something was up. Her mother was usually all about family and being together. "Mom, what's up? This is so unlike you. Are you okay?" Maggie's question left silence.

Maggie heard the ice cube jingle in the glass before her mother began slowly. "Well, honey, there's a certain gentleman caller I've been spending some time with." Maggie's jaw dropped. What was she hearing?

*A gentleman caller? Am I living* A Streetcar Named Desire*?*

"His name is Stan, and he's a retired fire chief. He's a nice man, dear."

Maggie made no response.

"Anyway, he's invited me to go to his daughter's on the twenty-second. We'll be home late on Christmas Eve."

Another man. What about Daddy? Daddy had passed away fifteen years ago. Maggie had never thought her mom wanted to find another man. Her mom had loved her dad, but she'd always been so critical of him when he was alive.

"Maggie? Are you still there?"

"What? Oh, yeah, I'm here. I guess you've surprised me a little. I didn't know you were seeing someone." *Seeing someone* sounded like something she would have said to her sorority sister at midnight after they'd come in from a night out.

Her mother's voice bristled. "Your dad's been dead for a long time. I'm lonely, Maggie. Stan is a good man."

"I wasn't saying anything against him. I guess as much as you complained about Dad when he was alive, I never thought you'd want another man around."

"What are you talking about? Complaining about your dad? He was a great man, and he loved you like crazy."

Things were escalating. *Tread lightly*. "Mom, I'm sure Stan is a wonderful man. You've caught me off guard, that's all. Not only do you spring a boyfriend on me, you're going to meet his family." *Boyfriend, really ... could I get more schoolgirl?*

With a small sigh, her mother replied, "I guess you're right. This could sound a little strange. As long as I'm springing stuff on you, can I bring him to Christmas at your house?"

In the two-minute call, not only was Maggie now hosting Christmas dinner for her family, but her mother also wanted to bring a date. Could life get any more bizarre?

"Okay ... yes, you can bring Stan to Christmas. Let me know what you'd like to bring, and I'll do the rest." Maggie closed her eyes for a second. "Mom, I know you deserve a life of your own. I didn't mean to sound otherwise."

"I know. Thank you for saying it, though."

Maggie hung up the phone and scratched her head.

"Everything okay?" The game was in its final seconds, and Dan's team had it locked.

Her eyebrows scrunched in uncertainty. "I guess."

"What did she say? Sounded like something about Christmas."

Maggie told Dan about them hosting Christmas. Then she told him about Stan, the boyfriend, or "gentleman caller" as her mother put it. She finished and then sat in silence trying to process it all. Besides not being ready for this news, she didn't know how she felt about it. Her mother had been a widow long enough. But while Joanna denied complaining about her husband, Maggie knew differently. Funny how death and time changed a person's memory.

"Maybe she'll soften up a little." Dan tried to help. Maggie wasn't convinced.

Maggie wanted to crawl into bed. "My list for the next three weeks just got a little longer. Think I'll make some tea and head to bed."

"We'll get it all done. I'll be up in a bit." Dan grabbed Maggie's hand as she passed. "I love you. Please don't let this spoil what has been the best day ever."

They both laughed. Yes, it had been a great day. Nothing, not even *gentleman callers*, was going to spoil it for Maggie.

# CHAPTER THIRTY-THREE

Maggie's lists had lists. She'd marked off several items. Christmas preparations were coming together. Never too far from her thoughts was what came after the holidays—the play. She would need to have her decision about continuing at the theater. She prayed for a clear answer. It would come and with it—peace. In the meantime, Maggie busied herself with holiday preparations.

She and Dan had scheduled two afternoons a week when he picked up the kids, and she could stay late at the theater. Nora was helping design the set. Jen was working with Cindy on costumes. Nora surprised Jen a little. It seemed Nora's style and prissiness hadn't changed but had softened, and her work ethic was strong. If Nora wasn't at her paying job, she was at the theater. Didn't she have family or friends? Jen had taken costume pieces home to hem. She and Nora were developing an unlikely friendship working together at the theater and meeting at the gym.

For now, Maggie was feeling good about herself and all her roles at the theater and at home. Order had returned. She started her mornings early. The house was quiet. It felt good to just be still and be thankful before the kids got up and the day's routine began. The schedule seemed to be working for everyone. Or so she thought.

The kids came bounding into the kitchen with only undershirts on. "Why aren't you in your uniform shirts?" Maggie shook her head.

Danny spoke up first. "I don't have any in my closet."

Emma followed. "Me neither."

"I know I washed them." Maggie headed for the laundry room where she found she had indeed washed them. Just not dried them. *Ugh.* Immediately she reached into the basket of uniforms yet-to-be-washed and did the smell test on a couple. One was a sweater, and one was a shirt. She tossed them in the dryer to warm and freshen them up.

"They'll be ready by the time you're done eating." The kids bought it and went about eating and getting their backpacks together.

Both were standing in the laundry room when Maggie pulled their clothes out of the dryer.

"Here you go, Danny. And here you go, Ms. Emma."

Tugging his over his head, Danny evaluated. "It's warm."

Maggie smiled. "Think of it as a warm hug from Mom." Danny taken care of.

Emma wasn't quite as positive. "Mom, this isn't mine. It's huge." Maggie looked over at Emma to see the arms of the sweater hanging below her fingertips and the waist band just below her butt. "It's Danny's!" Emma started to cry. "I don't want to wear his clothes. Where's mine?"

Maggie rooted through the pile and found a shirt of Emma's. Holding it up, she noted the huge chocolate stain down the front. That wouldn't work. Failing to find another one of Emma's shirts, Maggie turned to her daughter who was wrestling out of her brother's sweater. A quick assessment—was it better to make her wear it or deal with her being upset when she was called out for not wearing a school uniform? She'd campaign for the former.

"Sweetie, your shirts are in the washer, soaking wet. I forgot to put them in the dryer last night." *What kind of mother am I?* "Let's roll the sleeves up a bit and pull the bottom up, and kinda tuck it in—" Maggie was adjusting and tucking, and Emma kept wiggling.

"Mom, nooooo. I don't want to ..."

Maggie clenched her teeth. She walked into the kitchen, took a deep breath, and went back to the laundry room. *How had she forgotten to move the laundry?*

She knelt down in front of Emma. "Sweetie, I'm sorry. But this is the way it needs to be today. No one will even notice. I promise I will get all your uniforms cleaned tonight and you will get to choose whichever one you want to wear tomorrow." A final fixing and she turned Emma around to show her in the full-length mirror on the back of the door.

Emma examined her look. She shuffled her feet and shook her head. Not convinced. Sniffling and wiping her eyes, she said, "I guess."

"Thank you, sweetie. Mom is so sorry." Maggie hugged her and kissed her on the forehead.

The three got their coats and gloves and headed out the door. The guilt hit Maggie like the frosty December air. *I have failed.* While the kids seemed to recover from the incident, all the way to school and on to the theater, she went over and over in her head how she could have let this happen. She felt compelled to confess. She called Dan's cell phone. He answered on the second ring.

"Hey, hon. What's up?" He got to the point. Was he in the middle of something? Maybe this was a bad idea.

"Well, I ... This may sound ridiculous ... It was a mistake. A simple mistake. That's all ..." *Why did I call Dan? Emma was practically over it by the time she got to school.*

"Mag, you're not making sense. Is something wrong?"

"No, it's silly." Maggie began discounting.

"Sweetie, I need you to tell me why you called. I'm not trying to be short, but I do need to head to a meeting."

Maggie's laugh was nervous. "I did the most ridiculous thing and forgot to move the laundry from the washer to the dryer. So, this morning Emma had no uniform shirts."

Maggie heard Dan sigh, but she continued. Dan listened.

"So, I gave her one of Danny's uniform sweaters to wear. It was a little big, but we got the sleeves rolled up and tucked in a bit. She'll be fine. She only cried a little. It'll be okay." Maggie was working hard to convince herself because Dan really didn't need any explanation.

She could hear his smile. "Sounds like you solved the problem. Do we need to pick up another shirt for her, so she has enough for those off-laundry days?"

Maggie almost cried. He didn't get mad. He didn't fuss. He listened. And he suggested another shirt to save Maggie some laundry time. "You are too good to me. I felt like such a failure this morning. Why did I forget the laundry?"

"Maybe you need another list." He chuckled. "Or maybe your armful of responsibilities tipped a little. Nothing hurt. Emma will be fine. And years from now around the Thanksgiving table she will talk about how her mother made her wear her brother's clothes."

Maggie smiled. "You're right. If I didn't screw up every now and then what would our kids talk to their therapists about when they're middle-aged?" She returned the tease.

Dan added an additional bit of reinforcement. "One other thing—did you tell the kids you loved them when they got out of the car?"

"What? Of course I did!"

"Then what else did they need from you this morning? You're a great mom who's juggling about a million things right now. Give yourself some slack. I've got to run. Can we talk later?"

With the crisis averted, Maggie's spirits lifted, and she turned her attention to her work for the play. She was going to meet Nora for lunch but first was meeting Jim at the warehouse. The old but climate-controlled metal building was about a mile from the theater. It was a sight on the outside—dirty and displaying the faded name of the previous owners on one side. There were two garage doors side-by-side. Jim was getting out of his SUV when she pulled in.

Maggie looked at the building. "You know, next summer we could get a group of Boy Scouts or a high school ball team to paint the outside as a service project."

Jim smiled. "Sounds great. Does that mean you'll be here to supervise?"

Maggie knew exactly what he was insinuating. She smiled but didn't answer.

Jim shrugged. "Just a thought." He unlocked the two locks and yanked on the handle. The door squeaked as it opened.

"I wanted you to see the materials and old backdrops we have. They may not mean much to you, but if you're familiar with them, you can help Nora sort through what can be repurposed. She and the lady she works with—what's her name?"

"Phoebe."

"That's right. I can never remember her name. Phoebe. Anyway, they've been great to do some designing, but I need to be sure they understand our limited resources. Once their plans are final, I can get a crew of construction guys to help build."

They spent the morning going through old props and set pieces. Maggie took copious notes. She had never done anything with set design other than a basic class in her major area of study. They finished up at eleven thirty, in time for Maggie to meet Nora.

"Call me if you're talking and have questions." Jim was locking both locks.

"Okay. I may want to bring her by some time to look over what you have."

Jim spoke quickly. "Have Nora call me. I'll meet her over here."

"Thanks."

"If you can, get her going on the set materials list. I'll finish reviewing the internship outline you drafted and get it back over to the university. Dr. Cosby would like it for his budget."

Just before Jim got into his car, he waved at Maggie to roll her window down. "I'm a goofy guy on some stuff, but do you know if Sara is okay? I get the feeling the dad isn't around. And I'm not sure how well she gets along with her mother."

"She seems okay. I'm trying not to intrude. She told me her mother was being supportive. The dad isn't in the picture at all. In fact, I think he's giving up his rights."

Jim grimaced. "Sometimes that can make it easy, and sometimes not so much. Listen, if you hear of anything she needs, or if I can do anything for her, please let me know. It seems a little weird for me to ask."

"No problem. See you Thursday."

"One other little thing. Tell Nora 'Hi' for me." Jim grinned and turned to get in his car before the full shade of pink crept across his face.

Nora was already seated. The locally owned restaurant had a rustic look but a modern feel. The tablecloths were linen, as were the napkins, but the atmosphere was comfortable. Nora stood to hug Maggie.

"Sorry to keep you waiting." Maggie pulled off her scarf and coat, sliding into the seat across from Nora. "Things have been such a whirlwind with the play and everything, you and I haven't had a chance to catch up."

A thin, young waitress with short hair appeared. Nora ordered a sparkling water and Maggie a sweet tea. The lady kindly gave them the specials and asked if they needed a minute. Nora and Maggie nodded, and she disappeared to retrieve their drinks.

Nora nodded. "True. How are you doing? I bet you're all ready for Christmas with house decorated and gifts wrapped."

Maggie draped the napkin in her lap. "Not exactly. I'm not used to balancing my own work, the kids, and a major holiday. But it will all come together. Tell me about your work. How's it going?"

"It's going really well. Better than I thought it would." Nora nodded thank you as the waitress set their drinks on the table. "I grieved so long, there were times I didn't think I would ever get back into a job or any kind of life."

"I admire you for starting over. Rebuilding your life."

"The grace of God really carried me through what I hope was the darkest moment I'll experience. Getting back to work, and thanks to you, getting involved with the play, has helped so much. Definitely feeling more myself." They took a break from conversation to check out the menu.

Maggie made her decision and set the menu on the edge of the table. "Stanton Designs. Aren't they pretty high end?"

Nora waved her hand and smiled. "I could tell you some things about the homes of our local wealthy. Money does not mean taste." The two shared a chuckle. Nora didn't give names, but told her about one home Mr. Stanton refused to do because the homeowner wouldn't take his advice and only wanted the tackiest mishmash of colors and patterns in upholstery.

"Have you done any homes I would know?"

Nora leaned in a little. "The mayor's is the highest profile I've worked on, but there are others you would recognize who are clients." Nora winked.

"Well, thanks for fitting the set design in. Sounds like you've been busy."

"Yes, but I love it."

"Glad to hear it, because Jim and I met at the warehouse this morning. Now that I better understand our resources, I wanted to talk about your draft of the set design."

The two enjoyed fresh vegetable soup and sandwiches and chattered about the set and the theater's limited resources. Then Nora changed the subject.

"So, uh Maggie, I want to ask." Maggie felt compelled to lean in, as if Nora was going to ask some big secretive question. "Is uh, the Jim guy, is he, uh ..." Nora sighed. "Oh, we're not schoolgirls anymore. Is he married or otherwise engaged? He is too cute." She sat back blushing. The two smiled.

"Oh, my goodness! He did tell me to tell you hi. And, to my knowledge he is not married or otherwise engaged. Unless you can count the theater as his mistress." Maggie smiled.

"Just wondering. He had a good spirit about him. I don't know..." Nora took a sip of her coffee. "He caught my attention."

"I'm no matchmaker, but maybe in the course of working together, you will have a chance to get to know each other a little."

"Yeah, it's weird, since Seth—" Nora's voice cracked.

Giving Nora a minute to regroup, Maggie said, "I bet Seth was an incredibly special man. I'm sorry not to have met him."

Nora smiled, "Oh, he was, and at times I still miss him so much. But it's been five years, and it's time to get on with my life. Never to forget him, of course." She wiped her mouth. "He was my best friend."

Maggie was experiencing a different side of Nora St. Claire. Yes, she was a quintessential prom queen, but she was also very real and more down to earth than when they were in college. "It's hard to let go of someone so dear." Maggie reached across the table and squeezed her hand.

Nora took a deep breath and, in a teasing tone, said, "So, if that cute guy Jim isn't otherwise taken, maybe I do need to get to know him a little."

"Maybe I can help prod things along." Maggie smirked and left the thought to hang in Nora's mind.

# CHAPTER THIRTY-FOUR

Gifts were purchased, cookies baked, and while the nightmares hadn't completely stopped, Maggie kept praying and moving forward, checking things off her list. Ten days before Christmas, Maggie had finished her day at the theater. She walked out to the reception area to get her coat. "Sara, I'm headed out." Sara was intently looking at her computer screen.

"Okay, Mag." Sara's normal happy tone was missing.

"Is something wrong? You don't sound like yourself."

Sara paused and shook her head. "I'm fine. Just tired. Mom says it's normal."

"Some tiredness is normal, but if it's excessive, you may be working too much. When do you see the doctor again?"

"Next week."

Maggie leaned against the tall desk, laying her bag on the top. "Be sure to let him know how you're feeling. He may want to check your iron."

"Now you sound like my mother."

"Sorry." Maggie laughed and picked up her bag. Lightening the connection, she said, "Just looking out for you, kiddo."

"Thanks. I'll be sure and ask him." Sara exaggerated her obedience.

Maggie was curious. "What are you and your mother doing for Christmas?"

"Our Christmases are pretty quiet. It's the two of us. We make it fun, though. Each of us picks a couple of our favorite appetizer snacks and makes them. Then we stuff ourselves and watch old Christmas movies."

The scene tickled Maggie. "Sounds delightful. You're welcome to join us for Christmas dinner. Bring your appetizers."

"Really? We wouldn't be intruding?"

"Heavens no, the more the merrier. The kids get up early Christmas morning, and we do gifts and Santa stuff. Then they play, Dan takes a nap, and I fix a turkey and ham dinner. There is always a ton of food."

"That sounds wonderful. I'm sure all three of us could help dig in." Sara rubbed her blossoming belly.

"Talk to your mom, and let me know. We'd love to have you. Are you about ready to go? We can close up together."

Sara surveyed her desktop. Made a couple of clicks to shut down her computer. "Yep, let's go."

The December air was cool but not freezing. The two hustled to their cars, parked side by side. Maggie dropped her bag in the back of the van.

"Hey, Sara. I didn't mean to overstep telling you what to ask the doctor. I'm sorry."

"It's okay. I was just bugging you. I appreciate all your encouragement. Raising this child on my own isn't going to be easy. I'll take as many in my corner as I can get."

Maggie crossed her arms around herself. "Any word from the father?"

Sara looked down at her feet. "Nothing ..." She raised her sad gaze toward Maggie. "We didn't date long. His family is a little uppity. They wanted him to date some girl from their country club. You know the story."

"Is that what he wants?"

"I don't know. I didn't think so, but then this happened, and he got real distant very quickly. He's pre-law. His dad wants him to follow in his footsteps." A catch in her voice. "I'm not a part of that plan."

Maggie reached out to give her arm a little squeeze. "It'll work out. You're a wonderful young lady. Not being a part of that child's life is his loss. And God will bring other good mentors and examples."

"You think?" Sara dropped her purse in the passenger seat.

"I know." Maggie turned to head to her van.

Driving home, Maggie felt a strong urge to pray for Sara. "Lord, she is so young and in college, trying to do well in this world. This baby was an accident on her part, but I believe you will do something great with the situation. Sara doesn't know you personally, but you know her and her baby. Would you carry them and protect them? Bring into her life a wonderful guy who will love them both. Be with her mother. May their relationship be strong and encouraging. Amen."

Maggie thought about Sara all the way home. Her thoughts led her to what Sara might need for the baby. Had anyone thrown a shower for her?

Their evening went as usual. Dinner. Homework. The kids took their baths, had bedtime reading, and went to sleep. Maggie settled into bed next to Dan. The eleven o'clock news was on, and Dan was reading his latest spy novel. Maggie always had a book going too, but lately, she had been bringing the script and notes from the play to bed. It was never far from her. Flipping through the script pages, Maggie stopped on the scene they had struggled with during rehearsal. The flipping pages drew Dan's attention.

"Haven't you memorized that yet? You read through it every night, seems like."

"I want to be ready for rehearsal tomorrow. With the Christmas break coming, we're trying to get this scene nailed."

Dan rolled over and reached around Maggie's waist. "You want to have it nailed, huh? How cool are you? Saying stuff like 'nail the scene' and 'hanging out' with all those young actor wannabes." He began to tickle her. Maggie squealed in laughter and swatted him away.

"Dan, quit it. You know I'm ticklish."

Dan backed off and then drew her close. "I love you. And I love your passion for what you're doing."

This was her opportunity. "Speaking of what I'm doing ..."

"Oh no, have they offered you another job? An expense account? Use of the vacation villa?"

Maggie heard the teasing and decided to bring up Sara's situation. "No, silly. The theater can barely keep their lights on, much less pay me or give me an expense account." She took a deep breath. Dan was not going to want her to take something else on. She knew it. And two weeks before Christmas. "So, I was talking with Sara today. You remember who she is, the young girl who's pregnant?"

Dan sat up and nodded. "Is she married?"

"No, she lives with her mom. The baby's dad doesn't want anything to do with her or the baby. She seems okay with it for now." Maggie shifted around to face Dan and took his hand. Dan's expression dropped. He knew something was coming.

"Maggie, what are you about to ask me? I know you. You've got that look like you need to go fix something or someone."

Maggie shook her head. "I don't want to fix anyone or anything. I'd like to throw a small shower for Sara." Before he could protest, Maggie continued. "She doesn't have everything she needs, her mother can't provide them, and it would be fun. Don't you think?"

Dan's smile lines returned, but he was shaking his head. "Maggie, it's two weeks before Christmas. You have the kids, the play, and our own Christmas to get ready for." His hands were waving above his chest, counting off the to-dos. "And now you want to plan a shower for a poor, starving, pregnant college girl. Call me crazy, but I only have twenty-four hours in my day. Have you found more?" His teasing crescendo had a tone of frustration. Maggie sat up, ready to have the discussion she figured they would have.

"No, I haven't found any extra time in a day," she sassed. "Yes, it is Christmas, and if at no other time during the year should we go out on a limb for someone in need, it's this one, wouldn't you agree?"

"Yes, but ..."

She cut him off. "I've thought about this, and looking at the calendar, you're right, there are only a couple of options. I could do it the Sunday before Christmas or talk to Jim about making it part of the cast and crew Christmas party. Then it occurred to me ... I've invited Sara and her mother over for Christmas dinner and—"

"Slow down there—you invited them over for Christmas dinner? Were you going to tell me about this?"

Maggie looked at Dan. *Busted.* She hadn't talked to him before inviting people he didn't know to their Christmas dinner. She should have started with that and gotten his agreement. She sheepishly grimaced.

Dan closed his eyes and shook his head. "Please slow down and tell me exactly what you want and what you're thinking for Christmas dinner."

Maggie took a deep breath. "Okay, I invited her and her mother for Christmas dinner. They don't have any extended family and all they do is make their favorite appetizers and watch old movies." She shrugged. "I just thought dinner and a family to hang out with would be good."

'Hang out' with—she had been around young people too long. She reached over and took Dan's hand. "It's Christmas, Dan. Please?"

Dan smiled. "I can't resist you and your giving heart." He took her hand in his and kissed her fingertips. "Let's do this. They're welcome to come to dinner. *Dinner*, Maggie. I still want us to have our morning with the kids and our time to play with their toys and ..." He made air quotes with his fingers. "'Hang out.' They can come over at about six thirty for dinner." Maggie tilted her head, and grimaced. Dan shook his head. "What? What's wrong, isn't that what you want?"

"Well, yes, but I was also thinking we could do her shower when they're here for dinner."

"A shower with just us ...?" He figured it out. Maggie wanted to invite others on Christmas night. "Oh no, Maggie, you are not going to invite others to come on Christmas night. You will be running around all day getting ready, and it won't be our family day. No. I won't agree to that. Besides, what are you going to tell the kids about her not having a husband? You ready for the big conversation?" Dan smiled.

Maggie relaxed a little. She knew he was right. Her eyes drifted to the drooping plant at the window.

Dan sighed. "What about this—you're going to be on break for about two weeks, right?"

Maggie nodded.

"Why not plan a shower either here or at the theater after Christmas? It's a slow time at the bank. I can take the kids out for bowling or something."

It hadn't been the scenario she was considering. "I guess it could work." She smiled. "About *that* conversation. Remember our deal—you get Danny, I get Emma."

"Was that our deal? Are you sure? You're so much better at that stuff than I am."

Maggie nudged him. "Dan Nelson, you know we agreed. Oh, by the way, you should be thinking about getting together with your son soon. He's ten and needs to know what's coming."

"I know. I'll put it on the family calendar." They both burst out laughing. "Really, though, you didn't have the office party on the calendar. I added it to next weekend."

"Next weekend? Dan, I've got ..."

Dan put his finger to her lips. "Stop. I need you at this party. It's everyone, including the execs and their spouses. You don't need to shop for it, you don't have time. Just wear one of your beautiful dresses."

"Of course, I'm sorry. It's always a fun party. I'll call Jen to see if the kids can stay over there that night."

"Ooh, a kid-free night? Maybe we *will* skip the party." Dan's eyebrows danced up and down. He kissed his bride. "I love you."

"I love you, too. Maybe I'll shop for something else special for that evening." Maggie tried to make her eyebrows go up and down like he did, but ended up twisting her face in a funny way. Their laughter turned to giggles.

As Dan reached to turn the lamp off, the silence between them hung in the darkness, each quiet with their thoughts. They said their good nights and settled in each other's arms for sleep. Moments later the silence was broken. "Dan?"

"Yes."

"What would we do if Danny or Emma came home in Sara's situation?"

Dan drew her close. "We would love them and help them any way we could."

# CHAPTER THIRTY-FIVE

Christmas day didn't feel rushed at all. The kids were up at seven thirty and the storm of gift wrap and bows had blown through the living room by nine thirty. Emma squealed and Danny whooped at the gifts they received. Maggie opened her gift from Dan, and her eyes sparkled like the sapphire-and-diamond earrings. Dan drew her near when he opened his gift, a tie clip engraved with a silhouette of each child.

Maggie's warm smile drew Dan's attention.

He reached for her hand. "Penny for your thoughts."

"This feels like the perfect moment. The four of us here with laughter, and you close to me. I love you."

Emma and Danny swam through the paper from one toy to the next. "Danny, look at what this does. Oh, what do you have there?"

Dan joined Maggie in the satisfaction of a blessed family. "You're right. All the junk at work or out in the world doesn't mean squat right now. I think we did good in our shopping."

"Yep, the new racetrack was a winner."

Danny had already pulled the track pieces out. He began to set up the grand prix in the living room.

"Emma, where's Barbie going in her camper?" Maggie got up and began to pick up the paper.

Emma replied, "I don't know, Mom, but it will be fun!"

"I'll get a bag. Let's put the boxes in the garage until we're sure no parts have gotten dropped." As Dan exited to the kitchen, Maggie slid back down into the overstuffed couch. Watching her kids play brought a peaceful grin. Knowing she needed to start the turkey for dinner, she instead relaxed and soaked in the moment. How wonderful the thought of her children, young, innocent, and satisfied with the toys they'd received. Dan returned but stopped in the doorway. Maggie met Dan's gaze. "Oh, Dan. How did we get so lucky?"

Joining her on the couch, encircling her with his arms, he said, "I don't know. We're two imperfect people who have two great kids. I pray every day that I don't do anything so terrible it would mess up their lives."

Maggie's eyebrows furrowed. "What could you possibly do so badly to mess up our children's lives? You're a wonderful father and husband."

Danny and Emma went back and forth with their toys. Danny engineered the pieces of the racetrack to start at the top of the table, free-fall to the carpeted floor, then zip across and up a stack of catalogs from the coffee table to whiz into the entry. At one point Barbie was strapped to a race car and sent careening down the track.

Dan settled on the couch with the paper, which was his prelude to napping. Maggie went into the kitchen to bake the cranberry delight and start the turkey. Within minutes, the house smelled of sweet cranberries, apples, oats, and plenty of sugar.

Maggie bustled about, preparing the meal and thinking about her mother's arrival with her boyfriend, Stan. Her dad had always made Christmas fun, spending the afternoon on the floor playing games and assembling toys. She missed him. Her mother cooked on Christmas, no time for playing. Now her mother didn't want to cook, and she was bringing another man to her home. Maggie hadn't considered all this when she invited Sara and her mother over. The day would be interesting.

The turkey was browning, and the ham was ready. The house was warm with the smell of comfort foods wafting through, tickling everyone's noses. Maggie plopped at the end of the couch, waking Dan. She leaned her head back and closed her eyes.

Sleepily, Dan rolled over and reached for her hand. "Hey, everything smells great. You've outdone yourself again." Without moving, she locked fingers with her husband. "Thank you. I need to go get cleaned up. Everyone will be here shortly."

She raised her head and surveyed the living room. "Danny, you and Emma need to pick up your track and go get dressed." With a pout, Emma began to pack her new doll clothes in the bright pink doll suitcase. Danny sent one more car down the track before gathering up his collection of vehicles, new and old.

"Dan, will you be sure the kids wear the outfits I've laid out?" Maggie climbed the steps, thinking about the unique mix of guests to arrive. In addition to having Dan's dad, her mother and some man, and Sara and her mother, Maggie had decided at the last minute to reach out to Nora. After their conversation about Jim, Maggie assumed the holidays might be a little lonely for Nora. Her independence since Seth's death was admirable. Maggie wondered whether, if she lost Dan, she could be alone with the same life balance as Nora.

Maggie checked her look in the full-length mirror behind the door. Dan was shaving in the kids' bathroom while they danced and pulled their Christmas sweaters on. Emma needed her hair braided. Dan sent her to Maggie with a brush and hair band. "Mom, Dad doesn't do braids well at all." Emma thrust the brush toward her mother.

"He doesn't do braids?" Maggie sat on the side of the bed and began to brush through her daughter's long brown hair. "Did you enjoy playing this morning?" The two chatted about Emma's toys and which were her favorites. Maggie smiled as she listened to her daughter chatter about how all her Christmas wishes that had come true. Finishing the braid that landed halfway down Emma's back, she turned her daughter around. Maggie gave her a quick hug and a small pinch at her nose. "You look maaaaarvelous."

Emma covered her mouth and giggled at her mother's teasing tone. Danny came running in and tugged on Emma's braid. The two were off to play.

As Maggie made her own last check, the doorbell rang. *Here we go.* She headed for the door and the invasion.

The eight adults all leaned back in their chairs after feasting. Joanna's friend Stan rubbed his extended belly. "My word, Maggie, you can cook! Thank you so much." Others around the table concurred. The meal included all the traditional Christmas trimmings. Conversation had flowed well except for a couple of times when Maggie jumped in to steer her mother away from talk of Sara's unmarried situation. Her mother could be very self-righteous at times. While she would deny it, Joanna could make someone feel about an inch tall.

"My Maggie learned everything she knows about cooking from her dear ole mom." Joanna shot a dart of the sideways compliment across the table as she dabbed the corners of her mouth.

"How about dessert?" Dan took advantage of the transition. "Mag, Stan is right on. You outdid yourself.

Mind if we take our dessert out for the second half of the game?"

"Not at all. I've set it up on the breakfast table. There are two pumpkin pies, a chocolate meringue, and brownies. Coffee is in there as well. Help yourselves. Please, make sure I'm not left with anything." Maggie stood with a small stretch of her own full stomach. "Ladies, I'll clear the table and we can have ours in here."

Dan, his dad, and Stan made a quick stop at the dessert table. They filled their plates and headed for the den.

Gathering back around the table, Maggie noticed her mother was hesitant to join the ladies. "Mom, if you want to go in with Stan, Dan, and Daniel, you're welcome to."

"No, I just want to be sure he is comfortable. He doesn't know Dan or his dad."

"He'll be fine. He and Daniel are about the same age, and Dan doesn't bite. Besides, with men around a football game, there are no barriers to conversation." The humor was lost on her mother.

Nora jumped in to chat about her big project at work. A true professional, she left out the names of the homeowners.

Joanna perked up. "I'm surprised you have so much energy for the set design after all day at work." She looked up as Maggie walked back into the dining room. "Have you dragged all your friends into this ridiculous play thing you've got going on?" Her mother's words stung.

Maggie closed her eyes briefly, opened them, smiled, and said, "Yes, I *dragged* anyone I could find into helping with the play." Her volume began to raise with strain. "Nora has no brain of her own—she just did what I asked. Are you kidding me, Mom?"

Dan appeared in the doorway. "Pie, anyone? I'm getting another slice. Glad to get you ladies some more." His eyes captured Maggie's attention, hoping to give her a timeout to collect herself.

Joanna sat quietly and spoke evenly. "No, thank you, Dan. We need to get going. I don't want to be driving too late. Stan? Are you ready?" From the den, oblivious to what was going on, Stan threw back, "What? I just finished my pie, and the game is getting good."

Joanna snatched her coat from the closet. "We need to go before it's too late. You can watch from my house. I've got the pie I picked up from the bakery."

A dig. The pie from the bakery was better than Maggie could bake.

"Mom, please don't go. I'm sorry I snapped at you. It's a sensitive subject."

As Stan assisted her with her camel-colored wool coat, Joanna said, "Maybe it's sensitive because you are sacrificing everyone else for what you want."

Gloves were off.

Again, Dan stepped in. "Not true, Joanna. I'm proud of my Mag and all she is doing. Please stay. The game just has a few more minutes."

Joanna handed him her coat, and she followed Maggie back to the dining room.

The spirit of Christmas was a little squelched. Nora spoke up first, waving them back toward the dining room. "I'm willing to help make sure Maggie isn't stuck finishing all these goodies. Ladies, another piece of pie!" With her fork in hand, she marched back to the dining room.

The evening was filled with Dan and the guys flipping between football games, the kids playing, and the five women chattering away. Joanna slowly joined the conversation. Sara's mother shared her journey from disappointment to excitement about Sara's baby. "It's not going to be easy, but she's going to be fine."

Maggie sat down with a brownie. "No doubt. Hey, let's talk about your shower. What kind of food do you want?"

Nora jumped in, ignoring her own childless journey. "Can I make the cake?"

Sara's mom smiled. "You decorate homes AND cakes?" They all laughed.

"Homes better than cakes, but I do okay with an icing canvas."

Maggie snagged her notepad from the counter. "I hope you don't mind, I invited a few friends of mine from church. They'll love you. And they're fun."

Joanna smiled with a nod. "You girls really are something. On the heels of Christmas, planning another party."

There was a look between Sara and her mother. Sara shifted in her chair. "I'm not sure church ladies would want to come, would they?"

"These ladies would. They run a ministry for single moms. They're all about loving on women who find themselves with kids and no mate for whatever reason."

Another look exchanged. Sara's mom spoke up almost apologetically. "That would be great. Please understand the ladies from my church weren't quite as willing to accept our situation."

"Around here, we have plenty of grace. I promise, these ladies are the best. They've walked alongside many single moms. They'll love you."

Sara smiled and nodded. "Of course. Thank you. I know it's going to be fun."

Maggie warmed everyone's coffee from the carafe—except for Sara, who had her favorite, hot chocolate with marshmallows. With a silly grin, Maggie turned her attention to Nora. "Now that we have Sara all squared away, let's talk about some sparks I thought I spotted when you and Jim were fine-tuning those stage designs."

The women all chuckled, and Nora blushed.

# CHAPTER THIRTY-SIX

Three days after Christmas, Maggie had the house ready for the shower. With Christmas decorations still in place, she didn't do much shower decorating. The extra ham had been sliced and made into little party sandwiches, and she baked sugar cookies, icing them in pink and blue.

Maggie had been talking to Emma all morning about being a good hostess. Emma didn't want to go out with the boys. She wanted to stay and be a part of the baby shower. It was a sweet morning of mother and daughter preparing. Maggie showed her the list and how she timed her food so that she could have time to go get dressed as well. When they went upstairs to get ready, Emma came in with the outfit they had chosen as Maggie was putting her lipstick on. Maggie saw Emma's intentional watching of technique to the point of rolling her lips as her mother set her lipstick. Reaching into her makeup basket, Maggie pulled out a light pink gloss.

"Today you are attending a big girl party. Would you like to try a little lip gloss?"

Emma's eyes lit up and, almost jumping but catching herself so as to behave maturely enough for lip gloss, she replied, "Yes! How fun! I can wear makeup."

Maggie showed her how to apply it—a special moment in the lives of both mother and daughter. She reminded

Emma that today was a special day. She would need to be older before she could wear makeup every day.

"I know, Mom. This is great. Thanks."

The guest of honor arrived right on time, but with someone extra. Jim followed Sara and her mother into Maggie's house. Hustling in out of the cold, the three of them shook the packed snow from their shoes. The two women shimmied out of their coats.

Continuing to dry her hands on her apron, Maggie welcomed the first guests. "This is a surprise. Jim, welcome to our home."

"Not to worry, Mag, I'm not crashing your baby shower." Jim blew into his red, dry hands to warm them.

"I told him he could stay but to be ready. The games could get a little competitive." Sara handed her coat to her mom. "Jim rescued Mom and me. We went by the theater because I forgot my baby notebook, and when we went to leave, my car wouldn't start. He's going back over to meet the auto club guy."

"Aren't you the knight in shining armor," Maggie teased.

Nora stepped in the door to hear Maggie, not noticing Jim.

"Who's the knight and shining ar ...?" She spotted Jim. She gave him a shy smile, her eyes twinkling. "That would be you."

"I don't know about knighthood yet. The car is still dead. Let's see how we do with the tow truck." He looked directly at Nora with a smile. "You look lovely this afternoon, Ms. Nora." Nora's face turned a few shades of Christmas red as Jim turned to Sara. "Don't worry about a ride. I'll be back in a few hours to pick you up, hopefully with answers about your car."

"Thank you, Jim. You're at least a lifesaver, if not a knight."

As Jim closed the door behind him, all eyes were on Nora. Maggie and Sara, both with wide grins, imitated Jim's compliment in unison. "You look lovely ..."

Nora turned to take her gift in the living room. "That will be enough of that."

"I'm sorry, you can't dismiss the little whatever that was with Jim ..." Maggie gestured with a twirl of her hand. "Is there something we need to know?"

Waving her off, Nora came back into the kitchen. "It's nothing, really ... innocent flirting, maybe ..."

Sara's face lit up. "This is great! Jim hasn't dated anyone in at least the two years that I've been around."

Nora cleared her throat. "He hasn't? Hum, I mean ... well, really? He hasn't."

Maggie raised her hands in protest and shook her head with a smile. "Forget it, girl, you can't act like it's nothing now. You're busted. But we won't bother you about it today. Today is all about this lady and her baby." She gave Sara a side hug. "Where's Jen? She should be here." As if on cue, the doorbell rang. "That must be her. Make yourselves comfortable. Emma, would you offer them a beverage?"

Maggie reached for the door ready to see why Jen was late. But it wasn't Jen. It was a young man. He wore a three-quarter zip sweater and slacks under a down coat. Wisps of blond hair escaped a knit hat. He almost looked surprised that the door was answered.

"May I help you?" Maggie asked. While it was unusual for strangers to ring the bell, she didn't feel threatened by the young man.

"Well, ma'am, I, uh." Hearing the voice from the living room, Sara came flying to the door. "Jake? What are you doing here?" She stood there in all her pregnant glory. Maggie opened the door for Jake to step inside. "Sara, do you want me to give you a minute? Or would you like me to stay?"

"I'm so sorry for the interruption, Maggie. I'm fine. Just give us a minute, and if you can keep Mom in there, I'd appreciate it."

Maggie headed for the living room as Mrs. Biddle headed for the door. "Let's give those two a few minutes."

Mrs. Biddle resisted for a minute. "Maggie, the boy keeps breaking her heart. I don't want her to go through it again."

"I understand. Let's give them some space, and if we hear voices rise, we'll go in." Stepping back into the living room, they awkwardly began to enjoy the snacks Maggie and Emma had made. Emma had flawlessly served each of the ladies punch. "Thank you for serving the drinks, Emma."

"You're welcome." The muffled voices from the side door continued. Nora looked at Emma's dress. "That is a beautiful party dress, Emma."

Emma stood and twirled and began to share about her shopping day with her mom. Maggie sat and listened to her daughter's take on the day. Emma talked about trying on multiple dresses and skirts. As she told the story, the women nodded.

The door closed and Sara came into the living room. Maggie got up and offered her a chair and some punch. "Everything okay, honey?" Mrs. Biddle looked on her daughter with compassion. "What did he want?"

Sara sat there slowly shaking her head. "I don't know. He's so confused."

"He's giving up his rights, isn't he?"

"Mom, that is so far from the issue right now," Sara snapped.

"Well then, why did he come here?"

Maggie stood. "Nora, how about we give these two a minute." As they walked through to the kitchen, Jen burst through the door behind a huge bunch of balloons. In an unbalanced, clown-like moment, juggling her appetizer and gift, she said, "Sorry I'm late ..." Everyone stopped and looked at her. "What, what'd I do?"

Maggie waved her into the kitchen. "The father of the baby just showed up. Jake. He and Sara talked for a few minutes, and then he left."

Jen snapped her fingers. "I knew I shouldn't have been late, but when I pulled up, I only saw one car."

Nora jumped in. "Jim brought Sara and her mother. Sara's car wouldn't start."

A grin danced across Jen's face. "Oh really, Jim was here?" She gestured with her hand, and winked at Nora.

Maggie looked between the two.

"Wait a minute, Jen knows something? How does she get to know something, and I don't?"

They all cackled.

Jen elbowed Maggie. "Well, sister, if you worked out at my gym and maybe let your friend give you some personal training tips, you, too, would know things."

Sara and her mother joined them in the kitchen. Sara looked a little tired but was ready for some fun. "Let's get this party going."

The room exploded with girl talk and baby chatter. The doorbell rang with other guests arriving. The next two hours were filled with laughter and Sara getting to know the ladies from Maggie's church. In addition to the diapers, little outfits, and blankets, Sara was given love and encouragement.

As Maggie was washing up the last of the dishes that wouldn't fit in the dishwasher, she heard Dan's car pull into the garage. Emma had plopped herself in front of the television, exhausted from all the "big girl fun." Danny flew in the door with Dan shortly behind.

"Did you guys have fun?" Maggie hugged Danny, who was clearly bursting to tell her about their adventure.

"Did we have fun! We ate pizza for lunch, stuffed crust. Then we went to the go-cart place. I'm finally tall enough to drive my own car!" Danny roared through the kitchen into the den, making tire-squealing noises. Dan shook his head.

"The next Andretti," he said as he kissed Maggie and picked up the last sugar cookie. "How was your party?"

Maggie had been thinking through the early events of the day—Jim and Nora sparks, Jake showing up. Thankfully, things had settled into a fun afternoon, and she decided Dan probably didn't want to hear the drama part. "It was fun. And Sara now has a good start on supplies for the baby. I'm glad I did this."

# CHAPTER THIRTY-SEVEN

The next day, Maggie pulled into the parking lot of the little theater. The white-clad exterior stood stark against the bare trees and the fresh dusting of snow. Nora and Sara pulled in next to her. The three got out of their cars with their coffee mugs steaming and their work totes full of files, notes, and fabric samples.

Sara caught up to Maggie. "Thank you again for throwing the shower. It was great. And I can't believe all the gifts!"

Maggie smiled and opened the door for Nora and Sara. "Our pleasure. Nice hair, by the way. Brown? That seems a little calm for you."

Sara nodded and smiled. "Yeah. A little."

The three hung their coats. Nora headed to the stage to get started, and Maggie followed Sara over to her desk. "If I'm prying, then tell me to stay out of it. But what did Jake want? And how did he know where I live?

Sara's eyebrows furrowed with a wrinkle of her nose. "A strange guy shows up at your house, you deserve to know. He's talked his dad into meeting me and my mom. He told his dad that he wants to be an active part of our baby's life. He said his dad is willing to talk about how we can make this work."

Maggie's heart flipped, but she didn't want to show her excitement if Sara wasn't excited. "How do you feel about this?"

Sara tilted her head and thought for a second. "I love the idea of it. I just don't know what it will be like."

"I get that. Kinda scary after you've been eight and half months going through this alone."

"Mom and I are going to their house tonight to talk about everything."

"Is that what the hair color change is for?"

Sara ran her hand through her hair. "Yeah, I guess. Thought having a more normal color might help with his dad's first impression."

"I'm glad you're meeting. We'll be praying for a peaceful outcome. But can I offer a little advice?"

"Sure."

Maggie looked into Sara's eyes. "You are a beautiful young woman, no matter what color your hair is. Please be your wonderful self. They'll love you."

"Thank you, Maggie. You have been such a great friend."

Maggie dropped her bag on the conference room table as her phone chirped. It was Dan. "Hi, honey. What's up?"

"Good morning to you, Mrs. Nelson." Dan's voice was light and reminded her of when he'd call her before he left school to come home for the weekend to see her. "How's your morning going?"

"I just got to the theater. So far, so good. How's your morning?"

"Going well. Still quiet around here with so many of our team on vacation this week. Listen, what's your schedule like this week?"

Maggie flipped open her calendar. "Well, let's see ... it's quiet around here, too. We're not doing rehearsals until after New Year's."

"I know it's late notice and all ... but, I was hoping to take you out on the thirty-first. Think you could find a dress that sparkles or flows or whatever you ladies like about getting dressed up?"

New Year's Eve. They never went out on New Year's. What about a sitter? The words of her father took center stage: *"When Dan wants to do something for you, let him."*

"Sounds like fun—a date for New Year's Eve. I'm guessing you're gonna want a kiss at midnight." Maggie smiled into the phone.

"I can only hope. Would you like to ask Jen and Mark to join us? We could go to one of those hotel parties with the balloon drop and champagne toast." It all sounded fun and exciting.

"That sounds great. Let me work on a sitter today, and we can finalize our plans tonight." Maggie hung up, already excited to do something different for New Year's Eve.

"What was that all about?" Sara was dropping her lunch in the refrigerator.

Youthful excitement overcame Maggie. Before she thought, she told Sara about Dan's invitation. As soon as the words came out of her mouth, Maggie's stomach knotted. "Oh, Sara, I'm sorry."

"What are you sorry for?" Sara's belly protruded past her long-knit cardigan sweater.

Maggie dropped her head "I'm sorry. Here I am talking about going out to have fun and you're the one who should be going."

"Please, Maggie. Don't worry about it. I'm good. Me, Mom, the baby, and my swollen feet are looking forward to pizza and movie night. Oh, and the ladies from your church were so kind. They invited me to their single mothers' Bible study in January. I've never known church people to be so understanding."

Maggie's heart melted. "I'm so sorry to hear that. We are all imperfect people in need of a perfect Savior. We try every day to show his compassion. Sometimes we do better than others. I'm glad they invited you and you're going."

The holidays provided a good respite for each of the women to have time for their families. The first morning back to school, they met in the parking lot, holding the café in Nora's van. Jen and Brian were running late, so after she walked him into school, she grabbed her hot tea and hopped in the van with Maggie and Nora.

"Are you okay?" Maggie asked.

"Yes, I'm terrible with being on time these days. It's not that I'm lazy and not getting up, it's that I try and do too much before we leave the house," Jen admitted.

"You've probably done more this morning than us," Nora said.

Jen looked at Nora with a look of surprise. "Wait a minute. You don't have a kid in this school. Why are you here this early?"

"Good to see you too, friend."

Jen started to backpedal. Nora held up her hand. "Save it, blondie. You of all people should know why I'm here."

With a gasp of excitement Jen squealed. "You got the job!"

Maggie joined in the teasing. "See, I don't have to go to your gym to get all the latest news."

Jen swatted at her.

Nora shared the details of her meeting with Mrs. Fitzpatrick and how she wanted to refresh the teacher's lounge. They had met over the holiday, and today Nora was bringing swatches and colors for her to choose from.

"I am so excited for you."

"Thank you."

"Of course, the *real* news we want to hear about is how the rest of your New Year's Eve went. You and Jim seemed to be having fun."

Nora's cheeks glowed. She shared with Jen and Maggie, her tone soft and a little melancholy. "You guys don't know how wonderful and weird this all feels. After losing Seth, I couldn't have imagined ever wanting to date. It was like a part of me died too." Nora shifted in her seat. "There are times I still miss him so bad it hurts. But I know he wouldn't want me to be alone or to bury my life in my work. Jim is quiet and kind." A smile drew across her face. "And he's fun to be with. He plans the best dates." Her tone lightened.

"Wait a minute," Maggie interrupted. "Dates. Plural. How many dates have there been?"

The blushing glow returned, and, with a coy smile, Nora murmured, "A couple."

The three had a good schoolgirl giggle.

"I do feel like my spirit is waking up after a cold, dingy winter," Nora said.

Maggie reached over and touched Nora's arm. "I'm so glad for you. And I'm thankful you've joined the craziness at the theater."

"Between the theater and the gym, you and Jen have me moving. Work is good. I'll start on the mayor's house as soon as the holiday decor comes down."

The three finished their morning hot drinks and conversation and headed on their different ways. As Maggie pulled out of the drive, she smiled as she thought about their conversation.

# CHAPTER THIRTY-EIGHT

Nora and Phoebe arrived at the mayor's house promptly at nine o'clock. They took their color palette and samples and rang the doorbell. Nothing. They rang again, being sure to allow ample time. Nothing. Then a scurrying sound with a muffled, "Coming" from inside.

Finally, the front door opened. Before them stood Mrs. Watson in sweats and a sweatshirt, both paint-stained. She had not a dot of makeup, and even her lips were bare. Her hair was in a ponytail.

This was a sight for Nora and Phoebe—one they would no doubt have to take to their grave if they ever wanted to work for her again. Were they supposed to ignore this freakish happening? Was she sick? Had something happened to the mayor? Or should they take this as a compliment that she was comfortable enough with them to not feel like she had to dress up? She was a woman who couldn't check the mail without at least lipstick on. Should they not react at all?

Mrs. Watson smiled. "Can I help you?"

She spoke as if she didn't know them and hadn't expected anyone. Then she recognized Nora and gasped. "What day is it? Do we have an appointment today? I thought it was tomorrow. Oh, my goodness, you must think I'm a sight."

Nora stuttered, "No, no, you're fine. I had Betsy confirm our appointment with your housekeeper on Friday. If this is an inconvenient time, we can reschedule."

"Friday, that's right. She left me the message, but she's off this morning, and I was cleaning out closets. My favorite chore after the holidays." She smiled and took a deep breath. "Well, come in."

The two stepped through the front door, and Nora said, "Mrs. Watson, you remember Phoebe, our office manager."

"Yes, yes, I do." Looking in the mirror at how messy she looked, she got a little fidgety. "Tell you what, ladies, I'll show you the rooms upstairs we're going to start and let you measure or whatever, and I'll go make myself more presentable."

"You don't have to do that for us. We both have homes with closets that need cleaning," Phoebe said.

Mrs. Watson stood up straighter. "Well, I'm not comfortable, so I'm going to clean up and then we will meet." She turned deliberately, and the two fell in line to follow her.

Nora shot Phoebe a look and a shrug. Mrs. Watson led them upstairs and showed them the two bedrooms with a Jack and Jill bathroom between. The larger of the two bedrooms had an extra nook. Then she left the ladies with a promise to return shortly.

"Okay, so that was weird," Phoebe said.

"Yes, it was, but I promise Betsy called Friday. I know we were scheduled for nine o'clock,"

"Don't worry about it. I'm sure the appointment was confirmed. And I think had Mrs. Watson not known, she would have gotten mad and sent us away. No big deal. You know, though, we have seen that which no one outside this house has seen," Phoebe grinned.

Nora looked at her. "What?"

"Mrs. Watson totally scrapped out with no makeup!" Phoebe said with a chuckle.

Both had a guilty laugh and went to work measuring the space, taking photos, and making sketches. Twenty minutes later, the mayor's wife joined them, dressed in a coordinated outfit and with her lipstick on.

"Okay," she said cheerfully. "I loved your proposal. Now let's talk details."

Nora took the lead. She pulled out their presentation boards and two portable easels. She turned both boards backwards so that she could do her introduction to the concepts before showing the color palettes. Mrs. Watson sat on the foot of the bed and listened intently, asking no questions.

When Nora finished, Mrs. Watson complimented her on understanding her style and what she wanted for the rooms. There were a couple of minor changes before the three went down to the living room to discuss the plans. An hour later, Mrs. Watson had asked all her questions. Nora and Phoebe were ready to move forward. As they were walking out, Nora and Phoebe's boss, Mr. Stanton, dressed in a well-tailored navy suit, was stepping onto the porch.

"Good morning, ladies. Don't mean to interrupt, but I was in the area and thought I'd check on things."

Mrs. Watson greeted him with a smile and handshake, and invited him in.

Mr. Stanton stepped into the two-story foyer. "How did it go?"

Mrs. Watson went on about the ideas and the colors and how Nora was in complete sync with the style of home and what they wanted. "We started upstairs in a couple of the bedrooms because I thought she might need an easier start, but her color scheme and decorating ideas are going to flow well throughout the house. I'm looking forward to having it done by Mother's Day."

"Mother's Day! You don't mess around." He smiled at Nora. He turned to Mrs. Watson. "I'm glad you liked her plans."

Mr. Stanton, Phoebe, and Nora walked to their cars. It was eleven forty-five. Phoebe was about to burst with excitement. "You were outstanding with her. You knew exactly how to read her and handle her. You made her feel like she was being heard. And when she wanted something that wasn't going to look good, you did great at steering her to the better choice. Wow!"

"Was she that good?" Mr. Stanton looked amused at Phoebe's excitement. "Let me buy you two lunch."

Nora felt flushed. She couldn't stop smiling. "Thank you. I enjoy our work, and with a client like the mayor's wife, it adds another twist."

The three headed off to lunch and back to the office to finish the sketches and plans.

Driving home that evening, Nora again felt a huge rush of excitement. A grin danced across her face, and her heart was full of thankfulness for a job she loved. It had been a long time since she felt this light and happy. An impulse to call Jim surprised her. She wanted to call him just to tell him about her day. *Why not?*

Maggie got to the theater in time for rehearsal. She pulled in to see Jen's van already there. She smiled. Jen had really taken to helping with costumes. She had decided to make a second pair of ruby slippers for rehearsals or in case something happened.

Maggie poked her head around the corner of the costume room. “Hey, you two, how’s it going? Are you ready for me to bring all my mending from home?”

“You’re too funny.” Cindy continued to fold the costume shirts.

“We’re professionals, you know. We may be recruited by Phantom of the Opera next month.” Jen laughed.

“Thanks for everything.” Maggie said as she went on to rehearsal.

Rehearsals had continued three days a week for the first two weeks of January. With Nora and Phoebe’s help, the set design worked perfectly. The guys building the set were amazed at how well their system for hiding the yellow brick road worked.

Jim reported to the cast and crew that he and the chairman of the board had several interviews on TV and radio later in the month to promote the theater and the play. They were going to count on Sara and Maggie to run some of the rehearsals. This was news to Maggie.

After the meeting was dismissed, Maggie caught up to Jim. “Are you sure you want my help with this?”

Jim smiled at Maggie. “I’ve watched you run lines, work with blocking. This is where you belong. I’m already reading scripts for the summer production.” Maggie wasn’t sure what to say. She nodded and walked away.

Driving home, worry invaded her feelings of satisfaction on the day’s work. *Do I want to make this a more permanent job?* “Lord, your wisdom, please. This has been a challenge for my family. I don’t know if they could handle more.”

In the silence, she was reminded to take one thing at a time. The nightmares had settled. Dan had come around. The wisdom of Mrs. Fitzpatrick had settled her thoughts about her father’s death—for the most part.

# CHAPTER THIRTY-NINE

Opening night arrived. The costumes were pressed and waiting for each actor to come and pick up, the makeup stations were in order, and the stagehands were ready. But no one could find Sara. Jim had tried calling her all day. Finally, two hours before the curtain, Sara's mother called to tell Jim that early that morning Sara had gone into labor. Jim found Maggie and told her.

"That's great!" Maggie said with a smile—and then shifted to frown. "She was helping backstage. I need to make sure someone else can cover things."

Jim's phone lit up. He held up a finger for Maggie to wait while he answered.

"Hello ... oh no ... okay, I hope she feels better." Jim hung up and looked at Maggie. She'd never seen that expression. Jim's eyebrows furrowed. "Well. You are on, hotshot. Janice, our good witch, has the flu. Dare I ask if anything else could go wrong tonight?" Jim rubbed his forehead.

"What? No, I can't." A look of terror crossed her face. She might puke.

"You must. You're the only one who knows all the lines." Jim's tone was as urgent as it was encouraging. "You've run the lines so much you could do all the parts. Come on, Glenda, the good witch, you know you've always wanted to be a witch. Tonight, you're the good one."

Maggie grabbed her clipboard and headed to costume. Jim would back her up on stage managing. On her way, she peeked out front to see her kids sitting with her mother. It was good to see her mother there. But where was Dan? Maggie had been so lost in her plan for the day, she barely remembered saying goodbye to him that morning. She did recall something about him having a five o'clock meeting but that he should be able to make it in time. *What if he doesn't make it?* Anxious butterflies flitted about her stomach like stage fright. Maggie walked into the costume room completely lost in the building swirl of a ridiculous, made-up scene in her head where Dan didn't come at all.

She stopped short at what she saw. Dan stood there with a single white rose. "The usher let me come backstage. 'Break a leg' or something like that. I'm so proud of you." Maggie ran into his arms and gave him a big hug and kiss. "Thank you. I couldn't have done this without you. But Dan, now I have to go on. Our good witch has the flu." Her breath was tense, and tears puddled in her eyes. "I can't ..."

Dan held her close. "Yes, you can, Maggie Nelson. You've got this. You could do this in your sleep."

Her sleep, her dreams, her dad. That was it. She couldn't be on stage, something bad might happen again. Dan? Danny? Emma? No! Her breathing didn't settle but became more anxious.

Dan pulled back and led her to a chair. "Maggie, what's wrong? You can do this."

Maggie was quiet with her head down, and nodded. "Dan, it's Daddy."

"What about him?" Dan nodded. Over the last month or so, he had noticed without saying anything about the shadow under which Maggie often awoke. "Oh, Mag, he was your biggest fan. He would be so proud of you tonight. He'd be on the front row. What did he always say? He'd be there with popcorn to throw?" A smile broke through her tears. "Baby, he's up in heaven and has found a spot to watch you take the stage tonight."

Maggie wiped her eyes. She looked into the eyes of the man who loved her and knew her as well as her father did. "Thank you, Dan. I love you."

He kissed the top of her head, and grasping her hands, he whispered a prayer of fun, confidence, and peace for Maggie. "Okay, you need to get dressed. And I need to go find some popcorn."

She laughed and swatted at him.

Dan slipped back out front to take his place with the kids, Jen, Mark, and Nora, who had a pink sweetheart rose stuck in the side pocket of her purse.

When the curtains opened, Dorothy and the munchkins were looking at the ruby-slippers on the feet of the dead witch. As Dorothy implored the munchkins for help, the fairy-like music sounded and Maggie as Glenda the good witch made her entrance. She delivered her lines flawlessly from the first scene to the last when she reassured Dorothy that she had always known the way home and instructed her to click her heels together.

The curtain closed and reopened to the cast taking their bows. Dan, Danny, Emma, and Maggie's mom all leaped to their feet, starting the standing ovation.

With the last curtain call, Jim stepped out on stage to thank the cast and crew, and make an announcement to the audience. "I've just received a text that we have a new crew member! Glenda Ann was born right after the start of the second act. She is the daughter of our receptionist, Sara Biddle."

There was another round of applause.

Maggie changed and ran to meet everyone in the lobby. Emma and Danny galloped up with big hugs, crying in unison, "Mom, you were great!"

Maggie returned the hugs. "Thank you. So, you enjoyed the play? What was your favorite part?"

Emma hugged her mother again, "You were. Do you get to keep your wand?"

Everyone chuckled.

"No, I have to leave it for the next time."

Danny jumped in with his favorite part: "The flying monkeys." He raised his hands and scrunched his face.

"Thank you for being my fans. I saw you sitting right up front." Both the kids hugged Maggie again, and Dan squeezed her hand.

"You were great, hon."

Joanna adjusted her coat and fidgeted with her scarf. She took a deep breath and looked at Maggie. "Honey, I was so wrong. You did an excellent job tonight. I sat watching you, so proud." She leaned forward and hugged her.

"Thank you, Mom. That ... that means a lot."

Joanna held her hand. "Thinking about all you've done in the last few months, and seeing how excited Dan and the kids are for you ... I shouldn't have doubted you or your ability to take care of your family and go back to the theater."

Wow! Was Maggie hearing this from her mother? Recognition for her accomplishment? *Thank you, Lord.*

Maggie hugged her mom again. "Thanks for coming tonight. Where's Stan?"

Joanna waved her hand and chuckled. "Men! Not sure I'm ready for another one."

They all enjoyed a laugh.

Maggie noticed Nora's rose, and grazed it with her hand. "From anyone I know?" Nora smiled but didn't need to answer. Jim, Jen, and Mark joined the group.

"Thank you, ladies, for everything. This evening was a success because of each of you, bringing your time and talent in a big way." Jim was beaming. "The seats were full. The audience loved the show."

As they were chatting, an elderly gentleman stepped up with Mrs. Fitzpatrick. He walked with a cane. His silver hair reflected the lines on his face that tracked a journey of many years. He walked around to Maggie and took her hand gently in his aged, worn hands. He looked at Dan. "Does this young starlet belong to you?" His voice crackled.

Dan stood about six inches taller than the older man. A proud grin flashed with respect for the elder. "Yes, sir, she is my bride."

Not letting go of her hand, but looking into Dan's eyes, the older man said, "You take care of this one. She's something special." He gazed into Maggie's eyes and said, "Young lady, you were absolutely stunning on that stage tonight. I'm coming again next weekend and sitting on the front row."

Maggie felt the sting of tears as she locked eyes with this old man she didn't know. His eyes were a clear blue. They were so familiar. They were ... just like her father's. Had he lived, her dad would have been about the same age as this man. He sounded like him—his tone, inflection, and his encouragement.

The words caught in Maggie's throat. She didn't know what to say. She stood there with the old man holding her hands and Dan's arm around her waist.

Mrs. Fitzpatrick spoke up. "Maybe I need to introduce your fan to you. This is my brother. He surprised me this afternoon with a visit, so I brought him tonight."

Dan reached out and shook his hand. The others joined in the introduction. Maggie stood silent, watching this captivating man who just happened to show up on opening night. In her heart, Dan's words were confirmed.

Her father had been watching from heaven. And this man reminded her of how he made her feel after a performance.

Dan, Mark, and Jim walked the girls to Maggie's van. They were going to take the kids out for ice cream while the girls went to the hospital. Jim and Nora lingered behind, holding hands. Their romance was out in public now and oozed sweetness.

Maggie, Jen, and Nora headed for the hospital.

Gently stepping into her room, they saw Sara with her eyes sleepy and brown hair messy, but they wanted to say hi. Sara's mother stepped out to let the girls have their conversation. The baby had been taken to the nursery, so she went to check on her.

"Thank you for coming. How did the play go?" she asked. "Maggie, I'm sorry I left you on opening night."

Maggie chuckled. "That's quite all right, you had something more important come up."

Sara looked at the three women and said, "Any advice?"

Jen shrugged. "Not sure where we would begin. So how about we just be available for you as you have questions or need something."

Maggie smiled in agreement. "Being a mother isn't easy, but it is the most rewarding job you will ever have."

"I hope I'm half the mom you are." Sara said to Maggie and squeezed her hand.

Sara ran her hand through her hair. "So, Jake was here for Glenda's birth. When the contractions started something inside me said to call him. I did. And he came."

Maggie waved her hand. "That's great. Does that mean the meeting with his parents went well?"

Sara nodded. "It did. They were nicer than I expected. We talked about the baby, mine and Jake's education, and how we can both finish our undergrad." She looked out the window. "They offered to help both with watching the baby and providing for her needs."

"Oh, Sara, I'm so thankful. Did you and Jake talk about your relationship?" Maggie reminded herself not to pry too much.

"Kind of. We know we care for each other, and we agree that right now we need to focus on school and our baby."

Jen chimed in, "That sounds incredibly wise of you both. Take your time."

Sara went on to share the birth story. Her droopy eyes told them she was ready for a rest. Maggie, Jen, and Nora said their good-byes. Little was said on the elevator. Nora broke the silence. "Children are one thing I missed out on with Seth. There are times I wish I had a little one. You know, a little Seth running around."

Jen and Maggie looked at each other. A mischievous danced across Jen's face. "You know, Nora, if you ever want to borrow a kid or two, Maggie and I could help you out. Not that they aren't always angels ..."

Nora took the razzing. "Yeah, yeah. I know kids can be a handful. Of course, I could take on the role of 'cool Aunt Nora.'" Her hands came up in air quotes. "The one who lets you stay up late, eat junk food, and talk about boys."

Maggie laughed, "Every kid needs a cool aunt. But if Emma starts talking to you about boys, I want a full report."

They stopped for coffee and then drove back to the theater to get their cars. The guys weren't back yet. Standing in the parking lot, they looked at each other.

Maggie looked at Jen and Nora. "I can't thank you enough. This has been a blast." She caught Nora's eye. "And to reconnect with you has been a huge blessing. Thanks for jumping in."

Nora nodded. "Thank you for asking. This has been a wonderful experience."

Jen smiled. "Maggie, you're always getting me involved in stuff I wouldn't normally volunteer for. And it's always an adventure."

"You know, it has been great to remember what the stage feels like, and the fun of doing a production. I missed it more than I thought. But being in that hospital room with Sara, I was reminded how important being a mom is. We've got a big job raising our kiddos," Maggie reflected. "One of the things we can show them is how to honor God in being who he created them to be. Let's face it, our men didn't fall in love with mothers—they fell in love with an actress, a designer, and a health nut."

They stood in the parking lot finishing their hot drinks and talking of their families, the new year, and wondering what opportunities it would bring.

## ABOUT THE AUTHOR

**Karen H. Richardson** has always observed the world as a running narrative and encounters with others as fodder for a story. Over the years her desire to put words to paper to tell a story has never wavered. While in school, she wrote for the school newspaper and yearbook. She has had several magazine articles published.

In 2009, she launched a blog, KK's Candor where she posts short slice of life articles meant to encourage others. As a life-long learner, in 2012, Karen joined a tap-dancing class for adults. And recently, she and her husband, Jay, learned to play pickleball.

She and her husband live in Louisville, Kentucky. She has one son, Cole, who recently graduated from college with a degree in music education. Karen has a BA in journalism from Western Kentucky University, and a professional background in communications, marketing, and project management. She is a current member of ACFW where she served as president of the ACFW Louisville chapter.

Connect with Karen online, www.KHRAuthor.com, or on social media @KHRAuthor on Facebook, Instagram, and Twitter.

www.ingramcontent.com/pod-product-compliance
Lightning Source LLC
Chambersburg PA
CBHW070637310726
48982CB00001B/311
* 9 7 8 1 6 4 9 4 9 8 8 3 0 *